SHADOW
OF THE
GYPSY

A Novel

SHELLY FROME

North Carolina

Shadow of the Gypsy
© 2022 Shelly Frome. All rights reserved.

Published in the United States by BQB Publishing
(an imprint of Boutique of Quality Books Publishing Company)
www.bqbpublishing.com

Printed in the United States of America

978-1-952782-57-2 (p)
978-1-952782-58-9 (e)

Library of Congress Control Number: 2022932184

Book design by Robin Krauss, www.bookformatters.com
Cover design by Rebecca Lown, www.rebeccalowndesign.com
First editor: Olivia Swenson
Second editor: Andrea Vande Vorde

PRAISE FOR
SHADOW OF THE GYPSY
AND SHELLY FROME

"By turns charming and chilling, *Shadow of the Gypsy* is that rarest of gems, a crime novel that curdles the blood, even as it tugs on the heartstrings. Frome keeps the reader on a knife's edge in this compelling tale of danger, betrayal, and the generational pain of a sympathetic everyman whose life depends on reconciling—and finally defeating—his past."

– Jaden Terrell, author of *A Taste of Blood and Ashes,
River of Glass, A Cup Full of Midnight,* and *Racing the Devil*

—··—

"Frome brings a keen sense of place, from Connecticut to the Blue Ridge Mountains, as Zharko hatches his dark plan for the innocent Sonny, who wants nothing more than to leave his past behind. Sharp writing, and a keen pace keeps this story rolling."

– Lee A. Jacobus, author of
Crown Island and *Hawaiian Tales*

—··—

"*Shadow of the Gypsy* is intriguing, complicated, and mysterious. Shelly Frome has created a puzzle that includes characters from different countries, with different cultures, who each have complex personal goals. Their thought processes are given to us in true life dialogs back and forth between each other.

Everyone's goals intertwine in surprising ways with life and death consequences."

– Tina M. Zion, award winning author
and international teacher of intuition

— · · —

"Shelly Frome writes from the heart . . . he creates strong characters who live in intriguing places . . . the plot is spell-binding . . . this mystery will hold your attention to the last page . . . well written!!"

– Henry McCarthy,
host of Poets and Writers, WEHC 90.7

— · · —

"Once you start, you won't want to stop reading *Shadow of the Gypsy* by Shelly Frome. It pulls you in on the wild ride as a reporter is forced to participate in a Russian mob crime because of a debt owed from childhood. On the edge of your seat, it sweeps you back to his old home as he tries to fill in the empty blanks from his youth when he witnessed a crime. Now as an adult, he must rise to take action to stop life from controlling him. Instead of reporting the story, he becomes part of it."

– Jana Zinser, author of
The Children's Train: Escape from the Kindertransport
and *Fly Like a Bird*

— · · —

"Shelly Frome is back with another mystery thriller. Josh Bartlett thought he could build a new life with a new identity in a backwater town in the Blue Ridge Mountains. But he learns that you can run from your past, but you can't escape it.

The novel careens from Appalachia to Connecticut. Frome has a masterful sense of place, capturing the look, feel, and sound of these diverse locales. The action never flags as Josh Bartlett pursues his demons and his destiny."

– Len Joy, author of *Dry Heat; Everyone Dies Famous; American Past Time; Letting Go;* and *Better Days*

—··—

"Shelly Frome has a lyrical ear for dialogue and uses his experience working in Waterbury, Connecticut, to bring the city, and the surrounding Litchfield Hills, to life in a dramatic fashion."

– John Murry, Publisher/editor, *The Waterbury Observer*

"With rich characters, a strong narrative voice, and high stakes, there is much to love in this new novel by Shelly Frome. *Shadow of the Gypsy* is a mystery that "makes blood run hot," the plot revolving around an old secret, the Russian mafia, and caught in the midst, Josh Bartlett, a man at a turning point in his life. With these components along with lively writing and lots of plot twists and turns, what results is a compelling story written with intelligence and Frome's distinctive humor. It's one to keep you turning the pages."

– Lucy Adkins, co-author of *The Fire Inside: A Companion for the Creative Life and Writing in Community*

For the pilgrims on this road.

ACKNOWLEDGEMENTS

I'm indebted to the following for their invaluable prompts and pointers along the way: Beth Terrell of Mystery Writers of America, acquisitions editor Saundra Kelley, and editor Olivia Swenson.

CHAPTER ONE

This time Josh Bartlet couldn't shake it off.

The heavy rain and howling wind had morphed into harrowing flickers from his childhood, then dovetailed out of the dream into shadows outside the bedroom window. All of it highlighted by a lightning flash and the sense it was finally catching up to him. Soon the room was spinning and didn't slow until he finally sat up, reached over to the nightstand, grabbed the standby glass of water, gulped it down, and ever so slowly took stock. With the electric clock flashing on the nightstand, he could see that the power had gone off and may have just come back on. Gradually the sound of the pounding rain began to taper off, the wind receding as it all faded at first light. It took several minutes until he could talk himself out of a sudden chill brought on neither by the weather nor the fact that the heat pump must have turned off. It was spring in the Blue Ridge, the climate temperate and a brief nighttime storm was no big deal this time of year. So there was no way to account for the chill. Applying common sense was his fallback position. It had worked so far and had gotten him to this point.

Bound and determined, sitting up straight, he reminded himself of the overriding plan. He'd give it another six weeks at the *Black Mountain News*, ask Paul, his editor, for a letter of recommendation, check with Molly back in Connecticut in hopes she was still unattached, and convince her he had turned the corner. He was no longer at sixes and sevens. He'd return to the Litchfield Hills and, if she would have him, forge a brand-new life. That's the deal, he told himself. It's been almost two years, for Pete's sake. For all intents and purposes he was free and clear.

But then it struck him. It was only yesterday when he could have sworn he caught a glimpse of Zharko. Or at least someone with those same chiseled features lingering under the eaves of the rustic community center at the edge of the lake. But it couldn't have been him. He'd been deported, or at least that was what Josh was led to believe. And what would Zharko be doing almost nine hundred miles south of his stomping grounds? Besides, it was only a glimpse. A glimpse and then the figure was gone. He must have been seeing things. At any rate, he'd managed to put all that behind him. The wind and the dream-shadows must have brought it all back. Flickers of memories he'd done his best to tuck away— what he'd seen, what he'd run away from since he was twelve.

Once again, he told himself to get a grip. His bent was to pull back, watch, and listen from a safe remove. He was good at watching and listening, probably one of the all-time best. It was simply the advent of another Monday and nothing of any consequence was going on.

Not a single thing was off-kilter. Nothing, zero, zilch.

He sprang out of bed and, though it was way too early, shaved, showered, and got dressed. "You are what you do," he muttered to himself as he combed unruly strands of his sandy hair. "Get off it, assess the damages if any. Make yourself useful."

His was a small one-bedroom frame cottage nestled in a grove of oak and hickory trees right off the country road to Lake Eden. A rental, which suited him fine, except for the fact that the owners were on the road half the time and he had to do minor repairs, which he wasn't half good at or, if need be, call somebody in. So, he would check for any damage to the roof and whatnot. Engaging in a task, any task, always did the trick.

Josh went down the hallway, opened the front door, and was

immediately confronted by a huge limb that had splintered off
the Bradford pear tree. There was nothing for it but to go out the
back door, circle around, climb over the porch railing, and tug at
the limb until it cleared the steps. Though he was slight of build, he
was young and healthy, and this task would accomplish something
and get him off his ill-founded anxiety. So he set about hoisting the
limb shoulder high and shoving it over the railing. Then it was a
matter of hauling and dragging it behind the woodshed and leaving
it propped against a rusty wheelbarrow.

Returning to the front porch, he looked up at the point where
the limb had been cracked open and severed, perhaps by the
lightning or the strong wind gusts or both.

With that settled, he reentered the house, moved straight to
the kitchen, and made himself a breakfast of bacon, eggs, toast,
and coffee.

Despite himself, he began to recall a recent interview with a
retired physicist who claimed that beneath the surface there were
restless factors at work, invisible sub-atomic particles and waves,
colliding and breaking apart, that he called quarks. The physicist
also claimed this theory had been thoroughly tested. An avid film
buff, Josh's thoughts drifted to the first sequence of *The Wizard of
Oz*. When the story opens on yet another pleasant day in Kansas,
Dorothy, her little dog Toto, and Auntie Em are happy as can be
out on the farm. Presently, Miss Gulch comes by on her bike,
snarling and snapping at Toto like always. It was all perfectly
normal. At this moment, Dorothy is totally unaware of what's
afoot. Has no idea the quarks are at play and it's the proverbial
quiet before the storm. This is not going to be just another day.

There he was, at it again. He got up and walked back onto the
front porch to check things once more and keep focused. Avert-
ing the remnants of the damaged limb, he saw that the overcast
skies and deluge of the night before had given way to a dry,

sparkling Carolina blue. The mountain range in the distance was glistening as the greening continued to move up the ridges, lighter shades eclipsed by darker shades, eventually culminating in a deep, vibrant emerald.

Still, the possible sighting of Zharko stayed with him. What he'd seen when he was twelve and the sight of the blade raising and plummeting down over and over while he stood stock still, deep in the frozen woods of Litchfield. A memory he'd all but erased.

The only thing for it was to stay on track and keep any thoughts of Zharko's nearby presence at bay. If he slipped up again, he'd return to thoughts of Molly and the overall plan. Unless something actually stood in the way. In reality. Here on planet Earth.

He shifted his gaze to the right and caught sight of Amanda, the tousle-haired eleven-year-old who lived next door, running to the mailbox in her bare feet. She plucked out what looked like a few greeting cards and waved them, shouting, "Hey, Mister Josh! Guess what?"

"I'll bite. What?" Josh shouted back, hanging on to a just-another-Monday mindset.

Amanda ran back, stopped short by her white picket fence, leaned over with her freckled face beaming, and said, "It's exactly the second week of April, right?"

"That's a roger."

"So, you know that community school down the road?"

"You bet." He'd done a piece on the theater director and the way he got the middle school kids to work together like one big happy family. "And you got a big part in the spring musical, right?"

"You bet. It's starting to all come together. How about that?"

"That's terrific, kid."

"Boy, is it ever. Got to run. Talk to you later."

He watched her dash inside her sunflower-yellow country

house like a shot from an old Disney movie depicting a perfect day of Americana. At the same time, he couldn't help but feel a twinge of longing. There was Amanda, her idyllic safe surroundings, her petite, cheerful mom who always sent over fresh-baked cookies, and her affable, lanky dad, investment banker and pillar of the community. The total opposite of Josh's jaded mother back in Connecticut, not to mention a father he never knew.

Determined yet again to remain objective, he walked off the steps straight over to the Bradford pear tree. The storm had managed to snap a few smaller branches and scatter a number of leaves and buds across the lawn. Perfectly natural in the clear light of day. No portents of dire prospects, nothing of the sort.

He went back inside, entered the den, and spent some time finishing his list of follow-up questions for self-help guru Noah Ackerman, newly arrived from New York. During the whole interview, Ackerman had peered over his bifocals, teasing him with little queries like, "So, never mind *me* for a minute. What is *your* background?" and "What brought you down here—relatives? Yes, no? So, talk to me. What is your heritage?" Not to mention, "Is there anything you're willing to share so this isn't some freakin' one-way street? Come on, come on, give."

"Mister Ackerman, if you don't mind, can we just stick to the interview?" Josh had countered.

In his signature pushy way, Ackerman had persisted. "Fine. If you've got nothing to hide, you acknowledge this is who you are and what you stand for. Otherwise, you do have something to hide. Simple. Am I right or am I right?"

Josh had managed to brush off every one of these probes and finally called a timeout. "Maybe if we give it a rest, we can resume and manage to keep things on an even keel."

Ackerman shook his head. "Maybe *you* need to give it a rest.

Maybe you're not used to laying things on the line, which is my
definition of operating on an even keel. You get my drift?"

At an impasse, they broke it off then and there.

Now, taking stock once more, he simply put it down to a first
encounter with a pushy guy who jumped at any opportunity to
ply his trade. Antsy, bored—words like that. At the follow-up this
morning, he would have to fend Ackerman off, zero in on the crux
of his profile, and take some photos. Then, once back home, come
up with a through line, polish the piece, and post it to the editor.
That would be that until the next installment of his Call of the
Valley series.

"Right," Josh muttered to himself. He'd committed to the story
because Ackerman had garnered a lot of notoriety. His pushiness
was the price Josh had to pay. Just another day's work.

Still and all, he couldn't help wondering what Ackerman was
really up to. Mountain Vista and its cluster of Swiss chalet condos
had only recently been built to accommodate newbies attracted to
the quaint tranquility of this setting. It offered the companionship
of fellow retirees, many of whom were also former professionals
like the physicist. Which still didn't explain why Ackerman kept
working on him. No one else had ever given him a hard time.
Perhaps Ackerman's behavior stemmed from his retirement and
treatments at the nearby neuro-center?

Yes. Balding, paunchy Ackerman was the one who was ill at
ease and Josh was perfectly fine, if only Ackerman could just stop
rocking the boat.

Josh quit stalling, swept Dorothy and *The Wizard of Oz*,
percolating quarks, and iffy portents under the rug, and moved
on to the follow-up interview.

Zharko was not catching up to him. He was still secure in his
overriding plan to reunite with Molly, and this *was* just another
Monday.

Absolutely nothing was stalking him out of the past.

He repeated this mantra several times until he almost began to believe it.

CHAPTER TWO

Somehow Ackerman had gotten even more pushy. Holding forth on his patio at the retirement complex, he kept fiddling with the tea tray atop the glass-top table while muttering such things as "Let's hope you're going to pitch in this time. Bring something to the party." He then checked to make sure no resident was within earshot on the other side of the basket-weave fence and said, "I'm talking shooting straight from the hip. Enough of this phony polite tap dance."

Josh didn't reply and continued to sit tight and wait for Ackerman to settle down.

Ackerman blew on his bifocals, wiped them off with his shirtsleeve, and added, "What is it, almost noon? If they're out, the neighbors are probably at the outdoor market greeting each other with a 'How are you this lovely day? Fine and dandy? Well, ain't that nice?' Anything to avoid the truth."

Finally, Ackerman gave Josh a steely look. "So, what do you say we quit beating around the bush and get right down to it?"

"Our unfinished business, you mean," Josh said, clicking his micro recorder on and sliding it in Ackerman's direction. "Absolutely."

"Damn right," said Ackerman, repositioning the recorder so that it was midway between them on the glass tabletop. "So, what is it with you? What are you, thirty, thirty-five, half my age? You're still all bottled up. Underneath, I'm talking here. Apart from the sandy hair, blue eyes, and nice guy, boy-next-door act. Look, you can trust me. I am a whiz at this. So, come on, humor me. What gives?"

Josh pushed the recorder closer to Ackerman again. "Anyways—"

"No 'anyways'," Ackerman said. "I've been here for four weeks and you're the only interesting thing I've come across. Back in the Big Apple we've got millions crammed into the five boroughs and leaking in from all directions, including the Hudson, the ocean, and all points west and south. It's a contest to survive even if you're only looking for a cab, trying to get a seat on the subway, or just crossing the street. You have to let off some steam. But you, you keep it close to the vest. Which is starting to get on my nerves. It's like being with the poster boy from the Boy Scouts who's got something else cooking."

"Look, Mister Ackerman, all I'm doing is trying to be accommodating so we can get through it and call it a day."

"Accommodating? Who needs accommodating? I let on how hung up I am, and what do I get? Nice and pleasant while harboring the nitty-gritty. More phony baloney."

"Listen—"

"No, you listen. Why you and me, and why now? I'm guessing some repressed Heidegger syndrome. Come clean and we're off to the races."

"The what syndrome?"

"Heidegger, Heidegger! The Nazi king of philosophy. 'Thrown in . . . thrown in' is what he was always raving about. He was thrown in, born into the Nazi thing. Everyone I've dealt with, it's always the same. Thrown into this situation. So, now what? 'If my father wasn't an alcoholic . . . if I had gotten as much love as my older brother . . . if my sister and I weren't tossed into a foster home . . .' Ya-tada, ya-tada, ya-tada. I mention your background—which has got to be the root of the freakin' springboard—and what happens?"

Realizing Ackerman wasn't going to let go, Josh said, "Okay, what is it? What are you doing? What are you really after?"

"Some action, what else? Shaking things up, getting to the bottom of things. Impressing you so you'll tell the folks around the boonies here what a whiz I am at digging beneath the surface. So people will drop the infuriating let's-make-nice Southern games. So things will pop, crackle, and fizz. So I can drum up some clients and we can all get a life, for crissake."

Josh had a mind to give up and call this whole thing off. But some part of him still wanted to get a handle on his own unfounded anxiety. "Okay," he said, "I'll bite. What are the telltale signs something is about to bust loose?"

"Look at you," Ackerman went on. "The body never lies. Trying to come off la-di-da but sitting straight as a board, trying your damnedest to keep the dam from bursting."

Shaking his head, with his thick lips curling up in anticipation, Ackerman shuffled in and around the potted plants, his hands in full motion now. "So, humor me. Toss off something about your past, your family. Then I throw in something about my old man who drove a cab. Keep it going. Five gets you ten, in no time we'll have liftoff."

At first, Josh just sat there. Then he blurted out, "'The past is a foreign country; they do things differently there.'"

"Where did you get that one?"

"A literature course I once took."

"Well, I've got news for you. The past is never past. And the longer you try to keep it at arm's length, the hungrier it gets, until one day, sure as hell, it's gonna get you. And then where will you be?"

"Not if you keep on an even keel and put it all behind you. You're forgetting this is the land of the second chance. I don't know about you, but I've got plans. So, can we drop it now? Finally?"

Rolling his eyes, Ackerman came right back with "Oh sure, why not? We can fake it like everybody else around here. Make nice, have a chat and some tea. What the hell?"

As Ackerman retreated into the condo, Josh couldn't help wondering why he selected him in the first place. There were dozens he could have chosen from who recently took up residence here. Among the notables was the soprano from the Chicago Opera, the popular children's book author from Ohio, the award-winning pastel artist from Boston, and even the well-known DC pundit. Why did he select a therapist? Let alone an aggressive New Yorker in need of therapy himself?

Ackerman returned with the kettle. He emptied the boiling water into the ceramic pitcher and stirred clockwise, careful not to crush the tea leaves. He slid one of the cups over to Josh, who added milk from the carton into the bottom of a cup and nodded to Ackerman to pour.

Ackerman filled the rest of Josh's cup to the brim, replaced the pitcher, and peered at him, breaking into that same quizzical look.

"What?" said Josh. "What is it now?"

"Never mind. Except . . ."

"Except what?"

"Except you wanted lots of milk first, guaranteeing the weakest tea possible before the pot has a chance to get going. All the time you're trying to water everything down while on the inside everything is bubbling up."

"Why are you doing this? Why do you keep this up?"

"I told you. Do I have to spell it out?"

"Yes."

Taking a page from Josh's own musing, Ackerman said, "Don't you see, don't you get it? Why do you think I agreed to this in the first place? Right off I've got your number because of my incredible sixth sense. Once I get you going, you are bowled over and get me instant recognition. Just like that, I get clients from all the repressed niceness around here. I'm back in the saddle. To hell with this nervous condition. To hell with calling me erratic, telling me I'd better simmer down. Next thing you know, I'm in business, baby!"

Josh shut off the tape recorder and got to his feet. Ackerman's eyes peered at him over his bifocals, more expectant than ever. Josh turned away and perused the area beyond the hedges and rolling grounds, cast his gaze further, and kept his focus on the tranquil scene in order to pull back and see it all from a calm remove.

A figure hovered in the parking lot in the vicinity of Josh's old Subaru wagon. He closed his eyes, then opened them. There was the hazy outline of the same figure in the exact same spot.

"You see?" Ackerman asked. "Like I keep telling you, the body never lies."

"As it happens, I am taking in your ambiance. Your chosen background."

"Sure you are." Ackerman pulled up a wrought iron chair, sat down, and poured himself a cup of the darkening brew. Like a wily card player who'd just been dealt a winning hand, he said, "So, what do you make of this ambiance? All this peace and quiet that's supposed to do wonders."

Josh said nothing and glanced once more in the direction of the far-off parking lot.

A few more hearty swigs of tea and Ackerman added,

"Supposed to do wonders but is somehow making you jerk your head and keep looking over your shoulder."

"I am keenly aware, that's all. That's my stock in trade."

"Sure it is." Ackerman nodded. "A perfect denial as it's all about to spill over and, just like that, we're off to the freakin' races."

CHAPTER THREE

Reaching a standoff, Josh cut things short once again. He'd rely on the press release he glommed off the Internet, plus whatever he could draw from their recorded conversations, call Ackerman for any fillers he might need, and finish up here with a brief photo shoot. Since his profiles were, in effect, a glorification of this special corner of the world, the best bet would be to capture Ackerman with the Seven Sisters mountain range as a backdrop to compensate for the sketchy text.

But he didn't tell him he wanted him around the front of the Swiss-cottage condos because someone might spot Josh sitting out here in plain sight. He was also hurrying things so he could check out the situation in the vicinity of his Subaru wagon under the pretext he'd need to retrieve his Nikon 18-300mm lens in his trunk. The sooner he brushed off this whole Ackerman episode, the sooner he could chalk off this glitch in his life from first light till now.

"So," Ackerman said, "now we switch gears, get a move on. Quick-fast cast a blind eye while you take off, then sprint around to the front of this place for a Blue Ridge ad and leave me high and dry. But it's no use, buster. I'm telling you it's no use."

"And I'm telling you, we cut our losses, it's over and out. I go home and edit the new shots so that you're embraced by the setting. All you have to do is sit tight for a minute."

"Right, sure, of course."

"I'll be right back with the optimum lens."

Leaving his camera bag, slipping away from the patio, keeping low like he did as a kid in the Connecticut hills playing Indian scout, Josh skirted the bushes. Then he circled behind the low-lying activities building and hunkered down by the near side of the visitors' parking lot. He got behind the tailgate of a red Chevy pickup and glanced around the edge of the truck bed.

Once again, he wasn't absolutely sure. The figure was still almost a hundred yards away, blurred by the shimmering sunlight. The guy could be on the grounds crew. He could be the driver of the pickup. There were countless wiry workmen in denim for hire in these parts, especially now that spring had fully arrived.

With his mind revving like crazy, he reminded himself that, in fact, his old nemesis had been booted out of the country. Josh had, again in point of fact, recently flown back to New England once or twice to make sure, to touch base with his estranged mother and, most of all, to see Molly, his erstwhile childhood sweetheart. As a result, he'd been looking forward to his overall plan, absolutely counting on it, the only thing that had kept him going. If he could damn well get his act together and hold out just a bit longer.

Yet, as the figure pivoted and headed in Josh's direction, all hopes and dreams were shattered. There, big as life, was the black denim, shiny cowboy boots, and red blouse protruding from an open Levi jacket. If nothing else, the twisted, sparkling earring gave him away. That and the furtive way he scurried around, trying to get a bead on the whereabouts of his quarry. His thin, chiseled face and high cheekbones alone were a dead giveaway.

Unbidden snippets of memory came rushing back to Josh. As a youngster, gazing out the window of his mother's cabin in the woods, catching sight of the gypsy van and that thickset, baldheaded companion called Vlad. Once, Zharko had berated his mother in that awkward speech pattern of his: "Your boy still tractable for sure, tell me true. He is like well-behaved dog?" And another time: "Day is coming when he will be useful. Not now but maybe soon because feds hounding me worse than ever."

And this moment could very well be that "maybe soon." Zharko Vadja was actually close by while Ackerman, no doubt, was gloating that something was up as he waited impatiently.

Josh remained frozen, hunkered down. As if sifting through his recollections could alter his perspective. Recalling that foray only a few months ago to touch base—to see how Molly was doing and learning she was teaching second grade at that very same elementary school they'd attended before his mother and Zharko shipped him off.

Truth to tell, he'd always loved Molly. He was attracted to her fair-haired wholesomeness and the sense she was always there for you, never once playing games like most other girls with their feminine wiles. However, his attempt to shield her from the fallout of a haunted past became a barrier—she sensed he was keeping something from her. And his name change years later to good ol' normal-sounding Josh Bartlet only made matters worse and dovetailed into that recent troublesome exchange:

"I have to tell you," Molly had said. "I've been dating. I think he's getting serious."

"Oh?"

"He outlined the reasons we'd make a good team. Both of us settled in a well-established school system. Both of us not getting any younger. Also, as my assistant principal, there'd be no problem getting maternity leave."

"Terrific. Sounds very practical."

"I am serious. And isn't it about time you came to terms with your own life? Why did you have to change your name? And why is it the only newspaper jobs you'll take have to be miles south of here? What am I supposed to do in the meantime?"

"I'm turning the corner, Molly, trust me. In only a few more months, I'll have a track record. Solid, reliable, non-controversial. I'll ask for a letter of recommendation, nothing hanging over my head."

"What does that mean? What does it ever mean?"

"Nothing, I swear. Just a slip of the tongue."

It was the same old Catch-22. Keep skirting around it. Talk yourself out of it. But, then again, some day it might still catch up to you. Which it most certainly had. Crazed, volatile Zharko had materialized less than twenty yards away, closing in. And there was no way to make him go away.

He crouched even lower and scuttled behind a brace of blue Ford trucks. With his pulse racing, he moved past a fleet of service vans to the back of a brown UPS vehicle, hoping the driver didn't come upon him and demand to know what he was doing within reach of her delivery packages.

Making a dash for it, he doubled back, carefully making his way over to his Subaru wagon. He unlatched the trunk, snatched the telephoto lens out of the box, secured the trunk lid, and took off for Ackerman's patio.

All the while, it wasn't lost on him that keeping his distance was automatic. All built into his lifestyle, along with getting lost in movies, being a good listener, and hiding behind the lens of a camera or notepad or tape recorder or what have you.

He focused solely on his pace and breathing, shutting out all recollections, especially that damned incident when he was twelve-year-old Sonny Korda.

Before he knew it, he was back on Ackerman's patio. He could tell Ackerman saw how breathless he was. Nodding again, like an old baseball scout who'd at long last come across a prime raw recruit.

"Okay," Josh said, pushing right ahead. "Ready? I'm set to take those shots with the perfect backdrop and perfect lens. Indicating

the ideal reprieve from the hustle and bustle of Manhattan. That
and the hopeful promise of the nerve treatment center that
brought you here."

Nodding yet again, Ackerman said, "Right, why not? He sprints
back like he's being chased and I'm supposed to keep casting a
blind eye. Give me a break."

Josh shrugged him off and grabbed his camera bag. He led the
way inside Ackerman's quarters and out again onto the stand of
hickory trees with the looming blueish-green mountain range in
the background.

Shuffling along in his sandals, Ackerman held still at each
juncture, offering a wan smile as Josh snapped away. After taking
a number of shots while glancing back every now and then to
make sure Zharko hadn't circled around, Josh shut off his camera,
unfastened the telephoto lens, and slid them both into his bag.

"Tell me this," said Ackerman as they traipsed back, "are you
expecting some redneck who's tracked you down because you left
his pregnant sister in the lurch? Or are there a bunch of alimony
payments you're behind on, or somebody gunning for you? And
you're using this interview as a stalling tactic until you decide on
the right tactical maneuver?"

Josh didn't reply as they came to a halt in front of the tri-
cluster condo. Ackerman reached inside his shirt pocket and
retrieved a business card.

"What's this?" Josh asked, continuing to keep an eye out.

"To reach me. When you're ready. My hunch is you'll be calling
any hour now."

"No need. I'm fine."

"Oh, sure. But I'd like to catch you while you're still on your
feet. Otherwise that'll ruin my whole scheme."

Unable to hold still a moment longer, Josh snatched the business card out of Ackerman's hand and pocketed it. In turn,

Ackerman asked for Josh's card. Reluctantly, Josh handed him one and said, "Later, okay?"

He left the patio and worked his way down and around to his Subaru wagon. Spotting no one in view except a sauntering white-haired couple who wished him a blessed day, he slid behind the wheel, gunned the motor, and tore out of there before Zharko had a chance to get a good look at him and jot down his license plate.

He couldn't help wondering where Zharko had stashed his gypsy van? Or had he driven down from Connecticut in a rental and was tooling around looking to snare Josh while remaining incognito?

At any rate, what difference did it make? Ackerman's neurotic scheme had a lot more going for it than Josh's naïve, wishful plan.

CHAPTER FOUR

By the time Josh got home, locked the doors just in case, and forced himself to settle down to work on his profile of Ackerman, the fatigue from the night before started to get to him. Regardless, he plugged in his Nikon camera to the PC tower, downloaded the shots he'd taken onto the ViewNX2 file, and cropped the best of the lot. But the knowing look he'd captured on Ackerman's face only made matters worse.

His mind was so scattered now, it reminded him of a movie he tried to watch the other night listed as "an engrossing slice of small-town life." Like a promo offering reassurance he'd made the right decision in opting for the safety of this mountain village. In fact, the opening scene focused on a teen not unlike himself back in the day: sandy hair; soft, nondescript features; slim-to-average build. In this instance, the teen caught a well-hit fly ball in the outfield during a high school baseball game, securing the win for his side.

But it didn't end there. The cocky guy who hit the long drive accosted him in the locker room backed up by his cronies, shoving and goading him for what they called "crawling out of the woodwork." The hapless teen got out of this predicament by agreeing with the bullies, going along just like Josh, doing his best to fade into the background.

But matters didn't end there either. In the next sequence, the teen was working behind the counter of a diner as a couple of hoods burst in, one beginning to molest a comely waitress while the other pulled a gun, demanding all the cash in the register. This time, instead of complying, the submissive teen flung a carafe of steaming hot coffee in the leader's face, grabbed the weapon, and managed to wing the molester and hold the leader at gunpoint while the waitress got hold of the local sheriff.

At this juncture, the lead hood threatened vengeance from "his boys back in the big city." The scene quickly shifted to a black limo cruising down the main street driven by a scarred, middle-aged thug accompanied by his flunkies. Then and there, Josh immediately switched channels in favor of an old Gene Kelly musical.

He didn't know it then, but that "small-town flick" was just another harbinger of things to come. Namely, the unexpected arrival of Zharko.

He retreated to pleasant movie images like June Allyson as the girl next door behind a white picket fence. He thought of Molly at the upper end of the lane, her wholesomeness and honey-blonde hair. More whimsical thoughts that were getting him nowhere.

Soon, though it was only midafternoon, his eyelids became heavy and he couldn't fight the grogginess any longer. He went into the bedroom, intent on lying down only for a moment to still this abiding anxiety.

—··—

In the dream, Molly was twelve years old again, trudging down the lane in the snow, a package in her hands tied with green and red ribbons. Josh caught sight of her through the icy crosshatched windows, hoping she'd make it down to this dead-end rustic cabin cradled in the looming fir trees deep at the edge of White's Woods. His mother Irina tapped away on that old typewriter of hers behind closed doors, the rhythm of her tapping more and more insistent.

His mother then appeared at the front door, her raven-black hair glistening, piercing eyes as dark as her hair. With a lit pencil-thin cigar in her hand, a shawl draped over her shoulders, her willowy form tensed as if she were about to pounce. Gentle knocking at the door gave way to his mother hovering over Molly's quivering angelic face, her snow boots slipping on the bottom step, his mother hollering, "No, no, no! No Christmas presents from nosy neighbors! On your way! Back where you came from! Leave us be!"

The heavy oaken door slamming in Molly's face dissolved to Sonny (as he'd been called back then) slip-sliding up the icy lane, calling after Molly. Her cries echoed through the canopy of trees in the darkening stillness, the snow falling steadily, the slope leading up to the crossroad becoming steeper still, Molly's house fading further and further away.

Desperately, he searched everywhere for the Christmas present. Perhaps she'd dropped it. Perhaps he could hide it from his mother and open it in secret, celebrate Christmas morning like the rest of the kids, and thank Molly the next day. Perhaps he could sneak off and make it all the way to the top and ask for her forgiveness.

But a van drove past him, spattering his shivering body with snow, headed down the slope. It was embossed with two horizontal bars: blue on top for eternal spirit, green below for open fields. A raspy voice shouted, "Stop acting like a gadzo, not of our clan!" The voice rang out under the starless sky. The voice rang out even louder. "Our clan roaming Eastern Europe, Romania, Hungary, circling Kiev in the Ukraine!"

He called back, "But I don't know any of this. I don't look like you, don't act like you. And who was my father anyways?"

There was no answer.

He followed the van down the snowy whiteness, though he didn't want to go back there, though there had to be some way to erase this whole story.

Back in the cabin, trying to tell his mother that was a cruel thing to do to Molly. His mother slapped him, threw a glass of ice water in his face, went back into her secret room, secured the latch, her typewriter clacking away as loudly as ever.

Quickly, he was outside in the snow again, searching frantically for the Christmas present. Trudging through the stands of evergreens in his slippers, shivering so hard he couldn't stand it, frozen crusted pinecones under foot till he spotted the van in a clearing. There were shouts and threats. There was a bloodcurdling scream. He thrust himself forward to see, though for the life of him he didn't want to see, didn't want to ever know. A dagger flashed in the moonlight. Zharko's hand raised up and plummeted down over and over, finally cutting off the screaming for good.

Spinning around, Josh scurried over the pinecones and raced off, shaking with fear and cold, searching for the Christmas present. Longing to join the kids beyond the woods, snug inside, embraced by their mothers and the warmth of the hearth, glistening presents resting under the tree laced with tinsel and garlands of spangled light.

He thrashed around, seeking this first-ever Christmas present that would make everything nice, but found only his pillow and woke with a start. He sat up. There was no going back to sleep, no opting for dreamy images of walking to school with Molly as the weather turned to spring, buttercups lining the path. No way to erase anything. He was left with the same chill from this morning, now turning into an ache that had no name.

An ache that was useless to gloss over.

He got to his feet, returned to the den, and drew the shades.

He booted up the PC and just sat there. Try as he might to return to the business at hand (his profile of Ackerman), images of Zharko's flashing blade remained fixed in his mind. Followed by recollections of being shipped off to prep school, out of the way, after his mother bargained with Zharko—"He will behave, he wants no trouble. This too will pass."

"For now," Zharko had said. "We shall see. Let it go, but only for now."

He was still motionless in front of the PC, fully into the realities of the here and now, when the landline rang atop his desk. The caller ID told him it was the paper. The sugary Southern accent told him it was Crystal the receptionist.

"Josh? It's me. I left a message on your cell. Did you get it?"

He'd had it in mind to check his cell messages later. At this point, all he could think of saying was "No, Crystal, I haven't checked my calls."

"How come?"

"All kinds of distractions. Just been one of those days."

"Well anyways," she said, sounding a little rattled, "this fella comes bustin' in here, dressed kind of funny, talking even more funny like."

"Glossy red shirt beneath a Levi jacket? Hawkish face, cropped salt-and-pepper hair?"

"That's him. Wanted to know if I'd seen you and where you could be reached. I told him you were on assignment at Mountain Vista and incommunicado at the moment. When he kept at it and wanted to know what Mountain Vista was, how to get there, and who exactly you were seeing, I said that information was against company policy to disclose. However, if he could state his business and leave a number where he could be reached . . . But he turned on his heels without so much as a by-your-leave. Well, I tell you. How rude. Did I do wrong?"

"No, you did good. You get a 'bless your heart.'"

"Well, that's a comfort. Guess I'll just leave you to it."

After a few more pleasantries, Crystal offered Josh a blessed evening and hung up.

As Josh replaced the receiver, all he could do was mutter, "Oh great. What now?"

But he had no idea what to do. He spent another stretch of time sitting there in limbo.

Presently, though it was the last thing in the world he wanted to do, with no other recourse in sight, he called Ackerman. Opting for some way, any way, to reframe things. His fallback position of sitting tight for only a little while longer was no longer tenable. He was just plain at a loss.

— .. —

"Theoretically," Josh said, pressing a little harder. "For the sake of argument, that's all."

"Go on," Ackerman said. "What did I tell you? Any hour now, any minute."

"Anyway. Say a person has always steered clear of trouble, gone out of his way, in fact. But just when it seemed it had paid off, that all the dark clouds had rolled away and he was on the verge of getting a life, out of the blue, trouble returns knocking at the door. Sitting tight no longer covers it."

"Obviously. And neither does denial, buddy boy. So, you're going to add your own experience to your piece about Ackerman, the quick-bang therapist whiz. Give me a yes."

"Anyways—"

"Enough with the anyways shtick. We cut to the chase. In your case and your lame boy-next-door routine, a good start would be checking out the old reliable hero's journey. Consider this clue all part of our deal. Speedy solutions to any predicament. Check out Wikipedia or whatever. And move it. The sooner my profile is plastered all over the next edition, the sooner my phone starts ringing and my nerves simmer down." With that, Ackerman hung up as quickly as he'd snatched up the receiver.

—‥—

As anxious as Ackerman, with nothing else for it and purely out of curiosity, Josh Googled "the hero's journey." In the process, quite by accident, he came across a line of poetry that stuck in his mind: *Take the journey, find your way home.* He had no idea why those words struck a chord, but there it was.

Letting that pass, he read a number of variations on the mythic odyssey. Creating a file, he earmarked seven common steps and replied as if he was taking a quiz:

1) *The ordinary world as a safe place.* Only in elementary school away from Zharko.

2) *The call to action for the sake of the community.* Never answered a call or belonged to a community. Never knew who my father was or what clan Zharko or my mother were affiliated with. Couldn't answer Ackerman about my heritage or what my mother was up to ever.

3) *The turning point—meeting a mentor to set you on the right path.* Never had a mentor unless you now count Ackerman who, at best, is a sorry substitute. Matter of fact, there's something ironic about a nerve-racked guy running away from the wilds of New York giving advice in the first place.

4) *Crossing the threshold into the unknown.* Have no idea.

5) *Tests, allies, and enemies, at least one major defeat.* Ditto.

6) *A great ordeal, putting everything on the line.* Can't imagine.

7) *Transformation into full selfhood.*

This last one really caught him off guard. It brought to mind a movie he once saw centering on a Lakota vision quest. All he could recall was a rite of passage by the time you're fourteen or so. You go alone into the wild, without food or water, with only a blanket and a sacred pipe, seeking strength and a strong spirit guide like a wolf or an eagle. When your spirit guide finally comes to you, you now have a new name. In this case, it was Standing Elk. In this case, the Lakota young man came down from the Black Hills as a brave who had grown up.

He mulled this all over and, after nothing seemed to directly apply to his present situation, got on the phone again.

"It's me. Anyway, just humor me, will you? I got on the Internet, read all about the seven phases."

"That's not the point, sitting on your butt, pondering over the whole roadmap."

"Okay. Then take the call to action."

"Exactly."

"I mean, how about coming down to earth and just considering some options. I mean something actually doable?"

"How about it? And while we're at it, how's my profile going? Are we on schedule or what? And speaking of making it doable, you got your little tape recorder handy? Add this and hype up the sales pitch to the have-a-good-day natives for my services. Got it? You ready?"

"Hold on."

Going along with him for whatever it was worth, Josh retrieved his digital recorder, scrolled to the current interview folder, hit the record button, and said, "It's recording. Shoot."

Ackerman began to carry on about a repressed Manhattan housewife who ironed her professor husband's shirts, went shopping at Saks Fifth Avenue dressed in the prim outfits he liked, cooked his favorite meals, took to drink, smoked over a pack a day, and got more and more depressed.

"She comes to me," Ackerman went on, "as a last resort, and we get right down to it. She quits ironing his shirts, shopping at Saks, cooking his favorite meals, smoking like a chimney, and guzzling martinis. Instead she goes to the gym, meets other women in the same boat, starts writing for a feminist newspaper in Greenwich Village, and tells her husband where to get off. This lady was my latest get-on-the-fast-track triumph."

Josh turned off the recorder, picked up the receiver, and said, "All right, cutting to the chase like you said. What if someone's out to get you?"

"It's the same thing. You get into gear. That's the freakin' call to action."

Hanging up on him, Ackerman left Josh still with nothing to go on while, at this very moment, his nemesis was doubtless out there, up to God knew what.

CHAPTER FIVE

A short while earlier, Zharko reached inside the hatch of the borrowed camper van for directions and cast his gaze across the lake. He caught sight of Vlad's hulking form seated on a bench by the water's edge, his shiny bald head thrust forward, his large hands tearing into a loaf of black bread. The arching wooden bridge behind him and the little island no more than a hundred yards in front formed an inlet, giving the ducks sunning themselves three options: stay put, slip into the water and wade toward Vlad and his breadcrumbs, or ignore the dark objects so unlike the ones they were used to and keep going under the bridge to see what else they could find. To Zharko's mind, Vlad was acting like an overgrown boy at play. As if Vlad was gentle instead of good for things like extortion—breaking legs if the seafood distributor on the New England coast hadn't paid up for protection.

But that was old news, as others besides him and Vlad had been caught on those waterways and deported. And Zharko had switched gears when the US government booted him out. Learned the ropes, as Yankees say, and other ways of dealing over there from Odessa to Kiev to Moldavia and whatever Russian racketeers could teach him. Or what else he could find or whatever came his way. How many visas, false green cards, or what have you to come up with for new operations in cahoots with the red syndicate? Never mind they were not his own crew in Connecticut. It is always what you have to do, new tricks of the trade or whatever works to be an outlaw like gypsy days of old. Not like his uncle

Groffo from the old country wanted of him: to assimilate, be like good Roma, get along with people everywhere like sheep.

Of course, Groffo did say old gypsy ways for some was in the blood. Running hot and cold, wild anger and smart thinking, figuring angles; free like the wind and pulling up short. Restless, always restless. And pride in keeping van with gypsy flag on the side hidden in the woods, returning to old stand in Connecticut, having van overhauled with rebuilt motor and what have you got. To hell with what other sell-out gypsies say who don't have the nerve, don't have the fire. Except he would stick out again like a sore thumb. Which is why he borrowed this camper and drove it down to play it smart right before big deal, using Sonny, who now is calling himself Josh, for cover. New scheme on waterways but with Zharko in charge this time—kingpin behind the scene running the cockamamie show.

Yes! But Vlad had not yet gotten it into his head. Why Zharko had his work cut out for him, to find Sonny and for sure pin him down so it was in the bag with strict guarantees. To strike fear into Sonny so he would make no bones about it after making Zharko go to all this trouble. Sonny would pay the price, which was only right after all these years.

Nodding once more, muttering "for sure" to himself, he went over to Vlad as the quacking lead duck left the tiny island followed by a half dozen more. Just as he reached Vlad's side, all the ducks were diving underneath the crusts of black bread, coming up for air and following the quacking duck under the footbridge out of sight.

In disgust, Vlad tossed the rest of the loaf past the waters' edge. *"Blin! Valyat duraka!"*

"English," Zharko said. "How many times I tell you? Speak only English so you keep practicing. So we get by. I speak only English even in my head, better and better like sharp citizen."

Vlad leaned back on the wooden bench, twisted his blocky head in Zharko's direction, and said, "Fine, yes. Finally you are back. So, you find him?"

"Close. I am getting close."

"Close is no good. Lost in this place I have never been is also no good. I am hungry again. Pretty soon afternoon sun is going down."

"Not lost I tell you," said Zharko, waving the map. "You want directions. You ask for directions. I show you directions all the damn way down to here."

Zharko cast his gaze all about even though there was no one around. Back at the parking lot there was still only a Jeep parked a distance away from the camper and a family of four: a mother and father and two little girls by the swing set and sand box making little noise. There was no problem on that score.

"Here," said Zharko, opening the map onto Vlad's lap, grabbing a stick lying in the grass and using it as a pointer. "Look. Only a month ago, we cross border from Canada into Vermont for last time, okay?"

"Last time? You swear? You promise? So many crossings. By train, by boat. Then Canada, United States, Canada, United States. Like gypsies of old but not our kind. Talk I do not understand. Always talk I do not understand."

"Enough of this. I tell you, enough! You are going to look and listen or not?"

Vlad hesitated. "Okay, I look, I listen."

Zharko gazed all around again to make doubly sure there were no new arrivals. Tanasi, Basili, Nitza, and all his own crew were scattered who knew where. Himself up to his neck in debt. Leaving him stuck with Vlad and who he could round up for a last-ditch chance, using Sonny, now Josh, as for sure perfect cover.

"This time," he said, "to hook up there was no border crossing, yes? We start in Waterbury near Connecticut hills, you see?

Waterbury is perfect. Waterbury I know. Dirty politics I hear about, gangsters I run into. Business start up, business go bust maybe overnight—moving and storage, garbage, junkyards, scrap metal, and what you got for supper. So, now we travel west and down Pennsylvania into South. On speedometer, borrowed camper is telling us it is first two hundred, then four hundred, six hundred miles. Okay?"

"From Waterbury?"

"We go west again into Blue Ridge Mountains we have never seen. Total eight hundred and more miles."

"But later? When trucks ready to roll? Why we travel so far out of way again? Why not straight down on coast to Florida Keys?"

"To throw off feds. To shift pipeline away from east coast, from Waterbury to Asheville. Place no one would guess, never in hundred years. Pick up Sonny now who change his name is killing two birds with one stone like they are saying. And soon, very soon, make run from Waterbury, then stop, then down to Keys way south in Florida. Okay? Is brilliant! Thinking, I am thinking all the time."

Slapping the map hard again with the stick, Zharko said, "And here we are, so near to cousin five times removed or so we say even though not true. So near to front we need. So near to clincher to come back to for midnight run."

"But still, how you know this is not wild goose chase?"

"How I know? How I know? How I know he changes name to Josh Bartlet? How I keep track he is still with no spine and well-behaved according to Suwannee School in Tennessee, college in Virginia, last paper he writes features for before this one whose boss tells me? And now, under gun, with clock ticking away, with promissory note, what you think will happen?"

Not giving Vlad time to mull this one over, Zharko nailed it down. "I tell you what is going to happen. We are now, for sure, so close, I can feel in my bones. Any minute, any hour before sun is setting, I say it will happen. We connect, I check with Ivan in Asheville—pretty smart detour way out of way to Asheville to throw off feds like I say, yes? To make snatching Sonny two birds with one stone for sure, yes? Lock in Sonny and get show cracking."

"And I will eat."

"You will eat and there will be only business set in stone."

Vlad stared at the map, then the calm lake water. "No more cold in old country or northeast states like you promise. No more winter. Islands past Florida tip, you said. Fishing and I can get sailboat."

"If you leave to me and stop all the time wanting to know. You are what you are needed as muscle for whatever is coming down the pike. You read me, damn it, finally?"

"If I see payoff signs. Real payoff signs is good."

Zharko tossed the stick away, patted Vlad's broad back and said, "Real payoff signs is beautiful. Like ducks in a row."

"Like what I see with my eyes. Not maps. Not words."

"For sure, Vlad. Is for sure."

—··—

Soon after, however, Zharko still found himself getting nowhere. Plus having to put up with impatient looks Vlad was giving him along with more mentions of hunger. Zharko himself was impatient and hungry. Studying the local map he'd gotten from visitor center, he guessed Sonny must be through with business at retirement place. His new name was not listed in phone book, meaning he must be renting. No apartments and tight market, real estate people told him, leaves a house he must be living at. A small house because no one outside of doctors, lawyers, or what have you got for supper could afford big house to rent or buy in this special mountain town. He found these things out from a place at the corner of business section as season for tourists was starting up again. Lady broker in fancy clothes was telling him there was remote chance (remote—another word he must remember) for guest cottage or seasonal rental off Lake Eden Road or scatterings on Blue Ridge Road, "which in itself was relatively hard to come by" this lady said, making Zharko as restless now as Vlad waiting in the van.

The other thing the lady broker gave out was that the Lake Eden area was "sparsely settled" once you get past the high school.

And so Zharko opted for seasonal rental cottage on Blue Ridge Road first.

Back in the van, with Vlad continuing to stare at him, Zharko cursed and racked his brains until he came up with a plan. He would not go knocking on doors being conspicuous or what you call it. He would go to one place where people all the time come in and out on Blue Ridge Road to get himself a lead. Plan B, as they call it, would find some place much the same on Lake Eden Road, if odds were paying off for him.

CHAPTER SIX

At a garage between a stretch of Blue Ridge Road, a red-bearded mechanic in overalls was giving Zharko a hard time. While Vlad waited in the passenger seat of the borrowed camper, the mechanic eyed Zharko and Vlad like they were suspicious characters. Then he ducked under the hood of a parked beat-up Chevy blocking the first bay and came up again with a paper towel dripping with dirty oil.

"Look at this, will you?" Redbeard said. "Plugs so filled with oil they dripped into the cylinders. Now I gotta put the old plugs back in and run the motor till the gray smoke fades outta the tail pipe, making what should've been an easy swap of plugs into a dang waste of time. Plus, now the likes of you coming along and asking fool questions as if I had nothing else to do."

"Forgive please," said Zharko as Redbeard retreated, ratcheted the old plugs back in, slipped behind the wheel, cranked the motor, marched straight back by Zharko's side and eyed the sputtering gray smoke.

"Forgive please," Zharko said once more, raising his voice. "But I show you byline from *Black Mountain News*, yes? I am only wanting to locate cousin five times removed from Connecticut hills. To locate him for quick reunion and big surprise. A lady broker tell me is a good bet he rents house on this Blue Ridge Road."

"Look, fella, I don't know where you and your pal here are from or what you're up to. If the gal at the paper didn't want to give out his whereabouts, the realty lady brushes you off except to mention this here road, then I don't cotton to furnishing information or directions to two fishy looking characters—information I ain't saying I even got. So why would anybody give you the time of day?"

"Smart question. But naturally I want just a little bit to know. Will settle for small lead to long-lost relative with proposition this cousin very much needs to hear."

Redbeard went back to the Chevy, killed the motor, and shouted back, "What is it you don't understand about the word 'no'? Is it the N or the O? If I was you, I'd get in that lame camper of yours and go back to the dang drawing board." He stuck his head under the hood again.

Zharko hesitated, clenching his fists. Looking around, he spotted a tire iron on top of a rusty dumpster, rushed over, grabbed it, and was about to hurl it at a tool cart by the Chevy's exhaust pipe when the blare of a horn stopped him. Redbeard sprang up, Vlad hit the horn again, and Zharko let the tire iron drop onto the pitted driveway.

Hurrying back to the camper, Zharko gunned the motor and, with the tires squealing, doubled back to the railroad crossing, crossed over the main drag as the light switched from amber to red, the camper's rear end barely avoiding a delivery truck barreling west across the intersection. Still cursing, ignoring Vlad's grunts and head shakes, Zharko made a sharp left onto old 70 and kept speeding twenty miles over the limit, pulled into a clearing next to a quarry, and killed the motor.

Despite Vlad's grumbling, which really got on his nerves, he got out, marched over, reached inside the box by the rear door, pulled out the paperback book of synonyms, a ballpoint pen, and an index card. Evidently, it was not good to be outsider in this southland like hunky-dory Waterbury, Connecticut, below sleepy Litchfield. Waterbury, with melting pot from old country, from Eastern Europe full of Poles, Lithuanians, Bulgarians, Russians, or what else you got, where Zharko could operate undercover with shady businesses opening up and closing down and not be damn outcast like here, for few days till operation is off and running.

But then again, Zharko had to keep reminding himself they had caught up to him and had him thrown out. Because he had no Plan B, like they call it. And even now he made assumptions because he was close to Asheville where people are wild and crazy but not close enough and damn people here in Black Mountain giving him much grief.

Getting hold of himself, he studied the dog-eared synonym book for choice words to get by suspicions, to make Josh who was Sonny seem like an all-American boy like he always came across. Like a pretend cousin five times removed who would appreciate being reunited (reunited, perfect word) in mind of those who read this notice. After many stabs at it, Zharko had a perfect calling card he could pass around and finally connect:

Please help find long-lost cousin
Writer. Nice, slim, fair-haired, and polite
Lives in modest house, keeps to himself,
Connecticut Yankee Reunion is most necessary.

To be doubly certain, in case Sonny tried to weasel out, he whipped out his cell phone and hit the speed dial for the Asheville warehouse. For past few days he liked talking to Ivan, a Russian with perfect American speech Zharko could try to match. A deep voice who spoke only few words like spies in old Cold War Zharko had heard about.

"One more thing," said Zharko the moment Ivan picked up. "Like I am telling you, I need assurance that front I must have leaves town and takes plane, on schedule, for sure."

"You got his address?"

"I will have it."

There was a long pause until Ivan said, "What is this? You pinned him down or not?"

"Almost there, I swear, my hand to God."

Another long pause before Ivan replied, "And I am definitely in on the pipeline?"

"When shipment is ready, all systems go, you get green light. You are on board."

"Exact same timetable?"

"Even sooner maybe, if I am having my way."

"And this front is clean, no link to the feds?"

"Can pass for pure white Anglo or what you call it. Is in my pocket, on ice as they say since way back."

"Uh-huh."

Ivan hung up on him, like on TV when police are trying to trace the call but need more time.

Zharko glanced again at the calling card he'd made, nodded, and told himself the chances were good somewhere this close by Lake Eden Road Sonny was working on just-finished meeting notes. Some place or people could give Zharko good notions where work place for writer's little house could be.

But, as the afternoon wore on, driving the whole stretch of Lake Eden Road provided no payoff. Huge pine trees stood on both sides of road, only giving way to tiny lanes here and there, left and right until the road ran out and he reached a wooden sign. The sign led onto a crossing with giant shade trees on both sides of a lake ending in a narrow structure on stilts. After crossing over, Zharko got out and walked around the corrugated steel building but found no one around. Getting back behind the wheel, ignoring Vlad's grumbling, Zharko turned around and told Vlad to keep an eye out for anything going on, anybody Zharko could show his calling card to ask where a small rental cottage could be.

Doubling back past the lake, hoping to at least meet a single car coming toward him on the cramped road as glints of fading sunlight flashed through the stands of trees into his eyes, Vlad suddenly sat up straight in the passenger seat and yelled, "Stop, back up! I see one more wooden sign!"

Putting the gear in reverse, Zharko braked, turned into a dirt track, noted the sign that read *Community School*, circled around, and pulled into a parking space by a rustic building. What caught Zharko's eye was not the auditorium marker but a lineup of girls, ages maybe ten to thirteen, very disciplined. Not like boys who had trouble holding still but also friendly before getting shy or silly or whatever gets into them over thirteen years. Good-behaved girl, friendly like girls in southland are supposed to be, not like Redbeard and white trash, was a good bet.

Zharko waited and watched as the girls peeked at his calling card and passed it on. Only the bouncy, blonde-headed girl at the top of the steps peeking through the auditorium door held onto the card—perhaps one chosen to signal others as a girl inside singing very loud was through with her number. Perhaps the blonde girl was to call "places" or whatever.

While Zharko hung on at the foot of the stairs, the bouncy blonde girl whispered, "Almost, almost" to the others, glanced at the card once more, looked down at Zharko, and passed the word: "If the man in jeans could hold on for a minute, she might be able to help, right after their dance, right before the moms pull in to pick us up."

The little girl close to the bottom step handed Zharko back his calling card and said, "That's Amanda at the head of the line. She's super friendly. We elected her dance captain."

Zharko didn't know what to say, looked up, and caught Amanda's eye as all girls followed Amanda's lead and scurried off past the thick open door. He glanced at his watch and waited through the sounds of scuffing feet on a wooden-plank floor and a piano keeping time. Counting on the tune being short for little girls, with no corrections from the piano player, with no stop-and-go.

Soon enough, cars began pulling in and parking to the left and right of the camper. He caught sight of Vlad slouching down in the passenger seat, taking no chances a mother would tap on his window and ask what he and the stranger waiting by the steps were doing here.

Shortly after, girls began running past him, hurrying toward awaiting cars. Amanda hurried by him as well, waved at a white station wagon, and turned back.

"You really Mister Josh's cousin? How cool."

"You tell me his hideaway please for big surprise? A small house, I bet you."

Ignoring the beeping horn, Amanda said, "If you tell him to come see me a week from this Saturday. I just found out I've got a solo. A showstopper."

Amanda spun around a few times for emphasis, arms open wide.

"Yes, yes, I promise for sure," said Zharko, worried that the mother would pull Amanda away before she gave him directions, once again remembering the way that local garage mechanic had treated him.

Spinning back in his direction, Amanda said, "How did you know it was a small house hidden away? Out of only two houses on our lane and—"

Zharko placed a finger between his lips, trying to shush her.

"Oh, I get it, big surprise, right." With the horn beeping away, Amanda added, "See ya."

About to lose it altogether, Zharko yelled, "Name of lane is all I need!"

"Gotcha!" Amanda yelled back. "Magnolia," she said, half

whispering. "Make a right, don't blink or you'll miss it. Mum's the word. I'll tell Mom you were lost and I was being the good Samaritan."

Zharko waited until everyone was out of sight. As the afternoon sunlight drifted lower, filtering through the pines, he drove carefully out of the school grounds. Telling Vlad to look carefully, it took only a minute until Vlad said, "There, green sign hidden by bushes."

He braked and waited a short while longer, making sure there were no cars on the narrow lane road who might catch him turning where he didn't belong, and also giving Amanda and mother enough time to get settled and not look out for the camper.

Despite Vlad's poking and prodding, he took his time easing down the dirt track, making only the soft sound of crunching gravel. Happy when spotting little house hidden back in the woods, like Sonny's mother Irina's cabin across from the killing long ago. Like Zharko planned it this way. Getting hold of not-Romany, polite, good-behaved boy with no stomach for taking care of business deep in woods or whatever crops up and makes blood run hot.

CHAPTER SEVEN

For a moment, the whirring sound of the blender obliterated all of Josh's concerns.

Without warning, Zharko and Vlad burst into his kitchen and drove Josh all the way back until he was hemmed in between the sink and the cabinets. Before he knew what was happening, they took over and made themselves at home while Josh was too shaken to respond.

As things progressed, Vlad pounded his massive fists on a floured piece of cube stake on the counter. In turn, Zharko whipped out his folding hunting knife with the glistening six-inch blade and was busy peeling, chopping, and coring apples and pears on the Formica side panel to Josh's right while he remained frozen, seated behind the kitchen table. Vlad had already fried up a plate of scrambled eggs, bacon, onions, tomato, and potato slices, and Zharko had guzzled a bottle of chardonnay and crushed a half dozen walnuts for a Waldorf salad. Mugs of hot tea simmered by the kettle, and Josh had yet to respond.

"No worries, I tell you," Zharko said, slicing and dicing some more in a half-teasing, half-menacing way, as if backing Josh into the corner was only a prelude. "Is all going to work out. Amanda is such nice, friendly girl making sure we don't get lost. And she also want to make sure you come see her dance week from Saturday. Can you believe? Exactly when you will be back in harness for me if you play cards right."

"Meaning what?" Josh said, finally speaking, raising his voice a tad over the sizzle of the steak frying in the pan behind him.

"Meaning like wages of sin, or what you call it, has come due. Promissory note, payment in kind for services rendered. IOU from you."

"By way of what we can use," said Vlad close by, struggling to slice the strip of steak with one of Josh's kitchen knives. "By way of hard roads, hard winters, dirty business, no rest, bad food. By way of up and down territories across ocean, down from Canada, in and out like running dogs."

"Quiet," Zharko said. "What I tell you?"

"What I tell *you*, Zharko. No more circles, no more chases. Through red-syndicate ways we have learned, goods arrive at Florida Keys, I wash my hands, get my boat."

"Enough, damn you, enough!" Covering up, Zharko brushed by Josh, flashing his knife for Josh's benefit. "Here, Vlad, try Hoffritz blade, highest standard, sharp as razor."

With a newfound glint in his eyes, Zharko said, "Watch. Folding hunting knife for cutting or self-protection, you see?" For emphasis, Zharko deftly sliced a pear in half, peeled it, tossed the skin in a waste basket, folded the blade, and touched a trigger mechanism that shot the blade open again like a street fighter's switchblade. "Beautiful, yes? You must agree."

Flinching despite himself, Josh tried to change the subject, or maybe reason with Zharko. But Zharko immediately noticed his involuntary shudder.

"You see, Vlad?" Zharko said, handing him the knife. "Like insurance, like money in bank. He still shakes, still remembers from old days. He would not like playing hide-and-seek again. Would not like my blade finding him if he welches on old, which now comes due, IOU."

Unable to take it any longer, Josh blurted out, "Tell me. What are you talking about? What do you mean, an old IOU?"

Taking his sweet time, Zharko retrieved the knife and

returned to the stand by Josh's right side. Deftly, he closed the blade, slipped his knife into a leather sheath by his hip, and reached into an inside pocket of his Levi jacket. He unfolded a thin sheet of paper and slapped it on the table.

Josh studied the old dated promissory note as Zharko seated himself and dug into his salad and Vlad continued to work on his steak behind and to the opposite side, chewing away while slurping on a mug of hot tea. There were two dates, different terms, and goods and services noted in lieu of interest held in perpetuity until an undisclosed future time. All told, it was unsecured and high risk in terms of whoever took this set of signature loans on. With his mind whirling, he recalled getting shipped off to the prep school in the Cumberland region of Tennessee right after the knifing in the woods and altercation with his mother over Molly and the Christmas present. If memory served, there was something about her claim she was taking out a loan to get him far away for his own good.

The reason for his own signature was more convoluted. He vaguely recalled his mother saying she was deep in debt . . . or had to fix up some property, run-down tenements in Torrington whose furnaces were defective, insulation wasn't up to code or some such thing. He was on scholarship and a work-study program finishing up his degree in Virginia. It was during a winter break; there was a snowstorm brewing and he had to take off and get back to school in time. His mother kept harping on the notion she was only buying time, and when had she ever asked anything of him? There were twinges of guilt on his part, the same old wish someday his mother would start to care about him, and the need to get out of there because who knew where Zharko might be lurking? But there was never any mention of the prospect of the promissory note being handed off to Zharko to be used some rainy day or whenever the whim struck him. Nothing of the sort.

"So, you eventually got hold of this," Josh finally replied. "Or were in cahoots with my mother all along and always have been."

"Watch your mouth," Zharko said. "You think we got time for this? After trouble I go to to find and nail you down? But all part of brilliant scheme comes to me when I find out where you live. So close to Asheville in Carolina, which makes perfect stopover nobody thinks to look. Where Ivan has old warehouse and wonderful junction. Killing two birds with one stone, yes, but causing long drive to first dig you up. So we are on tight schedule with window of one more day and drive back to same factory town of Waterbury you know too well. But couldn't be helped and in long run is goddamn all working out."

As if on cue, Vlad pulled up a chair to Josh's left and plunked down his mug of tea, wiping his mouth with his shirt sleeves. "Yes, pipeline to Asheville to fool feds but too much aggravation till payoff."

Vlad leaned in but caught the pained look on Zharko's face, backed off, and said, "You will obey. Or tell him what happens."

"No need," said Zharko. "Bright college boy can imagine what happens to mother Irina and maybe girl he is still sweet on, Irina says. Bright, good-boy Sonny who changes name to Josh. So, okay, Josh it will be. Josh Bartlet name is perfect for final big score to make us whole for long, long time."

"Is funny, no?" said Zharko, switching gears. "He is in hiding, I am in hiding. To find him, you look for newspapers in little towns close to where he goes to school but not too far to go see Irina and girl. Oh yes, Irina tells me you still in touch. To track girl down, I have no time but have ways. To track me down, someone look to Waterbury for sure but not to old haunts like Hungarian restaurants and what feds know about. Plus you never look to Josh Bartlet running show as front. So my front good-boy-Josh only need schedule, which he will find inside business briefcase in short order."

"But—" Josh muttered.

"Cell phone number you will hand me on business card now."

Too distraught to argue, Josh handed him a press card from the *Black Mountain News*.

Placing it inside his pocket, Zharko went on. "Good. So far is good. Bright good boy who is reasonable must only hand in work he does so far for little town newspaper. At same time, he asks boss for leave of absence for two weeks, giving excuse he makes up why he must hurry back to Connecticut. Airplane tickets business class will be in mailbox tomorrow, Tuesday, for early Wednesday flight to Hartford. Which leaves time to rent car to Litchfield Hills where good boy stays at inn with other WASP businessmen while set for playing perfect front down in brand new Waterbury Transfer and Trucking very next day. Here you go, see? Connecticut schedule and map also all set."

Without missing a beat, Zharko reached inside his Levi jacket again, waved a folded list and handmade map of downtown Waterbury, gave Josh an instant to glance at the two items and, as quickly, jammed them back in his jacket.

"But how we know?" said Vlad, rising up. "How we tell for sure?"

True to form, Zharko's high cheekbones began to twitch as he rose up and started pacing, switching gears yet again, punctuating his argument with his bony forefinger. "How many times, Vlad? How we know? How we tell? Because he behaves! Behaves is all he knows. Give him threats, behaves is all he could know. Since very beginning, since everywhere you look, everyone you ask. He goes here, there, but always sends Irina birthday cards, New Year's card to keep in touch. Cards signed Sonny but with return address of Josh, Black Mountain last two times. Right now he behaves, you see? Is money in bank. Is cinch he washes plates and pans clean while he cannot refuse."

"But maybe—?"

"Is done! What you want from my life? We camp by lake, get rest, and check things out first thing. Did Ivan get airplane ticket? Will he put ticket in mailbox here in good time? We are on the road Thursday morning, start of whole new show is on the road. So, back off finally, yes? Sonny, now Josh, need time to digest and do what he is told!"

That said, Zharko looked Josh in the eye, pointed a finger, lingered for a moment, and prodded Vlad out the door. It took practically no time for the sound of the camper's engine to rev up and tail off, leaving a palpable stillness.

For a second, Josh thought of calling the police. But that had as much validity as a twenty-year-old memory of a scream and glimpse of a flashing blade in the frozen woods. That very same unfinished business that had always been hanging over him. Zharko doubtless footed the tuition bill at the prep school to get him, an eyewitness, far away. Zharko later must have gotten Irina to con Sonny into cosigning the promissory note as an insurance policy and future leverage. The past is never past. It was all one never-ending IOU.

At this point he could have thrown in the towel, accepted his fate, and busied himself cleaning up the mess in the kitchen as Zharko's well-behaved foil. Instead, out of force of habit, he got out his pocket-sized digital recorder and shifted to a new folder. Habitually, he would note the holes in a subject's story—dates, places, motives that may have led to certain turning points in their lives. In this case, there were countless holes but there were also a few leads.

He hit the record button and muttered, "Red Syndicate . . . pipeline from Waterbury Transfer and Storage . . . fake trucking business shifting west to Asheville with Ivan as the contact . . . proceeding all the way down to the Florida Keys."

Unable to go on, he shut off the recorder and gave in to that same chill running up his spine. It was payback for unwitting sins of omission that, as Zharko put it, had finally come due.

In the stillness, all that was certain was that his dream path back to Molly was all but untenable and his dangling days were done.

CHAPTER EIGHT

J osh spent the rest of that Monday evening cranking out the piece on Ackerman with no inkling how to pursue that elusive call to action. Still knowing full well if he acted true to form, he'd be looking for some way out.

Halfheartedly, he posted a hastily contrived piece on Ackerman to Paul, his editor, leaving out Ackerman's desire for a personal plug raving about his speedy solutions. He edited the photos he'd taken with the mountain ridges in the background and emailed six of the stills along with the essay to complete the assignment. He dozed off for a couple of hours, thankful only that there were no dreams.

The next morning, he got up and made himself a meager breakfast he had no interest in and attempted to still his growing anxiety in a number of hopeless ways. By nine o'clock, he was so stumped he couldn't help snatching up his cell phone and speed-dialing Ackerman one last time.

It wasn't until the third ring that Ackerman picked up, out of breath and definitely in a hurry. "Don't tell me they're moving my glowing profile up a week."

"No, nothing like that. But I still need something tangible, some guideline to see me through when all else fails. Needless to say, the hero's journey is way too mythical."

"We covered that. You're still confusing the roadmap with getting out the door and taking the goddamn trip."

"But—"

"Look," Ackerman said, "as it happens, time has run out and

I've got to get a temporary license otherwise I'm stuck here. The choice is, the hassle and traffic from here to Asheville and the end of Patton Avenue or the crazy mountain passes east to some backwater called Marion. If I take off now, there'll be no wait, but I'll have to take a vision test. But I can't pass a vision test if I can't find my stupid glasses!"

This outburst was followed by the sound of drawers opening and slamming shut leading to a shout of "Aha!" and the padding of returning footsteps. "Got it," Ackerman said. "You see? Even dealing with inanimate objects can be a hassle. Everything is a task in this life. Always a contest, a battle. The key is having enough tools, enough ways and means to cope with the constant frustration. Whatever's handy, you use it."

"Fine. But what if you're completely in over your head? What does the action directive do for you?"

"Do me a favor, will you? Do us both a favor. Everything's getting on my nerves today. So from now on, save us both a lot of time and energy and get your advice from Teddy Roosevelt. You in your way, me in mine. For my part, I'll just hang on a bit, wait for the next edition of your paper, and take the town by storm."

"Teddy Roosevelt?"

"You heard me. The twenty-sixth president."

"I know, I know, but what does that have to do with anything?"

"Teddy nails it plain and simple. Speedy, remember? So get off it, check it out, and cut the freakin' tap dance." With that tag line, Ackerman broke the connection.

More put off by Ackerman's nervy tone than ever, Josh poured himself another cup of coffee and came to the same dead end.

With nothing to lose, he got on the Internet, Googled Teddy Roosevelt quotes, skimmed through them all, and came up with the kicker. Then watered it down to something concise he could keep in mind:

The credit belongs to the person who is in the arena. Who strives and errs and comes up short again and again. A person who, if he fails, at least fails while daring greatly. His place shall never be with those timid souls who neither know victory nor defeat.

Then and there, it was painfully obvious that Zharko had always discounted timid-soul Sonny. After doing background checks in tracking him down, it was readily apparent that Sonny, now posing as Josh, hadn't changed one bit. He'd made no fuss as a bystander at the killing; made no fuss after they shipped him off to the prep school in the Tennessee boonies. He'd even made no fuss as Irina got him to cosign the promissory note. All told, Josh had systematically sold out and made do with hiding out and biding his time.

Therefore, as far as he knew, even Teddy Roosevelt's simple dictum was beyond him, much less putting up any resistance to Zharko's instructions.

And so he moved on to face his editor. He recalled Southern ladies in these parts could frequently be heard telling their children, "Now don't you go making a scene, you hear? Y'all need to be well behaved. Plain and simple."

But at this moment nothing at all was plain and simple. And that was the only glimmer of hope. Teddy Roosevelt seemed to be asking how much agency do any of us have under pressure? Once we take it on, once we've entered the arena, what are we actually capable of?

—··—

Like himself, Josh's editor Paul could be counted on to act consistently. A slight little guy, fortyish, balding with a grayish brush of a goatee affixed to his receding chin. More often than not peering over his bifocals, busying himself with last-minute decisions over the layout prominently displayed on his desk. That image certainly applied every Friday around five right before they both sauntered over to the Trailhead eatery around the corner. Taking his fallback position, Josh would humor Paul, listening to his tales as an investigative reporter back east before his paper went digital and had no more need for the luxury of newshounds. As a result, Paul wound up on this "homey, small-town beat" and, according to the powers that be, should consider himself lucky even though he'd much rather be tracking some dicey breaking story on the urban streets.

But this was Tuesday, not Friday, close to high noon. Papers were strewn all over Paul's desk, and Josh's interruption of his routine, let alone the anxious way Josh was standing there trying to get Paul's attention, only added to the tension.

Paul finally glanced up, stopped editing a printout which, in fact, turned out to be Josh's profile of Ackerman, and handed it back. "Well," said Paul, "as long as you've dropped in, this part about a New York professor's wife who found her true self by ditching her husband isn't going to fly in these parts. As if you didn't know. You'll have to change it. Say she gently spoke up and the couple came to an amicable understanding—something along those lines. Something a lot more down-home and easy to swallow."

"But that's not what happened and that's not Ackerman's style."

"What does that have to do with anything? Our readers want to be reassured, not agitated. We've got flocks of churchgoers here as you well know. Folks who believe in the sanctity of marriage."

"Except that's the crux of Ackerman's method. Helping everyone bust loose."

"Not on my watch. Not here."

"Okay, then you change it," Josh said. "It's your call." He was trying to be agreeable, trying to get along as usual, but had no idea how he was going to wangle a sudden leave of absence without getting into a hassle.

"Come again?" Paul said, obviously taken aback.

"Look, I don't know how to broach this, but something just came up. I've got to go back to Connecticut."

"All of a sudden?"

"Yes. Out of the blue."

Paul leaned back in his swivel chair and fell silent. Josh was obviously in for it. Paul had a keen sense of order and would brook no hedging or impracticality. Which, as far as Josh could tell, was why Paul flittered from one relationship to another, opting for a quick fix while the lady in question wanted a bit of understanding. Time after time, Paul would complain about feminine wiles and whims while Josh nodded, knowing full well Molly wasn't like that but playing the perfect listener to keep things amenable.

Predictably, Paul was taken aback by this glitch in the scheme of things, cut through the silence, and said, "Okay, okay, let's have it." At the same time, he reached for a thick rubber band and began twirling it around his fingers. "What is going on?"

"I'm not exactly sure, which is the whole point. You could say the upshot is that it's all a mystery."

"Come on, come on. Let's have it, Josh. Someone sick, had an accident, might have to go into a nursing home? That girl Molly you mentioned, is she in trouble?"

"No, as far as I know she's fine. I do need to have it out with my mother, and probably her lawyer if it comes to that. It's a matter of an old IOU. But even that's not the half of it. I really can't go into it."

"Terrific." Indicating his growing impatience, Paul snapped the rubber band, stretching it in and out of his fingers and releasing it. "Will you quit wasting my time and give it to me straight?"

"I can't, I tell you. I'm in a rush and have to get organized as long as the plane tickets are in my mailbox. But, then again, if they're not . . ."

Paul discarded the rubber band and stood up. "Good grief, what has gotten into you? You never get rattled. You sit back, take things in stride. You certainly are never hell-bent. Which is why I hired you in the first place. Mild-mannered, duly vetted and corroborated by every paper you've worked for."

"That's me, yes sir. Look, I'm only asking for two weeks. Maybe less. If I get through it somehow, I'll be right back."

"Terrific." Paul yanked open a file cabinet and came up with a bunch of stuffed manila envelopes. "You see these? Resumés. Every week I receive at least a dozen from college grads, hacks, longtime reporters who've been laid off because their paper was gobbled up by some conglomerate. There's no patience for a developing story, so the pile of resumés keep mounting."

"Unless," Josh blurted out, having no clue where he was going with this.

"Unless what?"

"They happen to get the whole juicy escapade in a nutshell."

"What are you talking about?"

Leaning over Paul's desk, too far in to back out now, Josh said, "Tell you what. Cover for me, fill in, hire a temp or an apprentice who wants to learn the ropes."

"Now why would I do that? Why won't I just fire you on the spot?"

"Organized crime, that's what. If I were onto something while I was up there attending to personal business. If I were privy to some dicey information. Initiated, as it happens, by a slip of the tongue from a Russian henchman who is an illegal alien. And so, of course, is his boss."

"Get off it. How in God's name could you be privy to or mixed up in anything?"

"Because it happens to be right in my face. Some kind of Russian Mafia connection, setting up an outpost in Waterbury, thirty-five minutes south of where I started from. I'm talking about a pipeline that veers off to a major junction in Asheville and on from there."

Catching a glimpse of the wary look Paul was giving him, Josh stopped himself and pulled back.

Paul grabbed the rubber band, put it back, waited for the longest time, and said, "Are you serious?"

"As it happens . . . more or less."

"This sounds a lot like one of those old, tired movies you're telling me about all the time."

"I know, I realize that." Josh glanced at his watch. "Then how about this?" he said, winging it again. "You take a temporary flyer on me even though it's a shot in the dark. If it pans out, you're in on it. The kind of stuff corporate in Asheville would jump at, especially if it went national. You'd have the Asheville connection. All I'm saying is, just think about it."

"Whoa," said Paul. "What do you take me for, some wide-eyed, wet-behind-the-ears newbie who, for some ungodly reason, will buy anything you can fabricate?"

"Never. Not at all, I swear."

Josh tried to come up with something more plausible. Though he'd barely glanced at Zharko's assignment and map, his part seemed to amount to no more than manning an office, acting as a front at some warehouse. And, by some stretch of the imagination, having an opportunity to catch Zharko in the act.

Off the top of his head, Josh came up with, "Let's do it this way. I wing it. It's Tuesday. By Friday, at the time you put the paper to bed and we usually saunter over to the Trailhead while you ply me with the good ol' days back in Baltimore. By then, I should have latched onto a lead or, failing that, have zilch to report beyond having it out with my mother."

"Zilch to report besides some fantasy subterfuge about a connection with infiltrating Russian Mafia. Nothing besides a load of bull brought upon by what's really going on in your heretofore placid life."

"Nevertheless, I call you by then and possibly feed you an irresistible lead. We keep going this way until it soon pays off in Asheville. If I don't call or you're not satisfied, all bets are off and I lose my job. All right? Okay?"

Paul sat still a while longer. Then he told Josh to go to the waiting room while he made a couple of calls. Paul drifted off. In turn, Josh dutifully made his way to the foyer.

In the meantime, Crystal, the pixie-like receptionist in pigtails wearing her signature bib overalls, came by the foyer with a cup of strong coffee. She also plied him with some of her little homilies, like "Whatever happens, Josh, it's all for the best" and "All in good time, Josh, all in good time." Then she left. Minutes later, she came back, retrieved the empty coffee cup and, as always, wished him a blessed day. Minutes after that, Paul returned.

"Against my better judgement, here's the deal."

Josh sat up straight, noting the effects of the coffee, which made him feel even more wired.

"I did happen to get hold of a stringer at the daily in Asheville," Paul said, sounding as businesslike as possible. "He's set to fill in for the next few days. Even if you do call me on Friday, I have no illusions whether what you've got going, except for some legal hassle up north, is remotely worth listening to. I can buy the fact that you may have overheard something lately or something's happened that's upset you. But that's surely as far as it goes."

"The deal, Paul, give me the deal."

"You resolve this thing with your mother. Then, calling your bluff, you provide me with the exact nature of this gonzo escapade, the precise why, where, when, and how. Plus a federal law enforcement officer, or at least a credible source, who can verify this information, including the pipeline to Asheville, including an imminent timeline."

"Oh, come on, Paul."

"Do I have to remind you I have to answer to the executive publisher in Asheville? That you can't play me? That this hometown paper is only a weekly and everything has to be strictly above board?"

Paul started to whisk back to his office, hesitated, and peered back over his bifocals. "As I said, the possibility of you being in any kind of jeopardy or even close to it has got to be bogus. But if you don't come to your senses, if you insist on pushing it, I will miss those one-way chats at the Trailhead. Guys like you who actually listen are hard to come by. On the other hand, I hate being jerked around."

Thrown for a second, Josh came right back with, "Don't sell me short, Paul. You just never know."

Paul may have heard him but there was no way to tell as he returned to his office as if the matter was closed.

Josh left the premises and took his time driving back to his rental off Lake Eden Road, secretly hoping there was no one-way plane ticket waiting in his mailbox. Some part of him would be more than willing to crawl back to Paul and tell him it was all a misunderstanding, asking for his forgiveness. His stint with organized crime had been called off, never existed actually. Nothing was hanging over his head.

But the plane tickets—a hop to Charlotte and then on to Connecticut—were waiting in his mailbox. Underscoring the

unfinished business that for twenty years had been waiting
patiently for this moment.

CHAPTER NINE

Unable to stall any longer, Josh busied himself with preparations the rest of the afternoon. Aware that Zharko and Vlad or someone named Ivan or all three were out there keeping tabs on him until he boarded the connecting flight from Asheville, he forced himself to keep at it. He attended to a bunch of tasks like withdrawing an ample amount of cash at his bank's ATM machine, booking a cab to take him to the regional airport first thing the next morning, dealing with the trash pickup, cancelling his mail service at the post office for the next two weeks, paying his bills online for the same period of time, and ordering a takeout to be delivered for an early supper.

At around three thirty, he braced himself to call Molly from his new cell phone outside the Dynamite Coffee House a few miles west of town. In his hurry to transfer his contacts, he'd listed her simply as M and hoped the number was still good. She'd changed it a few times, and it had been a little while since they'd been in touch. He figured she'd be home from tending to her second graders by now, but he had to calm down and decide what to tell her. The anxious gear he'd shifted into was the opposite of the one Molly was used to, the one he'd adapted after having convinced himself Zharko was out of his life. But now his pulse was racing and he had no idea how to play it.

He slowed his breathing as best he could and decided on a message that was brief, open-ended, and short on details. And he certainly didn't want to hear any more about her fielding proposals from the assistant principal. If nothing else, he needed her to be free and clear while he grappled with this mess. And he certainly didn't want to appear to have relapsed back to the same old Josh: distracted, flippant, often feckless, and adrift.

She picked up after only three rings. Skipping any small talk or explanations, he played the standard I've-only-got-a-minute card.

"Hi, Molly, listen," Josh started. "Something's come up and I've got to fly back to Connecticut tomorrow."

"Really? Something happen to your mother?"

"No, but that's part of it."

"I don't understand. Part of what?"

"Can't talk now. I'm in kind of a rush. Got to finish making arrangements. But if things work out—legal stuff, Waterbury, some old business hanging over me—I'll be staying at the Litchfield Inn and have a window of a week more or less."

"Josh, will you slow down? I can't begin to follow you."

"I know, I realize that. But, though it's a long shot, maybe there's an outside chance for some closure. By some miracle, maybe even get back on track."

He knew he was babbling, tossing out the first thing that came to his mind, but he couldn't help himself. A few more sputtering exchanges and he finally came out with, "Just bear with me, okay, and leave everything open, and I mean everything. Tell me you're okay and we'll touch base around this time tomorrow."

"This is weird, Josh."

"But you're okay, right?"

"Yes, but why can't you talk to me?"

"I'll do better when I see you. Promise."

He took the long silence as an indication she may have given him the benefit of the doubt or at least didn't summarily brush him off. He ended the call offering to somehow make things up to her, half wondering why she ever put up with all his vacillating in the first place. She provided him with an "I guess" as they both got off the line.

He hastily placed a call to his estranged mother, hoping she was out attending to her tenements or whatnot in some dilapidated section of Torrington, and left a message that he'd be dropping by to go over the bind Zharko had him vis-à-vis a promissory note. That is, he'd be dropping by if he couldn't get anywhere with the lawyer whose address was listed on the IOU.

After leaving this clipped message, he had second thoughts about the way he put it. How would she take it? What would Zharko think about it if she told him? But he'd set things up and that was that.

By the time he got back from his chores, circled up Lake Eden Road and pulled in, Amanda was home from play practice from the nearby community school. It was now around the same hour she'd shepherded Zharko and Vlad to his doorstep the day before. Among the ironies as he caught up with her by the white picket fence was the fact he was about to employ her to keep an eye out for intruders while he was away. If she hadn't been so trusting, Zharko and Vlad wouldn't have intruded on his life in the first place. Zharko's pressing timetable would have never been met in his hell-bent attempt to flush Josh out, and everything would have been quite different.

Pressing on, he barely got Amanda's attention. No matter how hard he tried to get her to hold still, she was too frisky to engage in a simple exchange. For starters, she insisted on demonstrating new variations on her dance solo in the musical, which now included twirls, high kicks, and a jazz move she called step-and-slap ball change.

"Isn't that cool?" she asked, returning to her side of the fence. "Dance lady added it 'cause she thought I could handle it and, like I showed your cousin, it might be a showstopper. How about that?"

"Pretty nifty, kid," Josh said, reverting as best he could to easygoing Josh.

"At my age, did you get to do stuff like this back in . . . where did you say you were from?"

Josh hesitated. Up till now he'd managed to keep everything about his murky past at bay. "Connecticut," he said. "Northwest hills. At your age, we only did little holiday programs."

"Did you take part?"

"Nope. Guess I missed out," Josh said, dismissing any thoughts about holidays.

Thrown for a second, Amanda came right back with, "Anyways, will you come see me?"

"Perform? You bet. Let me know when."

"Didn't your cousin tell you? Dress rehearsal a week from Saturday at ten, matinee at two, evening show at seven, and last show on Sunday at two. You can't miss."

Abruptly changing the subject as she did a perfect cartwheel, Josh said, "Wow, look at that. Pretty soon all you'll need is an agent."

"You think so? Hey, I know what that is. They send you out on stuff. Speaking of which, Mom said if I keep it up, she might take me to auditions for *Annie* in Asheville. You know what that is?"

"The Broadway musical from the comic strip *Little Orphan Annie.*"

"That's the one. Boy, you sure are up on stuff. Anyways, it's got a humongous bunch of parts for kids. Now wouldn't that be something?"

"Sure would," Josh said, unable to help noting the total difference between himself and Amanda when he was her age. "Listen, I'm going to be out of town for the next week or so. I'd like to hire you to keep an eye out. Make sure of things, like checking for poison oak crawling up the trellis by the back porch. There are spray cans in the shed. Ask your mom what to do about other things like keeping the bears away now that they're out and about."

Scrunching up her freckled face, she said, "So, taking off, huh? I get it. That's what your cousin said. I mean, after looking high and low for you. 'Cause something came up. Big surprise."

"That's right," Josh said. "Something came up. Big surprise." He continued to keep everything light, just a little chat between an easygoing neighbor and a perky little girl next door. A sweet bit of MGM Americana nestled in a spacious, idyllic neighborhood embraced by the Blue Ridge and the rosy hue of twilight afterglow.

But, as Josh might have known, Amanda would have none of it. She came right out with, "Say, how come you act so different?"

"What do you mean?"

"Well, your cousin pops up, talks funny, and doesn't look anything like you. No light sandy hair and smooth, nice face."

"Actually, he's not really a cousin."

"Really? Then how come—?"

"Some connection with my mother."

"Oh? Does your mom look anything like that too? And talk weird, foreign, like she doesn't have the language down yet?"

"No, she talks short and plain."

Josh was having the hardest time sloughing this off. It was as if this little girl was determined to fill in the blanks to keep her world normal and nice.

More and more puzzled, Amanda screwed up her face and said, "Then does she have light hair too?"

"No, she doesn't."

Not about to let go, she tried even harder. "But what about your dad? Me and Mom and Dad all look alike. And so do just about all our relatives. There's a resemblance and they get along real good. Which I do too, mostly."

Cutting in just in time, Amanda's mother called out from the railing of her front porch. "Amanda? Now, you quit pestering Mister Josh. Come in and do your homework, you hear?"

"Yes, ma'am!"

"She'll be right there," Josh called back.

"I tell you, sometimes I don't know what gets into that child. Talking to perfect strangers and all like she did yesterday."

"She's just outgoing, Mrs. Wilson."

"Too outgoing," Mrs. Wilson said for Amanda's benefit as she eased back inside.

Josh reached for his wallet, but Amanda held up a hand like a traffic cop. "No, sir. I'll be happy to check in and look out for stuff. All I want is your definite promise you'll come see the show. A week from Saturday is the first matinee."

"Do my best, kid, like I said."

"You better. I'll be counting on it." With that, she started to run back, stopped, and did another couple of cartwheels the rest of the way. Josh clapped. Amanda skipped up the porch steps, spun around and curtseyed, spun back, and rushed inside.

The rosy-tinged afterglow began to fade from the tops of the ridges along with any vestiges of comforting seclusion.

Presently, he noticed an object leaning against his garage door. Upon closer inspection, it turned out to be a thin, black attaché case, the kind frequent flyers on business trips carried. He released the latches. As promised, among the papers, fresh notepads, pens, etc., was the handwritten schedule and prescribed duties and a crude drawing of downtown Waterbury. There was also a red check mark indicating a warehouse and parking lot off the exit close to the crossroads of busy Routes 8 and 84. No doubt the case also served as an identification carry-on for watchdogs making sure he not only boarded the short hop but the direct flight to the Hartford/Springfield terminal as well.

He closed the case, put dealing with its contents on the back burner, and walked around the bushes, ascended the front steps, and entered the modest frame house. He couldn't get his mind around the way he got in touch with Molly and tried to slip by the realities. By the same token, he also couldn't dismiss the fact that he'd pressed Paul as if he suddenly had it in him to try his hand at investigative reporting.

At the same time, he thought of Zharko's veiled threats against his mother and his ability to track down some girl his mother told him he was still sweet on. Some girl it wouldn't take much to identify.

Then he recalled that line of poetry: *Take the journey, find your way home.* And Teddy Roosevelt's call to enter the arena. And the Lakota Sioux ritual to take on the wilderness sans everything but a blanket and water. To descend only when you were ready for manhood.

Something else crossed his mind. Starting with the bolt of lightning before dawn, the shattered limb, and the nightmare, everything had been conspiring to get through to him so that even the mercurial quarks were part of the call.

In short, like it or not, his charge was to face up to it. Get to the bottom of this, all the way back and up to the present dilemma. Fill in everything he'd cast a blind eye to and take it from there. That was the price of even a chance at a normal life with Molly. That was his mission, though he was the absolute wrong person for the job.

CHAPTER TEN

By the time Josh was settled in business class on the direct flight to Hartford, it might seem to the scattering of other passengers that Josh fit right in, dressed in his blue blazer, white button-down shirt, and tan slacks. There were over a half dozen neatly dressed young men also seated next to a vacant seat on which they placed their identical attaché cases. After the plane reached cruising altitude, they all focused on printouts and other material they'd displayed on the open tray tables in front of them. It was as if Zharko had planned it this way based on TV ads he'd seen so that Josh would arouse the least suspicion as he proceeded to adapt to his given role in this charade.

However, Josh's lack of sleep and the stress it took to make it to this point in Zharko's game plan only made him restless. Almost immediately, he missed the slower pace and clarity of the crisp Carolina sky during early spring. Not that the weather was always perfect, but something about the leisurely seasonal pattern and affable residents, despite Ackerman's loopy objections, was reassuring. Like the cheery folks at Ingles Market and the vivacious lady teller at the bank who wanted to know how your day was going. There was also the sense of belonging as folks around the little shops told you how much they enjoyed your latest feature.

He was taken by the fact that even perky little Amanda could tell he was no longer the same laidback neighbor. Something else was going on.

Buffered by the drone of the plane's engines, he recalled

Sam Spade's classic line in *The Maltese Falcon*: "Everybody has something to conceal," and Spade's struggles throughout the ordeal with femme fatale Bridget O'Shaughnessy—"You aren't the sort of person you pretend to be, are ya, sweetheart?" Meaning that Josh, too, would have to cut through the surface and all the games people played. Meaning that everything was grist for the proverbial mill.

Soon the plot of that other noir classic, *Out of the Past* starring Robert Mitchum and Kirk Douglas, came to him. In this crime caper, Mitchum was first seen in a small town running a gas station harboring the notion of marrying a nice local girl. Actually, it turns out he was hiding out. Before long, Douglas and his cronies came nosing around and caught up to him, forcing him to face up to the IOU he'd tried to turn his back on. Flashbacks ensued, detailing exactly where it had all gone wrong, how he'd gotten involved with gangster Douglas, and now he had to face up to it.

It didn't take any pondering to see that this plotline was painfully apt and easily added to all the signs and signals, including little Amanda next door shaking her head over his vague linkage with Zharko. You can use the refuge of a small town for only so long.

And so, in the forty-five minutes or so before preparations for landing, he opened the attaché case, pulled down the tray table from the back of the empty seat in front of him, and placed a blank notepad on the flat surface. Given the fact that he had his work cut out for him, he gave it the heading "Things to do." For starters: adding up what led to this sorry pass. Second assignment: digging up as much background on Zharko's criminal dealings as possible and scoping out the true origins of the IOU. Lastly: all things considered and despite his shortcomings, making some kind of move.

Pen in hand, he made a start by jotting down images from

the time he was twelve, including the knifing, his mother's awful treatment of Molly, the search for the discarded Christmas present in the snow, etc. Some twenty minutes later, he added earlier instances, scouring his memory for the foggy beginnings. When he was three or four, small enough to hide behind old wooden furniture, watching and listening. Catching the gist of the words he overheard, never knowing where he was or what was going on.

The words came from Zharko. The words were so cold and harsh, he kept still so he wouldn't give himself away. All the while, there was shadowy Zharko, dark complexioned and bony, chiseled face; straggly coal-black hair; and sparkling gold earring. Zharko darting here and there like a crazed dancer, making little Sonny feel even more lost and scared hiding behind the humongous chair. In this moment, some of the words began to come back to him:

What you want from my life, Irina? Little boy bastard is maybe accident but mostly what you deserve.

He is gadzo, not Romany, no good for nothing unless you use it or lose it, so they say.

Flashing forward, a little older this time, perhaps six or seven. Wakened from his sleep in his musty bedroom in the cabin in the middle of the night. The words outside his bedroom as harsh as the earlier ones:

Shut your mouth, Irina. Is business, always business. Get him before he gets you is what they are saying. Winners and losers.

And one last time when he was twelve:

He is eyewitness. Ship him off to private gadzo school in South, far away. Bury him down in nowhere until payback. Someday is payback, I tell you. Payback for goddamn sure!

Josh added a logline: *This is the tale of a kid trapped in somebody else's story.*

Try as he might, nothing further came to him. Out of sheer frustration he said aloud, "That's it. What else can you say?"

A few of the passengers glanced over as a stewardess walked up the aisle past him, making her way forward to announce preparations for landing. He shook the peering onlookers off with a halfhearted smile. In return, they too offered fake smiles and gathered up their busywork.

Glancing at his jottings, all he could decipher was a life stacked against him from the get-go.

CHAPTER ELEVEN

L eaving the airport in a compact rental, Josh was immediately confronted with a chilly drizzle, the total opposite of the sparkling spring weather back in the Blue Ridge, forcing him to concentrate on his driving as the wipers thwacked away. He'd mistakenly assumed the drive westward to the Litchfield Hills would give his overworked brain a much-needed rest, lulled by the easy backcountry dips and curves and dense green foliage of a comparable early spring in New England, nestled within little stretches like Paradise Valley.

But he realized everything was up for grabs, prodding him to keep his mind open to the twists and turns of ongoing reality. The gray sky, rain-spattered windshield, and the strain of getting used to a smaller new car and being careful not to lose his way or get into an accident was not the half of it. Along the way, he was reminded that the route only gave the illusion of skirting the hell-bent traffic and workaday push-and-pull on Interstate 84 south in Hartford, New Britain, Bristol and, soon enough, the melting pot and old factory town of Waterbury. Not to mention the schemes being played out day to day. In Waterbury alone, he recalled a history of corrupt mayors and a native son governor who spent time in federal prison. The whole Naugatuck Valley was rife with the dicey elements that awaited him by noon tomorrow.

Despite his best intentions, his whole things-to-do list was problematic. He didn't even know how he was going to break it to Molly, how much he would hide in an effort to keep her out of it, let alone how she would take any of it. And how he could possibly keep her on the string until he solved what was nearly impossible to solve. All told, at this point he actually didn't know much of anything.

A return to his on-again, off-again unease led to the uncanny feeling he was being followed. He'd first had this sensation back in the Blue Ridge, wondering if someone, possibly this Ivan character, was making sure he took the flights as ordered and carried on in his ploy as a businessman. But now it was the weather spooking him, or fatigue, or anxiety, or all three. Maybe it was his overactive imagination having entered an area replete with shady characters and double dealing. At any rate, just the notion of someone tailing him was starting to get to him. He slowed below the speed limit and hoped the drizzle-spattered beams shining in his rearview mirror would swing by his left, take the next passing lane, and dissolve out of sight. At times it happened that way. Other times a trailing car stuck close behind for miles.

Eventually, he came to the four-lane expanse of Route 8 running north and south: north to the gateway to the Massachusetts border and the tourist enclaves of the Berkshires; south for a speedy thirty-five-minute drive competing with the rush of traffic to Waterbury, Naugatuck, points east and west, and the bottleneck south into New Haven. Hitting the accelerator, he barely managed to maneuver around the on-ramp to Route 8. He kept it up, circling around, going a few miles out of his way. A few minutes later, he pulled over, waited for a dozen or so cars to pass him by, and proceeded at a crawl until he was fairly certain he was in the clear.

Traveling south on Route 8 for a few miles, caught up in the speeding traffic, he got in the right-hand lane and swerved onto the exit lane for Route 118. He veered right, gunned the motor again, and took on the steep climb that would take him high above to the preserved semblance of old eighteenth-century Litchfield.

Once finally there, he eased back and pulled over for a minute. He took in the stately elms, file of colonial Federal style homes on both sides of South Street replete with their low-pitched roofs, flat façades, and black, louvered shutters. The sight was not only familiar, for a second it became reassuring even in the foggy drizzle, like many an old-timey village in MGM movies.

He quickly realized he was recapturing that moment when word had gotten out that Zharko had been deported, perhaps for good, back to Eastern Europe or wherever he originally hailed from. He now knew that Zharko and his henchman Vlad were not that far away, in fact at this very moment driving up the last leg of their trip from Western Carolina in a rented vehicle. The old gypsy camper might very well still be nestled in the woods barely over two miles from here, waiting patiently down the dirt lane to a cul-de-sac across from where Irina's cabin lay. His nominal mother was still in cahoots with Zharko for all Josh knew. A gypsy camper also conveniently located not far at all from the inn where Josh was to carry on the role of a fellow businessman; an ideal location from which Zharko could keep tabs on Josh, cruise down to the warehouse in Waterbury if need be, and scurry back to his hideaway.

With a shrug, Josh put the car in gear, passed the picture-perfect village green, and kept going. Here the village retained its storybook façade adding the white congregational church on the corner with its Christopher Wren steeple leading onto West Street, the old brick shops, village restaurant, past the rows of Victorian houses with their pilastered front porches and attached shutters in homage to last century's Colonial Revival. He'd spent the first twelve years of his life here, returned those few times mainly to see Molly, but in the drizzling foggy rain this setting might as well be a flimsy Hollywood set that wasn't fooling anyone.

Momentarily, he passed by the pale-brick elementary school

on his left. Molly was undoubtedly reading something bright and beautiful to her second-grade charges to see them through this dismal day. Thoughts of his own second-grade experiences flittered by: out on the playground trying his best to blend in, deflecting any questions about his parents or religion; seated close to the front row, dutifully paying attention to the teacher, keeping a low profile. Even at play. Even at every encounter. Like being called upon in class, thereby being exposed. Being on was to be avoided at any cost. Keeping in the background his adapted fallback position, his survival ploy.

He proceeded on the mile or so stretch to the outskirts of the village, keeping an eye out for the large emblematic sign for the inn on his right, well before the dirt lane leading down to the woods. Pangs of loneliness began to creep in, but he managed to ward them off and locked his mind on the business at hand.

He pulled into the long, winding drive, noting that the old wooden structure had given way to a smooth, white façade, making the once rambling building look more like a bank. He parked, grabbed the attaché case and suitcase, entered the lobby, and went up to the glistening front desk.

A few suits around his age milling around the coffee bar and trendy armless divans nodded to him. He barely nodded back. All he could think of was connecting with Molly and spending a little time with her. Maybe if he could get around her disappointment with his evasiveness, he could return to the inn, study his so-called duties at the Waterbury warehouse, get some sleep, and take on whatever awaited him, armed with the thought she was close by and hopefully still unencumbered.

Once ensconced in his single-occupant room, he hastily scrolled down to the M on his cell phone and dialed. Her tone all but matched these pristine surroundings as she answered with a cool, "Hello."

Countering as best he could, Josh said, "Look, I know you probably just got home from school and I never told you exactly when I'd be arriving and all. But if I could touch base for a few minutes, give you some idea of the bind I'm in . . . The thing of it is, after the drizzly, foggy drive from the airport, I could really use a little human contact and some of your special hot herbal tea with a touch of honey."

Molly hesitated. "As it happens, George and I had a set-to last night. It wasn't a row or an argument, but I'm still not past it and not very good company at the moment."

"George? Wait, don't tell me," Josh said, encouraged that things were indeed still unsettled. "The assistant principal, right? The guy you spoke about last time? Very practical, about forty or so, some ten years older who hinted that you'd make a good team."

"That's not very funny, Josh."

"Okay. Look, I'm only asking to see you after coming all this way and feeling completely disoriented."

"Oh, I see. You're offering a moment of honest disclosure."

"What do you want me to say, Molly? It's hard enough the way things stand, as if I actually knew how things stand."

Another pause until she said, "Okay. We'll just touch base then. Only for a little while."

"You bet. You got it."

This little negotiation was followed by directions to her place. It seemed she'd sublet a cottage tucked away on Norfolk Road a half mile beyond the colonial mansions on North Street and the Green. The owner of her place was the art teacher at the elementary school, on leave in France and Italy, taking in the notable sites and museums. How this move on Molly's part came about was news to Josh, who assumed she was still living in her parents' guest house high above the lane running down to his

mother's rustic place. Once again, even that assumption was
falling by the wayside.

He hastily unpacked, donned a rain jacket, left the inn, got
back in the car, and contended once more with the cool drizzle
that had picked up another notch. Making his way back to the
Green, he turned left and kept his eyes focused through the
spattered windshield for the turnoff onto Norfolk Road, all the
while wondering what was up with Molly. Had she really become
standoffish since they last met or was this a momentary glitch in
the life of a generally cheerful young woman? Was there nothing in
this world he could count on while coming smack up against what
Teddy Roosevelt called the arena?

Immediately after the turnoff, he came upon another series
of idyllic homes set back among groves of maples. The one in
question was too cute for words: a sparkling white Cape Cod,
steeply pitched gable roof, perfectly centered chimney, upstairs
gable bedroom window prominently peeking out. Not to mention
a white picket fence and cobblestone walkway leading up to the
front porch. The house even had a polished-oak central front door,
flanked on either side by multipaned windows and the requisite
lacquered black shutters. If anything was designated as a Disney-
like retreat from any semblance of reality, this was it.

But despite her wary tone over the phone, he couldn't help
hoping for at least a hug. He hurried up the steps and was about to
ring the bell when the front door swung open and Molly ushered
him inside. Instead of any sign of affection, there was an "Oh my,
you must be soaked. Here, let me take your jacket. Sit by the fire
and I'll bring you the tea and some nice cinnamon toast."

"Okay," Josh said. And then simply, "Thanks."

Seated in a rocking chair by the crackling fire redolent of
pungent apple wood, he took in the cozy interior as Molly busied
herself back in the kitchen. She did look exactly as he imagined

she always did with her soft blue eyes, honey-blonde bob, cream-colored sweater, and beige skirt outlining her trim figure. But the hint of a frown every now and then matched that same preoccupied tone over the phone and her rushing about only generated more small talk like "How was your flight?" and "The kids were really restless today, as you can imagine." All these quips underscored the obvious fact she had something else on her mind. As if she hadn't quite figured out how to broach the subject but would get around to it as soon as she finished with the obligatory pleasantries.

He took in the décor as he waited her out, beginning with the curved-leg, hard-rock maple end table by his side. In fact, all the furniture was made of hard-rock maple, including the dining room set across the way. The paintings on the walls were originals but of the typical red barn New England countryside variety. The ornaments resting on the mantelpiece were so carefully placed it was a wonder that anyone actually lived here. Which, as soon as Molly placed the laden tea tray on the end table and pivoted again toward the kitchen, prompted him to say, "Is this where I promise to be extra careful and not spill anything on the braided rug?"

But she avoided anything approximating an affectionate exchange and went about retrieving the plated toast, honey, and jellies, left him and returned just as quickly and offered to pour the herbal tea into his porcelain cup.

Josh nodded, added some honey, stirred, and took a sip while she stood there holding the pot a few feet away.

"Okay," Josh said, not able to take anymore. "What is it? Me dropping in on you like this or you still mulling over your falling out with George?"

"I didn't say that. I never said anything specific about me and George. I only hinted that . . ." Holding onto that offhanded tone, she said, "Oh, never mind. Just eat your toast and have your tea."

With that, she headed back to the kitchen.

This time Josh got up and followed right on her heels. "All right, let me guess. George wanted to know what's going on with this Josh person? Who he is and what's your relationship? And how can you have a relationship over the phone every now and then and a few trysts up here?"

"George is very sensible."

"That's right. What are Josh's plans? he asked. What are his career objectives? What is the story here? And how can this wayward person possibly compare with the prestige of an assistant principal who will doubtless become principal of the high school in the very near future? A mature man who will provide you with a real home close to the green. There is absolutely no comparison."

"Maybe," Molly said, turning away from him, getting out a towel and drying dishes that were already dry and placing them back in the cupboard. "The same question my folks keep asking along with everyone else. I thought his name was Sonny, they say. Sonny Korda. Why did he change his name? What's his real background, for pity's sake? Isn't it high time you knew?"

"Good point."

"Speaking of his background, what kind of mother has it in for the Christmas holiday? To this day my folks have never forgotten that one. And every time you show up, they ask what is he doing down in Carolina working for some paper or other where he has no relatives or roots? Why does he stay down there when he's originally from Litchfield? What is the draw deep in the mountains? They just don't get it and, to tell the truth, neither do I."

With no ready answer at hand as usual, Josh merely nodded.

"And why is he suddenly back here? What are these legal matters with your mother that suddenly bring you to Waterbury

of all places? A town you've always kept shy of? And a whole bunch
of questions I never got to ask as you cut me short over the phone."

"I was in a rush."

"Oh, really?"

"It's hard to explain."

She put down the towel and looked straight at him. "That's it,
keep deflecting. Isn't that how we all get by?"

"That's not it."

"Oh, tell me about it. Never a time goes by that I don't have
to make the children happy along with their parents. There's
nowhere I can go without running into them, plus keeping in mind
that I'm now up for teacher of the year. But if you yearn for a real
relationship, if once you let your hair down, talk to Josh, ask him
anything of any consequence, he'll shrug it off somehow."

"Not always."

"Just about. We lose touch. Then, out of the blue, you show up
again with a new name without a care in the world. You even play
chaperone for me on a field trip to the Waterbury museum, that
very same area you've always been wary of."

She was referring to that very time he'd found out Zharko had
been deported and thought maybe he could steer his way clear.
Actually make plans and think of living a normal life. But he only
wanted to make sure and couldn't tell her that. Couldn't tell her
why.

"And here you are again," Molly said, pressing a little harder.
"Should I wait, keep biding my time? The funny thing is, I keep
telling the little girls in class not to settle. Get cracking now, every
chance you get. I say they can be anything they put their minds to
and have a happy ever after."

"Okay, okay, I get the message," Josh said, going back to the
parlor and retrieving his jacket. "I just wanted you to know
that I find myself on the brink. A blast from the past has stirred

everything up, sent me back here, and I don't want to drag you into it. At the same time, I feel lousy stringing you along like this."

He struggled with his raincoat, edged toward the door, and said, "You see, it's hard for a wary guy like me to answer a call to action. A person not at all used to going up against anything. On top of that, this weather is making it even harder. I know I have no right asking, but if you could see your way clear, if there was any way you could put off this thing with George for a little while till I either pull through or throw in the towel and wind up flat on my face, it would mean everything."

"What are you saying, for pity's sake?" Molly asked, framed in the kitchen entrance way. "Can't you ever just talk to me? What has gotten into you all of a sudden?"

"Let's say I'm not up to going to Waterbury tomorrow. But, if you don't mind, I'll try to brace myself and then touch base around this time. Thanks for the tea and toast. It was great seeing you—I mean it."

Giving her no time to respond, Josh slipped out the door. With the rain beating down more heavily, he hurried across the cobblestones, past the picket fence to the car. Sliding behind the wheel, he couldn't help recalling all those times he'd fantasized what he could've or should've said. But never coming flat out with the admission he simply wasn't good enough for her. Had never gone far out into the wilderness with just a blanket and water, had never come back with a spirit guide or entered the arena. Never had grown up, to put a fine point on it, or gotten over his abiding fear expertly covered up by a nice-guy façade. But at least he'd indicated things were a whole lot different for him caught in this realm of chance and runaway quarks.

CHAPTER TWELVE

As he drove away that night, he was still despondent, heartened only by the fact she didn't end things then and there.

He kept driving for a few miles out of town, fighting off the darkness and rain-spattered windshield until he pulled in at a familiar roadside diner. There he treated himself to a large bowl of clam chowder, a grilled cheese sandwich, and a mug of hot cider from nearby March Farms. Afterwards, he drove back to the inn, went straight to his room, and flopped down on the bed, so completely out of it that he dozed off immediately

Hours later, he awoke with a start and checked the clock-radio by the nightstand. It was only six in the morning. He had at least a few hours before he was scheduled to turn up at the warehouse. Not only that, there was a newfound edginess brought on by intimating to Molly he was going to start confronting things.

He showered, shaved, and got dressed in the same casual uniform he wore on the plane. Armed with the attaché case, he went downstairs to a maple-paneled pub, glad to see that it was much too early for his counterparts. He settled for a light breakfast and coffee, opened the attaché case, and began to decipher Zharko's notes.

From what he could make out from the scribbling, he was to act as a front man linked to an Eastern outfit called Gulfstream Transfer. The Waterbury locale, judging from the crude map of a loading dock, was a waystation for the transfer of goods. What the payoff was, was anyone's guess. His role was relegated to using his "good-boy smarts" to ward off any hitches and to field inquiries.

If anything minor cropped up, a guy named Sal was in charge
of opening, closing, and running the place. The order for today
was the removal by a work crew of all remnants stemming from
a former wholesale produce distributor. Josh was to report to
Zharko via cell phone at the end of each day's activity. Since today
was devoted to mopping up, Josh was not expected till noon.

But that was only part of Josh's own agenda for today.

He glanced at the contract he'd unwittingly cosigned way back
then. He thought again of intercepting some telling, incriminating
detail by five tomorrow and passing it on to Paul, his editor. A
prospect so dubious given Paul's response, Josh wasn't counting
on it. Failing to make any kind of headway, he'd be left with the
vague hope something else would turn up as an escape valve from
criminal entanglement with Zharko's scheme, e.g., going along just
short of being an accessory before or after the fact. A possibility so
hazy he couldn't begin to get his mind around it.

Nursing a third cup of coffee, he pondered over his initial
things-to-do agenda, which amounted to beginning to catch up
and catch on.

He glanced at the promissory contract one more time. The
only option was to contact the Waterbury lawyer who drew up the
IOU, provided he was still around. Then go through the motions at
the warehouse, make today's report to Zharko via cell phone, drive
back to Litchfield, and have it out with his mother (provided he'd
gotten something out of this lawyer and was armed with a way to
confront her grab bag of secrets). Afterwards have tea again with
Molly, make amends for the way he'd stormed out last night, and
juggle anything she may naturally want to know, hold back any
information that would put her in harm's way, and generally play
it by ear.

Then he pulled back. There was still no telling whether he was
up for any of it and what the fallout might be.

At this juncture, the other suits had trickled in, creating a buzz around him as they chatted away and downed their breakfasts. Their nervous energy coupled with his own misgivings spurred him out the door. *First things first,* he told himself, as if this old bromide would in any way do the trick.

CHAPTER THIRTEEN

A s expected, the drive down into the heart of Waterbury still unnerved him. The gigantic clock tower hovered overhead like a granite shaft, the clock itself appearing like a peering eye topped by eight menacing she-wolf gargoyles. Like some Palazzo Publico during the reign of the villainous Medici, the sprawling granite façade of the train station below the tower seemed to block off any easy exit. Just the thought of the city put him on edge under the best of circumstances, and the prospect of reentry under these circumstances rattled him no matter what pep talk he gave himself.

Under the lingering gray sky, caught up in the speeding traffic traveling south on Route 8, he continued to picture this urban hub in terms of entrances and avenues of escape. After the downtown exit and a quick jog, the warehouse would appear set back to his right. Around the corner there would be the "Palazzo" itself, including the clock tower and railroad station augmented by the headquarters of the *Waterbury Republican American* newspaper just in case.

What the paper might mean was beyond him at the moment except as a temporary refuge. The adjacent train station was not a barrier but also an outlet if he got there in time to board and head south to New Haven and other havens beyond.

He added to his list of options should he find himself on foot. Diagonally across from the clock tower stood the library on one side of the street and the courthouse on the other. Or, making a run for it, starting from the warehouse, instead of dashing around the corner, he could sprint left and then right, headed for the Waterbury Green. Except the Green itself was a long rectangular strip hemmed in on both sides, starting from an imposing gray-granite church and proceeding all the way across to a city college shaped like a sprawling office building, with constant traffic in both lanes, buildings wedged together like a wall of row houses.

Beyond this downtown setting, he'd been told of sections like Town Plot where members of the Mafia were said to still reside, plus a scattering of ethnic neighborhoods vying for prominence with their own restaurants, meeting halls, and the like, reminiscent of the "old country."

However, he was aware that the WASPs, the white Anglo-Saxon Protestants who spread these rumors back in the Litchfield Hills, were prejudiced and his just-in-case agitation was merely the product of his own longstanding hang-ups. For all he knew, the denizens of Waterbury were brimming with civic pride and his old perceptions were totally warped.

Pulling himself out of this little bout of paranoia, he switched his focus to Sorin Novac. The old contract had listed the attorney's home and office addresses on the letterhead. Zharko wouldn't have been so cocksure of his legal rights and the iron clad hold he had on Josh if Novac wasn't around to confirm it all. So, assuming Josh was on target, the best tack was to hope Novac hadn't moved, catch him before normal business hours, do his best to disarm him, and start to come to terms.

He took the Waterville exit before the main drag and eased down to a ridge perched a few blocks above the Green. If memory served, according to the museum photos, there, nestled among the old estates of the captains of the brass and copper industry, he'd find the landmark Benedict-Miller House embossed on the letterhead of the IOU perched above Hillside Avenue.

And there it was. Under the canopy of gray clouds, set far apart from the other mansions on the street like some gothic Queen Anne Victorian, it echoed the muted tones of the overcast sky, designed to afford its occupants complete seclusion. At street level, gazing up the steep rolling front lawn, he noted an endless jumble of peaked gables, turrets, and chimneys fronted by narrow balconies, the lot of them stretching all the way across from slanting roof to slanting roof, floor to floor, topped by rows of chimneys. Perhaps during Victorian times, passersby were impressed by dark wooden residences like this and imagined them to be ultra-cozy with each fireplace going full blast during harsh New England winters. Josh assumed Novac had gotten hold of the place during a downturn in the economy—a prestigious piece of the city's heritage to impress his clients. Then again, he may have amassed enough coin over the years with a burgeoning practice. But what difference did it make except to indicate that Novac was living comfortably and not some fly-by-night shyster.

The second Josh spotted a flickering light under a third-floor gable, he got out of the car, snatched the attaché case, climbed the steep row of brick stairs in the center of the lawn, and took the front porch steps as quickly as he could. Finding no front doorbell or knocker, he tried the brass handle of the thick oaken door, eased inside the enormous mahogany-paneled entranceway and foyer, and called a greeting. No answer.

There were spacious rooms right and left and a huge, hanging glass chandelier in the center. All the rooms were filled with leather couches and armchairs, but there was no one around. He drifted forward, located a curving staircase highlighted by a polished mahogany railing and waited. Soon he heard running water two stories above. He called again, still received no answer, and climbed the carpeted stairs, following the running water sounds through the pipes till he reached an alcove. Through the alcove, he spotted a brass nameplate heralding the home office of Sorin Novac.

He called once more, trying a friendly "Hello?"

This time a voice called back. "Come in, come in. I was expecting you. And I must say the timing is excellent. Excellent indeed." The voice sounded as if it belonged to someone who had taken speech lessons to overcome a foreign accent. Or to indicate he was educated and to convince any foreign clients he was well-versed and could surely navigate the ins and outs of this country's legal system.

Passing through the open doorway, Josh came across a chubby little man in a rumpled beige linen suit, sporting a carefully trimmed white handlebar mustache and a full head of thick white hair. The way his beady little eyes darted around as he fiddled with a grow-light while standing atop a step ladder only added to Josh's first impression. When he said, "Well, don't just stand there, young man—enter," the stagey command clinched the deal.

Apparently, after receiving Josh's phone message, his mother had warned the lawyer her son might be coming by his home in regard to the promissory note, and thus the little man was primed and ready. Or so it seemed, given Novac's cheery greeting.

Josh entered a spacious room with a high, angled ceiling. The view through the dormer windows down to the street were obstructed by a jutting iron railing, just as Josh expected. The only surprise was the sight of bamboo everywhere you looked, including a bamboo coffee table and recliner with fluffed-up coral pillows and a scattering of bamboo chairs to the left of where Josh stood, all resting on straw mats. To the right, a bamboo bookcase full of coffee table books took up the opposite wall. The central attraction was a display of colorful orchids set on white metal stands, another glowing lighting fixture catty-corner to the one

Novac was adjusting shooting down on the rest of the plants. The only items out of place were the old-fashioned steam radiators in the far corners and a second alcove leading to a bathroom past where Novac was perched. He scurried down from the ladder, exited, and returned with a watering can.

"Excuse me," Novac said, "only for a moment. Then I can give you a short time before I must go off to the courthouse for a bit of litigation. All in moderation, you see. All in good time."

Hovering over the array of pink, orange, yellow, and white clusters set in ceramic pots, he lifted each one, murmuring something about silvery roots are a sign a plant needs more water, green means it's just right. "Ideally," Novac added, "in their natural habitat in the tropics hanging on trees, the fluffy clouds come by, the rain douses them, and the rain water flows to the earth. There, the lighting and warmth are ideal and you don't have to go to all this fuss."

Novac darted around faster despite his "all in good time" spiel, speeding up his watering ritual as his voice became more fake ingratiating.

"I know, I know what you're thinking," Novac said. "I'm looking for some escape. But you see, each time I return in late March from a Caribbean cruise, a few weeks of dank, gray, chilly Waterbury and I long to return. But I can't. So many clients, so much litigation to catch up on. So there is only this one delightful solution."

"Great," said Josh, "but isn't there some way we could do this while you're tending to your watering?"

"Yes, yes, you need to be reassured, I'll wager. We all need to be reassured and worry-free."

"Look, I only want to get a handle on things. I admit I don't know much of anything about loopholes, what's binding or not. But if you know my mother, that's par for the course after my being kept in the dark all this while. It seems all the loose ends have led to some kind of reckoning, but you can't discuss anything with the likes of Zharko either. So that's the long and short of why I'm here."

When Novac didn't come out with "Who?" or indicate he didn't get the gist of Josh's concerns, Josh assumed he was getting through.

Novac plunked down the watering can, scurried over to the bookcase lining the far wall, plucked out a bright picture book, ushered Josh over to the coffee table on the other side, sat him down, and motioned for him to put aside his attaché case. "There, you see?" he said, deflecting like crazy. "We all have our dreams. All in the same boat, no pun intended."

He flipped the pages, pointed to sailing boats skimming across an island inlet in the tropics, and said, "I showed this to Vlad once. Have you ever met Vlad? I'm sure you must have. And even he, in his gruff manner, was impressed. Said this was his goal as well, hopefully in short order. There, you see? It's all a matter of finding common ground."

As if, in this roundabout way, he'd pushed it too far, he added, "What I meant was, I am certain we shall all come out of this just fine if we follow the most reasonable course. Keep things on an even keel. And you certainly look the part of a reasonable young man which is, of course, half the battle."

Beginning to wonder if Novac was in on the deal or at least in cahoots with Zharko, Josh put aside the picture book and flipped the latches of the attaché case. "Do you mind if we get down to it since we're both in a hurry? For instance, I'd like to know how I was supposed to realize what I was signing. As far as I remember, there was a snowstorm coming, and my mother, who never explains anything, hit me with this as I was about to rush out the door. So, how about being sucked in under false pretenses or extenuating circumstances? And there's the matter of my signature. I changed my name. I'm legally Josh Bartlet now. I chose a Cape Cod–sounding name so I could go incognito and get away from all this subterfuge."

Josh stopped himself. There he was blurting things out again like he had with his editor Paul, still having no idea how to play it under trying circumstances.

Novac scuffed back over to the watering can, ran his stubby fingers through his mop of white hair, and returned to Josh's side.

"What is it? The plane ride?" Novac asked. "This is not exactly the young man I was expecting. True, I did hear you changed your name. Nonetheless, I was expecting someone well-mannered who was only curious about the open-ended terms."

"Well, I'm sorry to disappoint you. But it's my first experience with something bordering on a shakedown."

Novac scrunched up his pudgy face, trained his eyes at the white plaster ceiling searching for a comeback, returned his gaze to Josh, and pointed at the document. "Call it what you will, but it is still a manifestation of mutual intent, which is the case with any binding contract. The intent is there, easily determined. The signature is yours, to which any handwriting expert will attest. To refresh your memory, at a previous time your mother needed funds from Zharko to pay for your boarding school expenses in Tennessee. You are a beneficiary of those expenses."

"The truth is, my mother needed to get rid of me. More to the point, Zharko had to get rid of me for reasons I'm sure you don't want to go into."

Countering once more, Novac's tone got more insistent. "Never mind any hidden motivation. Legally, according to this document, Zharko was willing to wait until such a time he needed your services. He advanced money free and clear. At the time of the signing, he advanced additional sums to bail your mother out.

And so, what we have here in lieu of payback accruing mounting interest is payment in kind. A few days of your time, which is exceedingly reasonable and generous. What it amounts to is simply a quid pro quo—if I do this, you will offer recompense to be determined by me when the day or need arises."

"The day or need has apparently arisen. Renege and you cause all kinds of trouble. In addition to being liable, given her own signature on this transaction as a co-signee, your mother will also find herself in court. Is that what you want? Say you do try to back out. In the meantime, not wishing to engage himself in any civil dispute, Zharko passes the note onto some unscrupulous person who has a totally different interpretation of payment in kind and takes Irina for all she's worth. Or Zharko himself produces documentation of all the money he's advanced. There go the tenements, there goes her house, her livelihood as a realtor. There goes everything and she's out on the street. Can't you see that? What is your problem?"

"Oh, nothing much," Josh said. "Just the prospect of ir-reparable harm despite your legal doubletalk. Because we're both probably in for it if you can't convince me to bypass the legality of forced engagement in a criminal pursuit. Because Zharko isn't going to hand this note over or anything of the sort. Meaning both of our necks are on the line."

Novac was clearly taken aback. Josh himself was surprised by yet another outburst on his part, this time spilling all over the place. He drifted back to the edge of the bamboo bookcase. At this rate, there was no way he was going to eke out anything.

Luckily, Novac also decided to change his tack. "Now, now, young man, this simply won't do. Won't do at all."

"I know. I guess this is what comes of overloading the circuit and losing your cool."

"Indeed."

On the other hand, Josh felt his accusation wasn't that far off and Novac had been in touch ever since Zharko had double backed to the states. Thus, Novac's chummy reference to Vlad's longing for a boat to sail away to the Caribbean. Thus, his notion that Zharko wouldn't want to come out into the open. Thus, Zharko's threats to the tune of "trouble for your mother" amplified by Novac's insistence on glossing over it all so he could probably tell Zharko, "No worries. Josh né Sonny duly took his mother's circumstances under consideration and was only curious about the open-ended terms."

"Tell you what," Josh said, breaking the silence. "Just humor me, okay, and we'll sweep all the subterfuge under the rug for now and call it quits."

He went over to the coffee table and plopped himself down on a bamboo chair. "You see, it's more than just the promissory note. Normally, a person would have had a nurturing mother, an understanding dad, a kind uncle—someone to fill in the blanks instead of shunting him and leaving him groping in the dark. I don't mean to get maudlin, but if you'd give me a lead, placate me a bit, I'll be peacefully on my way."

"Give you a lead?"

"My mother has never been open with me and it would help to come to terms if I had some idea where she's coming from. What's her background? Who is she really and why treat me that way? Why all the holes in my story?"

"Well, if you don't know, what can I tell you?"

"You can tell me something. For instance, how did she get here? What's the deal with her and the gypsies? What's the deal with her and Zharko?"

"Listen, young man. I am a lawyer, not a depository of family history. At best, I could offer only an inkling."

"Great. An inkling will do me just fine."

Novac gave Josh a weary look, went back to his watering can, and slipped between the lineup of orchids and the front window. With the warm beams of grow lights glinting off his white hair, he gazed up yet again at the ceiling, then began to speak as he finished his measuring and dousing chores.

"Now don't hold me to it. It was such a long while ago."

"I understand. Whatever you can come up with."

"Well . . . as I recall, my distant cousin Groffo, who was living outside of London at the time, knew of a displaced girl from Romania. It seems she emigrated to the English countryside at the age of nine or ten."

"And . . . so?"

"There was some talk about missionaries, who lived by Victorian greenhouse values, linked to a world-wide welfare agency hospitable to select orphans."

"Select? What do you mean by *select*?"

"Promising. Thereby, they would be more than willing to take Irina in."

"By Victorian standards?"

"Yes. The theory was that exceptional children needed to be enclosed in a greenhouse, so to speak. Far from the influence of loose morals and modern ways. Taking a few of them in so that, under the proper conditions, they can be rehabilitated into proper society."

"Okay, so she got transplanted to a Victorian greenhouse system."

"But you have to remember it's been a number of years since Groffo explained it all to me."

"Okay. But how in the world did she wind up around here?"

Novac examined a few thick, glossy orchid leaves and turned his attention to a set of pink-dotted clusters before responding. "All I know is, this denomination had boarding schools around the world. When she was about fourteen, Irina turned up in a secluded prep school in the Litchfield Hills, west of where she is living now."

"Which explains her thing about boarding schools and shipping me off. But how do Victorian values and Zharko fit in? Come on, you can tell me. What's the big deal?"

Novac sighed and finally came out with it. "It seems there was a riding stable close by. Zharko was related to Groffo. But he was wild. Once had a knife-throwing act in a carnival in Bucharest. Constantly getting in trouble. Running with gangs, getting into knife fights."

An involuntary shudder ran up Josh's spine. The harrowing image of the flashing blade in the snow dovetailed into Zharko's slow fruit-peeling act with the "sharp as a razor" Hoffritz knife in Josh's kitchen. He tried to shrug it off, but Novac noticed.

"It's the weather," Josh said. "The damp, the cold. I'm not used to it."

Along with Novac's watering, the room was not unlike the steamy tropics the older man was so fond of. Novac glanced at one of the hissing radiators and said, "Yes, indeed. The damp and chill. Now where was I?"

"The riding stable?"

"Yes, yes. Zharko was always good with horses. Something to do with bareback riders. Groffo then calls me long distance. We decide, perhaps if he gets far away, a whole new world."

"Right. Close by the missionary school where transplanted Romanian Irina and her classmates partake of wholesome, greenhouse-like riding lessons. Good for the mind, body, and soul of impressionable young ladies."

"Perhaps."

For a moment Josh was stumped. The notion of wholesome, transplanted young Irina didn't at all jive with the jaded mother he knew. "And then what? What about this whole gypsy thing?"

Novac sighed once again and said, "Here," putting the watering can aside and scuffing straight over to the bookcase. He plucked out a dog-eared book and handed it to Josh. "It just so happens I helped him with his English, which was atrocious. Through contacts, I got him the job at the stables and insisted he read this when he found himself longing for his ventures with gangs, the knife-throwing act, and what have you. I lent him this book so he could gain a wider, more wholesome Romany perspective."

"And how did he take it?"

"He scoffed, dog-eared a few pages, and gave it right back to me. We stayed in touch now and then over legal matters."

"Like devising an unsecured promissory note for future consideration."

"Never mind. Are we finished now? Are we through?"

"Wait a second. Was Groffo an integral part of this Romany network? Are you part of it too? Rehabilitating orphans like Irina and misguided young men like Zharko?"

"Enough, I said!" Novac pulled back and buttoned his rumpled jacket. "Now, if you will excuse me, I have wasted enough time and simply must be going."

Taking the cue, Josh put the book on Romany life in the attaché case, latched it, and got out a calling card from his wallet. "I'm leaving my press card on the coffee table. It's got my cell number in case something pertinent jogs your memory. But I do really appreciate the information."

Starting to leave, noting Novac's beady eyes darting around again, Josh added, "No problem. No worries, see? I'm back to my old mild-mannered self."

But this flimsy attempt at defusing things got him nowhere. He retreated to the winding staircase. The irony that Novac chose a Victorian mansion for his residence wasn't lost on Josh.

It also registered that from now on he'd have to do a much better job disarming people. Especially in light of a date to touch base with Paul by five tomorrow in possession of evidence linking an impending mob scheme and the city of Asheville.

A conflicting lawless/Victorian thread as well as the dubious prospect of placating Paul stayed with him as he headed to his opening gambit at the warehouse.

Keeping score, he still had no understanding of the rules of the game—or if there was any. He had gained an inkling of the backstory though. To his credit, he had made a start.

CHAPTER FOURTEEN

By the time Josh reached the loading dock, things were in full swing. Three identical box trucks sat idle. Crews from two cleaning outfits could be seen through the open triple-wide steel rolling door operating their noisy machines, scrubbing, burnishing, sweeping, cleaning, rinsing, and drying the multi-surface flooring. A few other workers wearing beige coveralls were busy coping with the residue, which included stacks of pallets. They continued to gather and deposit the debris in dumpsters at the far end.

Josh reached for the attaché case. A stocky guy with a shaved head and droopy eyelids appeared out of nowhere, grabbed hold of his arm, and steered him up the ramp, past the workmen, and into a cement-block office furnished only with a space heater, metal desk and chair, phone, computer, fax, and printer. A prominent bulletin board was affixed to a wall.

"I take it you're Sal," said Josh, releasing himself from Sal's grasp.

"You got it."

From his gruff, no-nonsense tone and the way he snatched the attaché case, plunked it on the desk, and took a cursory inventory of the contents, Josh assumed he'd be better off letting Sal take the lead rather than attempting any normal exchange. And, sure enough, after announcing he was the operations manager, Sal proceeded to rattle off the status quo, including the fact that the federal and state permits were in order, as were commercial driver's licenses, liability insurance, DOT, IRP tags, and IFTA decals (whatever that all meant). Plus federal heavy highway use taxes and such—all of which was beyond anything Josh had ever encountered. But he nodded anyway.

Then Sal said, "So, I oversee all the loads, what needs to be picked up, when and where it's going, the charges and manifests, which I give to the drivers. When we're operational, that is, which, say, give it a couple of days. You copy?"

Again, all Josh could do was nod. But when Sal gave him a funny look, Josh added, "Gulfstream Transfer, right? That's the name of the outfit. And I'm some kind of agent for the parent company."

"Lookout, more like. Point man to do all the talking and such. Zharko says you come off as white collar." Sal looked him up and down this time. "Smart college-boy type who'll cause no suspicions on the part of whatever."

"Okay, but what do I do?"

"Troubleshoot. You been listening or what? Like if the recorded message machine don't handle it, you pick up the ball, smooth it over. The spiel goes something like this: 'At present there's only maintenance, a makeover conversion to this new operation.' Words like that. Then trial runs begin. But as I said, we're not open for regular transactions and the like for a couple of days, give or take. You got it?"

Josh nodded once more, translating this to mean that in the next few days Zharko would have put his scheme in motion, transferring heaven-knows-what across state lines, zigzagging over to Asheville, and then down to the Florida Keys. Leaving only an answering machine at this location and maybe Josh or, then again, maybe not.

"Except," Sal said, "if the call is from Raul. You jot down the message and relay it to Zharko when he checks back in with you at the end of your shift."

"Checks back in?"

"Calls you on his cell like he told you. What do think, he's gonna risk showing his face? Get with it, will ya, fella?"

"Right."

"So—and this is the kicker—if somebody actually comes poking around, maybe winos, deadbeats, guys with nothing better to do, or characters linked up with the old produce outfit—steer them away. It's a whole new thing, under new management and such—period. No time to blabber. Everything is above board, like they say. Time is money. Putting it simply for you, I run the operation on this end. You keep anything and everything outta my way and it all keeps tickin' like a Swiss watch, ba-da-bing, ba-da-bing, ba-da-boom."

"Because you're on a tight schedule."

Sal didn't answer this time. Josh recalled Zharko's henchman Vlad used that phrase. He also recalled other snatches and incriminating odds and ends. But the smart thing to do was to keep from tipping his hand. This wasn't affable Josh drawing out folks who were dying to tell their tale. This was the complete opposite.

"Running a tight ship," Josh said. "Anyone can see that."

"Hey, whatever. You spot anything, you come across anything, it's your play. Then all you gotta do is list the glitches. Read them off to Zharko along with the day's word from Raul. That's it. And no outside calls. Zharko wants a tight lid on this whole operation. Incoming is strictly your lookout. You pick up the phone and it's other than Zharko, you make like a recorded message. Keep a close check every which way but loose. You follow?"

Sal pointed to the bulletin board. "And keep track of this, got it?" With that, he turned on his heels and left.

Josh went over, noting the mock schedule for the next few days hanging by a pushpin and the dated empty sheets pinned the same way, awaiting possible entries.

He closed the door and sat down at the desk to take this all in. Only muffled humming, buzzing, and whacking sounds seeped through the closed door and walls. His duties still seemed vague apart from acting as some kind of buffer. Besides mulling over Sal's directives, he had absolutely nothing to do.

Totally hung up, he rethought the choices he'd made that brought him to this pass. Choices that amounted to nothing more than playing it safe, which amounted to making no choices at all. He thought again of Teddy Roosevelt's credit to those who dared. Who failed many times but still managed to pick themselves up and keep on. *But who gives you this credit? After you did what? And who is monitoring things besides yourself?*

Just for fun, he gave himself points for wheedling information out of Novac. But that wasn't at all the kind of confrontation Teddy was talking about.

More sitting, more feeling totally hung-up.

Nevertheless, he had the prospect of getting back to Paul by five tomorrow and coming up with a direct connection with the mob. But given only Sal, the operations manager's possible characteristics, there wasn't even a possible link. Except Vlad, of course, who at best was an enforcer, not on any mob payroll, and wasn't even around.

He reached into the attaché case, got out his pocket digital recorder, hit the record button, and forced himself to get on track. Recalling and underscoring a few glimmers, he began to dictate the situation so far: *tight schedule . . . Red Syndicate or maybe some other syndicate but no tangible connection . . . pipeline of goods to Asheville from Waterbury transfer and storage operation still a possibility . . . plus a deflection to Ashville with some guy named Ivan as a contact . . . and a handoff all the way down to the Keys . . . or it's all a front just like me.*

Prompted by Vlad's purported response to photos of tropical

sailboats on Novac's coffee table, Josh added, *But you can't discount Vlad dead set to get the boat he longed for.*

Taking stock of only the realities, he noted that Sal was in charge of cleaning up the residue from some former produce distributor and the pace of the cleanup indicated they were on a tight schedule.

Josh shut off the recorder the second Sal jerked open the door.

"She's back," Sal said. "You're on."

"What do you mean?"

"I mean move your feet."

Sal left as quickly as he'd burst in. Josh got up and weaved his way past the din of the flooring machinery and traipsed down the loading ramp.

He had no idea what Sal was referring to until he spotted an old Army jeep pulling in from the side-street traffic into the entrance. As the driver braked, killed the motor, and sprang from behind the wheel, all he could tell was the supposed target was comparatively young. Moving closer, he saw she was slim with tomboy features, had short, disheveled, dyed brindle hair, and wore a black leather bomber jacket, jeans, and combat boots. Assuming she was headed straight for the ramp to have it out with Sal, Josh hurried over to intercept her.

"Excuse me. Hold it, miss, if you don't mind."

"Miss? Don't mind? What is this?" Glaring straight at him, she asked, "You some kinda choir boy, junior executive type? Where'd they haul you in from? Yale? You sure as hell ain't from around here."

"None of the above. Anyway, if you'd—"

"Anyways, pal, if you'd just get out of my way."

Josh held up his hands in mock surrender and stood his ground. "Look, as I was saying, if you'd calm down, I'm sure we can work something out."

"Oh yeah? What do you know about it anyways?"

"Nothing, not a thing. As it happens, this is my first day. My first hour, in fact. I haven't even begun to get the lay of the land. So, in a way, we're in the same boat."

"What is that, a joke? If I was you, I'd get out of my way, sit down someplace, and get your head on straight."

She peered past him at all the activity and watched workmen scamper off the dock carrying more shards and pallets and toss them into the dumpsters. "Jeez, will you look at that? It's all that remains of Uncle Fredo's wholesale supply. That's it, for crissake."

"What are you saying?"

"I'm saying my Uncle Fredo tells me to forget about it. Is he kidding? I had three restaurant chains lined up. One in Watertown, one in Torrington, and one in Naugatuck for the finest fruits and vegetables. And he tells me it's off. He's got a black eye and an arm in a sling. I come by here the other day and there's nothing doing. The place is shut tight like a clam. Next day I come by and run into this Sal character. This morning I go over to Fredo's place, he's all slumped over nursing some booze, which is weird 'cause he don't even drink. He's shaking his head saying, What am I gonna do? He tells me some stocky Russian who can hardly speak English says his legs are next if he don't cool it down after all he did was complain a little. You got the picture now, choir boy? So, where'd this bozo Sal take off to?"

She took in the scene once more and brushed by Josh the second Sal reappeared on the loading dock. But before she could move toward him, Josh swung her around and steered her back to the Jeep. "What do you think you're doing? Asking for an apology for what Vlad did and demanding Sal restore your uncle's business? Come on, missy, use your head."

"It ain't missy, pal, it's J.J., dammit!" she yelled back, leaning against the rusty hood of the jeep. "And where do you get off? How do you know the Russian's name? What's your play here anyways, telling me what I should or shouldn't do? I mean, what's the score here, Jack?"

"Josh. My name is Josh. Apart from business matters, I don't know what the deal is. And I'll never find out if I flunk my first test as a lookout."

Thrown for a second, she peered up again at the loading dock and then back at Josh. "So, you're in with bozo Sal and you know the hood who put the muscle on Uncle Fredo. That is just terrific." She spun around, slid behind the wheel of the jeep, and fell silent.

Josh turned back and noticed Sal in the near distance giving him a thumbs-up and moving out of sight.

"I got news, pal," J.J. finally said. "Maybe I can't mix it up with Sal. But I got an acquaintance who's a fed and like that, who got me off the streets. Got me into a youth program and steered me clear. Like a Big Brother so's I'm well connected. You get it?"

When Josh turned back to her, she jumped in even stronger. "That's right, Mister Josh. A fed name of Mike. I can get hold of him any time I want. He told me to play it cool, keep a sharp eye out, check back any time. Which means, now that I see how this game is playing out, I can get in touch. Tell him all about you and Sal and this Vlad creep. Tell him about what happened to Uncle Fredo. Have him scope out this whole operation from top to bottom. Now what you gotta say?"

"I say, you do that and you ruin any chance to step in. The second this Mike person starts nosing around they'll shut the whole thing down, heads will roll, and there's no telling who else will be in for it."

"Who said? How do you know all this?"

"That's not the point."

Josh stepped back, realizing he was dealing with a street person, a total stranger at least ten years younger. But then again, he needed a liaison with some kind of law enforcement.

J.J. went silent, banged her fists against the steering wheel, and said, "Okay, okay. Maybe. But I'm telling you, I can't sit still for this. I gotta do something."

There was a long delay until Josh came out with, "Then how about this? You track this Mike guy down. Ask him what he knows about a red syndicate still operating in this area. Tell him what happened to your uncle at the hands of a Russian named Vlad."

"Oh, yeah? And trust you to boot? Fat chance."

"Try it. What have you got to lose? We'll meet first thing tomorrow morning and take it from there."

"Like hell. I don't know you from nothin' and from all I do know, you are handing me a load of bull."

"Listen to me. If I have something to go on . . . maybe even get my boss down in Carolina on board . . ." Josh fumbled for his wallet, flashed his ID from Gannet Media, and slipped it back in his pocket.

"Hold it, hold it. Now you're jerking me around with a reporter ID and working for this Sal, which don't figure six ways outta Sunday. What if this is your thing, conning anybody stupid enough to let you take them in?"

"All right. Just tell Mike a deportee is back and up to no good. A deportee who's running this show. Tell him that and let him decide whether working with me might be a good idea."

She shook her head, reached into her bomber jacket, and pulled out a crumpled pack of cigarettes, stuck one in her mouth, and sat there motionless.

Spotting Sal reappearing and waving him off, Josh banged on the hood of the jeep, leaned over until his face was almost touching hers. "Look, you better beat it before Sal comes over and messes everything up."

"Oh yeah?"

"That's right. We can't meet anywhere around here to hash this out, but how about around nine tomorrow morning in front of the gray-stone church? The one at the corner of the Green, catty-corner to the museum where I once helped chaperone a teacher's second grade class."

J.J. gave him a wary look. She didn't give him a yes or a no. She got out a lighter, lit the cigarette, and took a deep drag. Hanging onto the wary look, she said, "I'd have to be pretty desperate to give a guy like you even the time of day."

"Except that, like you, I'm in a bind."

"Right. Oh goody, tell me another one."

"At nine tomorrow. Don't forget. A deportee and his flunky are back."

"Yeah, terrific. Don't hold your breath, pal."

He could have given her Zharko's name but couldn't risk the ramifications—her spreading the word, people pressing her where she got this hitherto bit of unknown information, all of it possibly coming right back to haunt him.

She gave him another suspicious look, cranked up the old engine, spun the jeep around, and tore out, heading back in the direction of downtown Waterbury.

He hurried up the ramp, raised his voice to combat the noise of the floor machines and told Sal the girl gave him a hard time and didn't believe he had any authority but finally gave up trying to argue with him. Giving Sal no chance to holler back, Josh weaved his way back to the cinderblock office, shut the door, and sat down. He couldn't help wondering if by some fluke this encounter with J.J. might actually lead to something.

He also wondered if some part of him that had been under wraps all these years was starting to burst through the seams.

CHAPTER FIFTEEN

Over the next few hours nothing else happened. The recorded message on the answering machine, stating when this subsidiary operation would be up and running, handled a few perfunctory calls. Though callers were asked to leave their name, nature of their inquiry, and a number where they could be reached after the initial setup was in place, no such requests were received. By four p.m. on that Thursday, however, the first call from Raul came through. In a distinct Latino accent he said, "So far, the weather is balmy, the Gulf Stream warm and swift, and the trade winds are favorable."

It was soon afterwards that Josh's cell phone began to jingle. The instant he picked up, he knew Zharko was on a tear and Josh would barely be able to get a word in edgewise.

"Is true you sneak into lawyer Novac's house this morning? No phone call to ask permission? Irina gives him heads-up behind my back but not me also? You both do this behind my back?"

"First of all, I didn't sneak in," Josh replied. "I knocked. There was no phone number listed on the promissory agreement or in the phone book. I had a few minutes to spare and only wanted to know—"

"What? I not make everything plain as daytime? I not warn what happens to you, your mother, girl you are sweet on, whoever, if you cross me, throw wrench into works? What you think I am running here? I got time for this? Answer me, bright good boy who is obedient for damn sure."

"That's all true except—"

"Quiet, I am talking here. Irina show me birthday cards you send so I can track you and then she calls Novac? Why? Besides, you are gadzo, not Romany, not gypsy of my blood. You, who only watches and listens, now wants to know about orphan mother from Romania? And how I fit in as if any of your damn business? Novac is nervous little man, not good at his age this questioning, which is why he calls me. What you do is not good for anybody. What, for sure, I am missing here?"

It struck Josh that this was something new for Zharko. In his volatile, cocksure way, he wasn't used to having to reevaluate anything. Apparently, Novac's typical reassuring ploy had fizzled over the phone. Zharko absolutely wasn't buying it.

"I only wanted to make certain," Josh said, taking a page from Novac, "that there weren't any contingencies. That compliance wouldn't go on forever. And what the deal actually was between you and my mother. What that was all about since she would never talk to me straight out. And I mean never."

"And he tells you? He tells you what Irina is maybe pulling?"

"Nothing like that. He only hinted she's on shaky ground."

"For sure. Shaky ground is good way to put it. So, you will go see Irina and draw clear, straight line. Guarantee there is no mix-up here, no funny business I have to worry my head about. No surprises or what you got for breakfast, around the corner, or whistling upriver. You will do this, you are reading me, yes?"

"Yes, I read you."

"What you are reading? What you understand?"

"I'm to see my erstwhile mother and make sure she knows she can't jerk you around. And you won't put up with either of us trying to pull a fast one."

"Ah. Shaky ground, pulling fast one—good words to keep in my mind. Maybe you are learning, yes?"

"Yes, I am learning."

Josh assumed this little altercation was over. But Zharko beat around the bush a little more before settling on the outcome of Josh's encounter with Irina to be relayed to him immediately afterwards. To humor him, Josh promised he'd get on it right away, leaving out that having it out with his mother after he left the warehouse was next on his fact-finding mission anyways.

"If there's a problem," Josh added, "some misunderstanding, rest assured I will keep you in the loop."

"Because you are fooling with me, you get ramifications. Good word Novac teach me many times. Watch out for ramifications every which way."

"You bet."

"We will see what Irina is maybe hiding, yes?"

"Or not. Absolutely, right away."

"So, good. Now give me number one message from Raul."

Josh glanced at his notepad. "'So far, the weather is balmy and the trade winds are favorable.'"

"Also good. And you keep in mind exactly who you are dealing with."

But Josh, of course, still didn't know exactly who he was dealing with. And about the dynamic vis-à-vis Zharko and Irina, apart from the stable-boy connection, and why she would warn Novac behind Zharko's back knowing full well it would get back to him. The only thing Josh could come up with was the possibility Irina and Zharko had a connection based on experiences Josh knew nothing about.

After Zharko hung up on him, he reached inside the attaché case for the tattered book on gypsy/Romany life. The one from Novac with the passages Zharko had earmarked. But before opening it, he took stock.

Based on what little Josh knew based on hearsay and the

rumor mill over the years, Zharko had various nefarious dealings that may have had links with Waterbury's past. Like the body they'd found in the trunk of a car in a junkyard in the Town Plot section and the flashy Lincoln limo dealership on the east end catering to mobsters. But that was part of the old Mafia and not, as far as he could tell, connected to any red syndicate of today.

Moreover, what he had gleaned from Novac pointed to a conflicted thread between Zharko's gypsy/Romany ways and Irina's proper Victorian values. How it factored in in terms of Josh's predicament was still beyond him. If he could better understand this odd Zharko–Irina dynamic starting with gypsy Zharko, he might at least begin to have a handle on things.

In the hour remaining before the warehouse closed, he started sorting through *Romany Life*.

Focusing solely on the pages Zharko dog-eared and scribbled comments on, and keeping in mind Zharko had read these pages early in his US orientation, Josh soon uncovered a pattern. Zharko wasn't at all interested in gypsies, per se. His aim was limited to popular myths, romantic stories, and anything that underscored wild, unpredictable behavior, thievery, and the outlaw life. Anything, in effect, that echoed the old Hollywood movie version of gypsies.

Zharko may have latched onto his stint as a riding instructor but was actually taken with tales of Nikolai the horse trader who "threw himself with much abandon into duels, love affairs, and derring-do, including the theft of prize horses under a magistrate's very own nose." Zharko underlined phrases like "cleverness and rivalries of the tribes." He made check marks next to passages like "because of their Slavic blood lines," "they will naturally throw themselves into war as into music or love affairs," and "the intensity being such that once launched was incapable of being held back."

There were also check marks alluding to the wandering nature of eastern European gypsies in the nineteenth century and their "contempt for furniture that holds you down." In one example, everyone in the band seats themselves around a legless table. After tea, the truncated table is removed, tossed back in the horse-driven caravan, the living space they'd briefly occupied once again unoccupied as off they go, leaving no trace of ever settling down. "Try as hard as you please to domesticate us," wrote one traveler back in the day, "the first chance we get we run off to the woods and our horses." Next to that declaration Zharko had scribbled, *Yes! Not let them damn ever nail you down!* obviously for Novac's benefit.

At the head of another section were references to Romany people finding themselves in a strange land treated as foreigners by the gadze. A feeling, doubtless shared by Josh's mother during the Christmas present fiasco, promulgated in all probability by Zharko. But that still didn't jive with her Victorian upbringing. Moreover, the authors of this book acknowledged the presence of racism, hatred, violence, prejudice, and discrimination suffered at different times in different locales. However, most of the book was dedicated to the commonalities of Romany people around the world, decrying the disparaging connotations of gypsy as in "gyp," fakirs, cutthroats, crystal ball reading cheats, and lusty, fiery women wearing hoop earrings and slit skirts, howling and dancing up a storm. As a counterargument, the authors featured photos of happy Romany families from all walks of life who peacefully settled in many regions of present-day Eastern Europe, Spain, and Latin America.

As Novac had indicated, Zharko wasn't at all interested in any of that happy, contented assimilation. Zharko had scrawled one more rebuttal on a blank end page:

Oh, for sure, Novac, you think I am going to settle down, sweet Romany life, grow crops, start business? Forget what I know from old country, corruption, paying protection money? Parasites (good word, no?) living off workers? Shell companies and shell bank accounts? As much or more corruption here in US lousy government, I hear. As bad or much worse everywhere you go—payoffs under table or what have you got. Race is too swift, so I hear. Winners and losers, zero sum game. This is what I know of life.

Josh put the book aside. The upshot was that Zharko was an outlier, a rogue gypsy hooked up with any breed or enterprise that was worth his while. The more Josh realized this, the more he saw there was a direct link between his catching on and Zharko catching on to him if he didn't watch his step. Especially with a tight window and a big payoff hanging in the balance.

As for Zharko's immediate concern, there was the matter of his relationship with Irina. Which gave Josh the opportunity to find out how it evolved. And more importantly, how things stood, causing Zharko to doubt her.

And so he got set to drive back up to the Litchfield Hills and confront his mother. Given their strained, impossible relationship, he had the disjointed correlation between her Victorian upbringing as a Romanian orphan and her dealings with a renegade gypsy to sort out. Now that he thought about it, what of his biological father? What was that all about?

As he drove, he took in the possibility that the deeper he delved, the more tangled the web and the more twisted this whole proposition. Which was why there were so many family secrets in this world. Better to keep everyone forever in the dark.

CHAPTER SIXTEEN

As he reached the exit and the long steep climb to the Litchfield village center, he reminded himself not to push it. Not to put her on her guard, like the time a few years back when he dropped in on her and couldn't help noticing how swiftly she moved, her willowy body darting out the door of the rustic cabin, brushing by him and then back inside clutching a realty folder she'd misplaced. Just before she reentered her study, he'd said, "That is so amazing. I mean, the fact that you never have to touch up your hair and there isn't a line in your face. Each time I see you, you never grow older." She'd glared at him with those dark piercing eyes and closed the study door in his face.

More recently, when he'd traveled up here under the pretext of checking out the newspaper publishing scene in the Litchfield Hills and the Berkshires, and offhandedly asked if it was true that Zharko had been deported, she put him off until he said, "I hate to break it to you, but there's a rumor going around that some mothers actually confide in their children. They don't always play things close to the vest."

As his frustration got the better of him, he added, "Not only that, but when the children are little, moms ask how they're doing. As a result, conversations take place."

In response, she had gathered up a sheaf of papers off her desk and said, "As you can see, I'm busy. Have to deal with complaints from the tenants. Make yourself something to eat if you're hungry."

And that was it. Nothing further was said.

Now, as the climb got steeper around the little hamlet of East Litchfield, he had no idea how he'd get through to her. The milky-looking late-afternoon sky held still, there were no wind gusts and little traffic, but that same edginess stayed with him. Zharko had forced the issue and Josh had come this far and couldn't back down. Josh Bartlet was a façade tacked onto another façade. A ploy that kept him endlessly skirting around. If he didn't cut through all the smoke and mirrors, he could wind up on charges as an accomplice, the IOU notwithstanding. Not only that, there would still be no telling what would happen to Molly and countless others who would wind up as collateral damage.

And his abiding, impossible dream of somehow earning the right to be with Molly free and clear would never be fulfilled.

He reminded himself that confronting Irina at last wasn't just an errand to appease Zharko. And it wasn't only an item on today's to-do list. What he'd unearthed so far were clues to all that lay beneath this whole mess.

Reaching the village, he cruised by the colonial structures and cozy brick-and-mortar elementary school on his left where Molly taught her second graders and life was safe and wholesome. A sweet refuge miles from Waterbury and other nervy urban hubs, if you discounted the goings-on deep down a certain lane. If you discounted everything else that was mounting up on him.

Once out of town, he came to that very lane, hung a left, and passed Molly's folks' old cottage on the corner. Almost immediately, the road turned into a gravel track, dipping deeper into the woods, narrowing into a dirt drive that swerved into his mother's rustic cabin and proceeded to tail off into a wall of hemlock and pine. He tried not to think of the prospect of Zharko's gypsy camper hidden beyond the tree line across the way and the carpet of pine needles that may very well lead to a shallow gravesite. He tried not to consider the possibility that only he and Zharko knew of the vicinity where the body was buried; that Josh, for all intents and purposes, was a material witness who had shut his eyes and merely gone along with being shipped far out of the way. He tried not to ponder the correlation between dutiful obedience and guilt.

He pulled over when he noticed a tamped-down opening where something had recently parted the brush, wide enough for an old camper to pass through. An old camper that could have been recently serviced for the long trip ahead to the end of the mainland and the Keys. For the moment, with ample food and supplies, Zharko could be lying in wait with Vlad.

Josh shut off the engine of the rental car, got out, and trod carefully forward. He'd never done this before. This was the exact opposite of stay back, keep out of the way. Like he'd instinctively hidden behind the truck back at the retirement center as a matter of course.

He shuffled forward. Though the sky was losing its milky hue and the late afternoon was quickly wearing down, he could make out everything as sharply as could be. He stopped the second he spotted the old camper dead ahead in a clearing flanked by a canopy of jutting pines. The camper was rusty in spots, but there was no mistaking the two horizontal bars embossed on the side: blue on top for eternal spirit, green below for open fields. Not for the Romany people of today doing their best to blend in. But perfect for Zharko's outlaw emblem of yore and his personal brand taken from his beloved horse thieves of legend.

Josh stood still, but only for a moment. To be able to stand your ground, to say, *Here I am no matter what*, would really be something. So was walking slowly back to the car instead of rushing. But he couldn't quite bring it off.

Back at the gravel track, he forced himself to get on with it. He slid behind the wheel, hit the ignition, and drove on.

Presently, he spotted his mother's old forest-green Subaru station wagon embossed with the white realty logo on the side panel. It was still light out away from the deep woods, leaving time enough to have this encounter. Then field Zharko's call regarding Irina's possible complicity. Then check back with Molly and reveal a couple of things so she'd find him more forthcoming and keep this juggling act going.

He pulled into the dirt drive, shut off the motor, and took in the stillness. With his work cut out for him, he headed straight for the weathered front door, grasped the wrought-iron knocker, rapped a few times, and eased the door open.

As a rule, she would be ensconced down the musty hallway to the left in her knotty pine study, on the phone or riffling through papers, paying bills, or tapping on the computer keyboard. And there, as he walked forward, was where he found her.

It wasn't the sight of her slender body bedecked in a white peasant blouse and ankle-length black skirt that made him pause before making his presence known. That outfit was de rigueur. Nor was the raven-black hair parted in the middle and severely pulled back unusual, the hoop earrings and the piercing set of her dark eyes at all remarkable. It was the fact that the burgundy window drapes were open and she was gazing out the window toward the vicinity of Zharko's camper. As if sensing Josh standing there, she pivoted sharply.

"I received a call from Novac," she said in that usual dry, clipped tone.

"That figures," Josh said. "But before you start in on me, I dropped by to get a little reassurance." Stepping partway into the cluttered room, he added, "You knew that, or at least must have assumed."

"He said you wanted a lot more. Why? What's the matter with you?"

Shrugging, he said, "I don't know. I guess something happens when you suddenly find yourself up against the wall. Tracked down and forced to come back up here before you were ready on your own terms."

"Forced?"

"What else would you call it? Dragooned, still perpetually in the dark, not knowing whether it was even legit."

She took this in, waited a moment, and then kept on the offensive.

"So you barged into Novac's home."

"Dropped by, I said. I didn't barge. Besides, he was expecting me, obviously thanks to you."

"To make a quick call, perhaps," she said, deflecting as usual, going to a file cabinet and shuffling through some folders. "Not to confront him."

"I was polite mostly. Good grief, do we have to keep this up? I only wanted to know."

"What exactly did you want to know?"

Josh hesitated. This was as close as they'd ever come to an actual encounter. Latching on to this opening, he said, "I wanted to know how I fit into this convoluted muddle."

"All you have to do is go along and then it's done. Is that asking too much?"

"Oh sure, la-di-da. How do I ever get through to you? Everyone I know, everyone I interview can tell you where they're coming from, or at least not harboring some glaring hole in their story."

He went over to the window and pointed. "Can it be? Was it the woods you've been looking at? At long last beginning to take it all in?"

"What are you talking about?"

Josh wanted to say, *Recalling the nightmares it must have given me*. But all he could bring himself to say was, "Remembering what I was privy to, that's what. The catalyst that led to everything."

She shook her head, grabbed one of the folders from the file cabinet, sat down at the desk, and riffled through the papers for the longest time. Unable to meet his gaze, she said, "Why bring that up? So long ago . . ."

Josh didn't answer, hoping the strained silence would do the trick.

Suddenly, she slapped the papers down on the desk. "His partner was embezzling. Zharko took care of it. Whatever happened, whatever you saw or thought you saw, all you had to do was let it go. Get away from here. It was all for the best."

"He took care of it? All for the best? Really? Is that what you think?"

Predictably, she cut the topic off then and there. She opened a desk drawer, searched around, came up with an ink pad and broker's seal, and was poised to stamp some documents.

"That's it," Josh said. "Just ignore me."

He abruptly left her, headed down the corridor to the kitchen, went over to the coffee maker with its ready supply of a European blend, grabbed the carafe, and poured himself a cup. Skipping the cream and sugar, he stood by the counter and sipped the strong, bitter brew until he calmed down a bit. Then he hurried back to her study, resolved to break through this time, come what may.

"Okay," he said, reentering, "this is the deal. As it happens, Zharko has so much riding on this shakedown, he thinks you put me up to it—touching base with Novac, I mean. Having something up your sleeve that could jeopardize his plans. So he's going to call me back shortly on my cell phone. I'll fend him off, come up with something to save you some grief if, and only if, you fill me in."

"Meaning?" she asked, pushing the documents aside, glancing up at him.

"Meaning," Josh said, moving in on her, "I can't take being jerked around with this humongous hole in my story. Meaning I just plain have to know."

"Know what? What is it you want from me?"

"The basics, the missing pieces. There I am, no father, no relatives, no guidance or religion to turn to. So I look to comic books, school, and movies, which doesn't exactly fit the bill."

He hesitated. Unable to tell her that to this day the little kid in him never understood why he was forsaken. He'd kept still, out of sight, out of the way, didn't he? Maybe if he was extra good she would let him stay and someday be nice to him, even care for him a little bit. If he stuck it out, in time Zharko might be gone and somehow, some way, things could get patched up. But he couldn't tell her any of this.

"What I'm saying," Josh said, "is you owe me something, don't you think? Some explanation how I got this way."

Her expression seemed to soften but she still didn't respond.

"Tell you what," Josh said. "We'll make it a bedtime story, a good ol' cautionary tale. I'll start and you take it from there. Okay? You don't even have to say *I*. Let's make it *she*. Once upon a time, *she*."

Giving her no chance to deflect again, Josh moved closer and began to wing it. "As the story goes, once upon a time there was an orphan girl from Romania who was so bright and so light-skinned despite her high cheekbones, dark hair, and dark eyes, she could pass for Caucasian hailing from just about anywhere. And so, because everything about her was so promising, she was taken in by a missionary agency in England. Time passed. She later found herself in another missionary boarding school across the pond, tucked away in the Litchfield Hills, still secluded, of course, from the evils of the world, located in a kind of Victorian greenhouse, speaking perfect English and looking just right."

Josh went on, like a storyteller who'd at long last found a receptive audience. "So, one day, she and the other bright-eyed girls began taking riding lessons at a nearby riding academy under the tutelage of a wild-eyed gypsy. Or to her mind, he seemed like a wild-eyed gypsy from way back then. But still and all, everything was perfectly fine, she fit in perfectly with her boon companions she'd known all this while."

Slowly, she opened a desk drawer and reached inside a tin of thin cigars with a wooden tip. She plucked up a match, struck it against a matchbox, and began inhaling as if the smoke was gently soothing.

Seconds later, cigarillo in hand, she rose, drifted back over to the window and began to speak, her tone wistful as can be.

"She was barely fifteen then," she said. "The headmaster's son, who was about ten years older, tall, blond, eyes of blue, read poetry to her . . . told her she was special, not like any girl he'd ever met. He also quoted passages from the New Testament. She thought he was like a fairytale prince come to sweep her away."

Another deep, soothing drag on the cigarillo. Then she went on. "But when she found she was with child, the headmaster sent his son away and she was no longer allowed to stay in school. With no one else to turn to, she told the riding master. He listened, he understood. He had funds but never told her from where. They tell you you're one of them, he says, but they lie. Make one mistake, they cast you out. Break one rule, they forsake you."

Another deep drag, her voice a bit harsher this time. "He arranged for her confinement, a cabin in the woods—everything. He thought the gadzo baby would fetch a lot of money on the open market. But she wanted to keep it because surely the head-master's son would return. She learned the missionary school had picked up stakes and moved far away. The gypsy still had plans for the child but later on, when the boy saw something he shouldn't have . . ."

"After the mother drove the neighborhood girl off," Josh cut in. "The one whose Christmas present reminded her of the missionary school. Reminded her of all her nice classmates who shunned her who had the same blond hair and blue eyes. Reminded her the unwanted son's similar features were exactly like the one who'd left her in the lurch."

But by now she had tuned Josh out, fully locked into her reverie, the tone of her voice growing defensive.

"More time passed," she said. "The gypsy came and went, gone sometimes for months at a time. Having to make do, she took a real estate broker's exam. There was the purchase of rundown tenements, maintenance, tenants who didn't pay and some who skipped town. Inspections. Liens, quit claim deeds, clients who forfeited . . . male brokers who swept in and snatched her commissions. But she kept at it. What could she do? Who else would have her under the circumstances?"

Josh watched her hand slip down to her side, still clutching the lit cigarillo. In the stillness, though they had never touched, he went over and patted her shoulder. But she was too far gone.

He eased back to the doorway and said, "Okay. I'll handle Zharko. I'll think of something."

She may have felt his touch, may have heard his offer—there was no way to tell. Her gaze remained fixed somewhere in the distance. Still drawn, perhaps, by something she lost and was still yearning for.

CHAPTER SEVENTEEN

J osh remained parked in front of the cabin for the longest time. A gaggle of honking geese flew by and dissolved into a roiling cloud bank, signaling how fruitless it was to go on grappling with his elusive childhood. The simple fact was that he had no roots to draw from. He'd gotten lost in storybooks, old movies, other people's tales. Under the cover of good behavior, he'd done his schoolwork. Later on, he'd interviewed others for whom everything came easy and polished their journeys. He'd watched and listened from a remove but was never able to squelch neither those fearful nights of remembrance nor that ache that had no name. A good part of that ache was yearning to be with Molly, a feeling of belonging, a sense of home.

At least he'd now filled in the gap and had to own every bit of it.

As a second gaggle of honking geese flew by heading for the roiling cloud bank, he thought of Lakota Sioux youth preparing for battle. He thought of John Wayne's adopted son in *Red River*, getting into a knockdown, drag-out fight with his surrogate father to earn his place among the cattlemen and drovers. It would have been nice to have had a father who showed him the ropes, gave him some advice, or even served as someone to go up against. It would have been nice to have had a doting mother who comforted him after every setback. But there it was.

In reality, by the time he was three, his nineteen-year-old biological mother was bereft, in debt to Zharko, and in over her head, which left little Sonny earmarked as a commodity on standby. Sold to the highest bidder or hung onto for some future bartering. As an eyewitness during the knifing incident, being so well behaved became a liability. Confronted by the police, like any obedient child, he'd tell the authorities all he'd seen. Better to ship him away to a boarding school like the one his mother attended, where his fear and compliance could be molded into a dutiful adult. Thus, the melding of the Victorian and the devious, and the final hook of the promissory note. Thus, his current predicament as a foil and accessory. No wonder Zharko was all for his change of name to Josh Bartlet. It was perfect for a docile front man who had to go along in a shady enterprise. It fit—all of it.

With nothing more to hash over, he hit the ignition, backed out, and began cruising slowly up the gravel track toward the main drag. He was intent on dropping in on Molly, hoping she'd be in, wondering what he'd tell her.

At the top of the rise, his cell phone began to jangle in his blazer pocket. He pulled over, shut off the motor, and got set to deal with Zharko, though he'd completely forgotten to come up with a deflection Zharko would buy.

No sooner had he answered the call when Zharko's gravelly voice bore in. "Now you will tell me. I call her myself, you know that?"

"No."

"But she cut me short. So, in world only of winners and losers from very beginning of earth and stars, what is story here? You playing me, is that what you doing? No way you are playing me, you hear?" Zharko sucked in his breath, apparently on the verge of going on half-cocked.

"Yes. Okay."

"What is okay? When was okay? Was okay when feds confiscate goods, deport me? Lock up goods but goods get on streets anyways? Price goes up and who is holding bag? Feds profit, kingpins profit. This is right? This is okay by you, spoiled good boy who never gets damn gadzo hands dirty?"

As Zharko carried on, Josh perked up. He recalled what he knew about Zharko's antics in Bucharest: in the carnivals, throwing knives within inches of a nubile target, training horses for the bareback riders. Branching out far and wide, getting in with gangs, eventually picking up tips from the Red Syndicate. Flaunting the image of a renegade gypsy. This was exactly who Josh was dealing with, factoring in rampant paranoia now that he was back in Connecticut and had to operate from a remove.

Still sucking in his breath, making a hissing sound through his teeth, Zharko noted things that ticked him off during his stint at the riding stable and ended with, "And you talk to me of okay, quiet boy who has dealings with nothing? No way anything is okay. Now you damn read me, good-behaved boy?"

"You bet," Josh said, realizing Zharko had no way of knowing what transpired between himself and Irina but had become so anxious hanging back in the wings, he was venting and grabbing any excuse to let off steam.

"Irina, who cut me short, tell you how I wait, wheel and deal, plus keep herself going? So now is my goddamn time? Answer me. And answer how Irina let Novac know so, real cozy, Novac let you in on ways you and Irina get off the hook. Maybe Novac is playing both ends, calling me but, at same time, you not so good boy after all."

"You're seeing it all wrong."

"Oh? So tell me how else I should be seeing this? Irina is only business, only cut and dried. So what is business this time she must call Novac? Business Novac, sharp shyster he is, cannot handle easy and needs Irina to talk over?"

Josh reached for some way out of this. Zharko's paranoia was getting worse by the second. "Look, it's no big deal. She's frustrated over tenement repairs, recent dealings with unscrupulous realty clients coupled with this old promissory note hanging over her head. Taken together, she simply wanted to give Novac a heads-up so he'd be all set to get me in line. In short, she has far too much on her plate right now."

"Is all about far too much for her?"

"Yes."

"For sure?"

"I just spoke to her. For the first time she told me all about her hard life and needs a break."

A long pause until Zharko said, "Then you stay away from her and from Novac is long and short of it. You swear to me. Cross your heart to gadzo Sunday school or what you cross your heart to."

"Fine. I will stay away from both of them."

"And never forget. You stiff me, you pay consequences worse than you imagine. This is not threat. This is goddamn, cockamamie promise." With that, Zharko broke the connection.

"Of course," Josh muttered to himself. "Toe the line and turn a blind eye. Like always."

As a tint of grayish-pink twilight came on, he headed to Molly's pristine sublet just off the file of historic homes. Along the way, he thought about where he and Molly had left off. She'd mentioned the abiding mystery of his background and his mother's aversion to Christmas. He'd mentioned he was in a bind but didn't reveal exactly what it was that suddenly brought him back here. He did say he'd try to do better next time and asked for a window of seven days or so while putting the assistant principal on hold.

Which left him where?

If nothing else, Molly clearly deserved to know about his origins. She might then grant his request to wait and see while he tried to get up to speed on his dubious road to redemption.

—··—

"I can only spare a minute, Josh," Molly said, calling from the master bedroom.

"I know, I know. You have a parent-teacher conference and I didn't give you any notice."

"Nothing beyond saying you'd check back as you slipped out, distracted as can be."

"That's me all right. Distracted as can be. One of the all-time greats," Josh said, keeping up the preliminary banter.

"This time I'm guessing it has something to do with your mother."

"That's right. Give me a second while I go over my closing argument."

Uncertain how to put it without rocking the boat, Josh took in the atmosphere once more with its sturdy hard-rock maple furniture. And the glistening oil paintings of red barns neatly hung in birch frames circling the living room. Not to mention the porcelain ornaments carefully positioned, resting on the mantelpiece next to where he was standing, reflected by the gilt-edged mirror above, keeping watch, making sure not one item was out of place. All of it the worst possible ambiance to come out with the shoddy realities.

But he had to level with her for once before she bolted; had to in some way find out how things stood, just as he'd done with his mother.

Taking a chance, speaking loud enough so she could hear him down the hall, he opened with, "What would you say if I told you I had broken through? Just come from brushing past Irina Korda's defense barrier all these years and appear before you now with the big reveal?"

This was flip, whimsical Josh, signaling he was skimming over the surface of something far too touchy. Though they had both dated other people over the past years, there was a tacit understanding that Josh only confided in her. Like the time he was accosted by a deranged derelict on the Waterbury Green. But he told her in this offhanded way.

Taking the utter silence as a sign she was giving him her full attention, he went on. "You see, as it happens, my biological father was tall, blue-eyed, handsome, and blond, at least some ten years older. Plus the son of a headmaster of a nearby missionary boarding school. In turn, Miss Irina was a starry-eyed teen, barely sixteen, an orphan from Romania by way of the UK. Taken in by this false Prince Charming, she found herself with child, jilted by yon prince, booted out of this pristine refuge by the headmaster who would brook no sinful behavior on the part of his pure charges. Thus, closing his eyes to his son's culpability. Not only that, but said boarding school soon after pulled up stakes and, alas, was seen no more."

Josh waited for a response. The stillness was broken by a soft, barely audible "Golly."

"Well now," Josh said, "unmarried with a toddler in tow, Miss Irina was still pining for the prince to return and make her an honest woman. If he had, little Sonny would no longer be disparaged, Christmas would once more be welcomed into the hearth and home, and there would be peace and good will toward all. But the longer there was no sign of yon prince, the more jaded Irina became, so that the snowy night in question when one Molly Hunter came rapping on the door, looking every bit like Irina's holier-than-thou old classmates, Molly's Christmas present was the last straw."

"Really?" Molly said, her voice a bit closer now. "This is all true?"

"Scout's honor."

"How awful. And where does this leave you?"

"Well, since there was some talk early on to sell baby Sonny to the highest bidder, it appears changing my name may have actually been a smart move. I mean, all I have to do is provide Josh Bartlet with a little spunk and a whole bunch of missing attributes and I may eventually have something solid to go on. Maybe to the point I can even rival George. That is, if Molly Hunter will bestow upon me that allotted grace period."

There was still no response to this proposition. Moments later, she came bustling toward him, honey-blonde hair slightly askew, brush in hand, dressed in a white peasant blouse over a beige flare skirt.

"Oh, how awful for you," she said. "I really mean it."

"Yup. However, mind you, the jury is still out."

"Which, I take it, still leaves some fending over this legal matter."

"Indeed. This thorny legal matter and its dicey consequences."

As she moved toward the mirror opposite him and applied a few finishing brushstrokes to her hair, Josh added, "One more deep dark secret my overly young mother kept from me. A promissory note that has come due out of the blue. Which requires poking around Waterbury to sort things out while avoiding the denizens of its mean streets. And that, lady, is the gist of it."

Molly stopped brushing, gave him one of those quizzical looks, and said, "And you ask me to believe your editor bought all this and gave you a leave of absence?"

Though the so-called arrangement with Paul was barely tenuous, he plowed ahead. "I'm to touch base and give him a call back in the Blue Ridge by five tomorrow. Let's just say I'm bound to do a better job putting it all in perspective by then."

Molly reached into her leather shoulder bag on an end table, came up with a tube of coral lip gloss, returned to the mirror and, while applying the gloss, said, "So, you're telling me you've got the kind of editor who puts up with this kind of intrigue."

"Rather took it all with a grain of salt, underscoring that this is nothing like the person he hired and he better come up with something a helluva lot more promising."

"Uh-huh," Molly said. "I see." But her tone indicated something entirely different and that Josh was apparently through with any further revelations. She moved away from the mantelpiece, deposited the lip gloss and brush in her bag, moved to the closet and reached for a matching beige spring coat. Josh followed her.

"Allow me." Josh took the coat off the hanger and held onto it for a moment. "Not to change the subject, but it would help if you held off like I asked. You know—putting George on the back burner for a couple of days while I see to it."

She shook her head. "As it happens, George and I are barely speaking. We only acknowledge one another politely in passing down the school corridors. That's the way it goes every time he admonishes me for biding my time and I, in turn, tell him how much I don't appreciate his patronizing tone. In fact, it usually takes a week until it blows over again. Now if you'll excuse me, I have to put on my positive, hopeful face and assure the parents that their little second graders have a bright future ahead of them, each and every one."

She adjusted her silver charm bracelet, allowed him to help her with her coat, patted his shoulder, and said, "Oh, Josh, I mean really. Whatever is going to become of you?"

With that, she retrieved her bag. He followed her out the door into the faint twilight afterglow, saying, "So, we'll keep in touch. Compare notes in regard to our respective ordeals."

"Very funny," she said as she locked the door. "I, for one, will put this down as a matter of an outstanding debt aggravated by a reckoning with your mom." With that exit line, they went their separate ways.

As he retreated to the car, what kept his spirits up was not the continuing on-again, off-again rift between Molly and George. It was the forgiving way she responded this time, coupled with her concern, all enabling him to forget his shaky circumstances for a few moments.

Moreover, she'd chosen to wear the silver charm bracelet while mingling with the sedate village parents. The very one he'd recently sent her for Christmas, replete with the dangling unicorn, seashell, and crystalized snowflake.

CHAPTER EIGHTEEN

His hopeful mood was short-lived. Back at the inn for a bite to eat, he couldn't help noticing that the pub-like den seemed cold and artificial despite the rough-hewn beams overhead. It was as if everything was colluding to make sure he never let down his guard. His room upstairs with its cookie-cutter wallpaper echoed the same business-like tone—e.g., you're here to close the deal.

Moreover, as Josh took a last sip of herbal tea and got set to leave a tip, he realized he was going to have to venture more deeply into the here and now of Teddy Roosevelt's arena. First thing tomorrow he would no longer just be skirting around. If he had any hope of making any strides, he needed to convince J.J. to put him on to Mike, her FBI acquaintance. That or permanently cross Paul off his list and lose any chance of some backup.

In terms of the actual business at hand, Zharko's scheme must emanate from his encounters in Eastern Europe and lessons he'd learned from his Russian associates, including setting up shell companies and dealing with illicit goods that got him deported in the first place. All of which doubtless readied him for some final upcoming big score from Waterbury across state lines down to the Gulfstream and restitution.

Which made sense. But what did he, Josh Bartlet, actually have to go on that would in any way get anyone's attention and come to fruition?

Feeling the pressure of filling this enormous gap, all he could do was get out his laptop, hook up to the inn's Wi-Fi, and surf the web. Then, by broaching the realities of organized crime, he might be able to make some headway with this world he knew next to nothing about. Not (as Paul pointed out) as some misguided movie buff no one could take seriously.

"Exactly," he said to himself as he left a generous tip for the waitress and moved on. "Right now, you're in no position to convince anybody of anything."

— · · —

Once settled in his room a little after eight p.m., he placed his laptop on the desk and went to work. This go-round he wasn't after a little background on an interesting hometown figure. This backstory centered on another universe altogether.

The first heading he scribbled on his notepad was "Deportation hearing and disposition re: Zharko Vadja." But no matter how he phrased it on Google, no matter what combinations he used, he came up empty. He assumed it was under the subject of Connecticut news but found no hits to pertinent arrest files.

The second heading he scribbled down was "Inklings of a red syndicate operating on the eastern seaboard." This time his goal was to dig up anything pertinent, list the results, and call it a night. Sleep on it and have his findings in mind bright and early for the encounter with J.J., assuming she actually showed up. Convince her he knew what he was doing so she'd be more inclined to give him the benefit of the doubt and get her fed contact Mike on board. Not for Josh's sake, but to come to the aid of her Uncle Fredo. That done, he'd keep a sharp eye on the day's goings-on at the so-called Gulfstream Transfer outlet, contact Paul by five, and endeavor to keep this juggling act going.

Flitting from link to link, it took over an hour before he came across a reference to the Organizatsiya or Russian mob located in Brighton Beach, a neighborhood of Brooklyn. From what he could make out, emigres from Odessa, a tawdry Black Sea port once the Marseilles of the Soviet Union, hung out there. Some were cited for Medicare and Medicaid scams, counterfeiting and drug deals. But most of all they were under surveillance for strong-arming extortion tactics—Vlad's stock in trade.

There was also a reference to the *vor zakonye* or "thieves-in-law"—a fraternal order of hardened criminals that dated back to the time of the czars. The Vor had a rigid code of behavior that included never cooperating with the police or state unless it was to trick them. In Brighton Beach, members were cited for running an extortion ring that brought in tens of thousands of dollars a week. According to one blog, victims ran the gamut from doctors and lawyers to shopkeepers and grocery store owners on Brighton Beach Avenue.

But these indications didn't tell Josh which members of the Vor brotherhood were incarcerated, deported, or still at large. Also, it didn't seem likely that Zharko was a card-carrying member of any outfit that required obedience. Perhaps an associate then. Nevertheless, these clues did validate the presence of the Russian Mafia operating in the northeast.

Continuing his search, Josh learned that Russian mobsters tended to be generalists, opting for any opportunity that afforded itself. By the same token, they'd enlist their services with other gangs or ethnic groups as long as the venture held the promise of a big payoff. It would seem logical then for Zharko, the Vor associate and maverick gypsy with a checkered past, to hook up with any offshoot of a red syndicate with Vlad in tow. But what Josh had turned up so far was limited to Brighton Beach.

He tried a bunch of other keywords, but it wasn't until he was having trouble keeping his eyes open that he came across another lead. There was a vague reference to FBI agents and a Russian organized crime unit "playing a bad game of catch-up," conducting investigations into money laundering at various large banks in Manhattan and branches in Hartford and Boston as the units poured over wiretap transcripts of suspected mobsters. This little tidbit didn't relate to Zharko directly, but it at least tied in the FBI with other cities closer by and thus, by extension or sheer luck, J.J.'s contact, a local field agent.

Another reference cited a smuggling operation on the waterways off the New England coast. There was also an allusion to a mobster named Sliva, who was deported on a visa fraud for failing to disclose his criminal past in the Ukraine. This citing took place during a New Jersey deportation hearing centering on Sliva's connections in Antigua, the dirty money center in the Caribbean. This tiny island harbored eleven banks owned by Russian organized crime and was noted as a key transit zone for laundering funds from fictitious companies. Gulfstream Transfer could very well be a fictitious company.

There was also something about an outfit called YBM siphoning money from the accounts of phony shell companies in the Cayman Islands and the Bank of New York. During a recent FBI raid, bank statements and shipping invoices were seized.

Josh's head was swimming while copying notes and saving the file. But he couldn't get over the feeling that he'd come close to scoping out Zharko's caper, possibly linking up with Raul and onto the Caymans or Havana or thereabouts, but still missing the kicker. Among the only conclusions he could come to was the fact that Russian criminality in and around these shores was rampant. Taking into account the previous hold he'd heard the Italian Mafia had on the city of Waterbury, Zharko may have very well sensed the vacuum and stepped in. Waterbury was probably ripe for a launching pad for a new venture employing a crew made up of mob offshoots including Vlad, Sal, and Raul, with Zharko at the helm plus fringe members from other outfits filling in the gaps.

But how in the world would Josh be able to pass any part of this on? J.J.'s field agent would make this old news coupled with Josh's predicament as way too vague. To say that Paul's response would be doubly incredulous was putting it mildly.

He spent some more time trying to make the case that something had to be going down in the next week or much sooner. But that still made him feel like a complete novice way over his head.

Much too tired to go on, he gave himself some more points for giving it a try and got ready for bed. He'd recheck the file bright and early tomorrow on the off chance some provocative clue that slid by him would have clicked in by then.

All told, he had the elements of a story but nothing concrete— no major crime caper in progress about to funnel into the city of Asheville, and nothing Paul would buy on the spot, much less post immediately to the parent company and executive publisher.

Getting much closer, maybe, but still no cigar.

CHAPTER NINETEEN

Josh parked by the side of the white-marbled Waterbury library and immediately sensed someone lurking in the shadows of the elms. He cautiously moved away from the library grounds, came to the pedestrian crosswalk, was about to cross the busy street, and hesitated.

Over to his left he noted the gigantic shaft of the granite clock tower topped by the menacing she-wolf gargoyles. The warehouse loading dock was located past the tower, adjacent train station, *Waterbury Republican American* newspaper building, traffic light at the corner, and three blocks west. It was highly unlikely that anyone from Zharko's outfit would be on the lookout this early on a cool and overcast Friday morning, much less traipsing about on foot keeping tabs on him. All he had to do was dodge the traffic, walk up the lane past a vestry till he came to the corner, and keep an eye out for J.J. If luck was on his side, as soon as she appeared at the entrance of the granite church that fronted the busy main drag, he'd approach her. Since there was bound to be no church service at this hour, they could mount the stone steps, stand under the overhang, and have their exchange muffled by the traffic noise. Which would leave ample time to return to his car at the library, maneuver a few blocks, pull into the warehouse drive, and resume his duties at the pseudo trucking company a few minutes ahead of schedule.

But once again, he sensed someone lurking, this time close behind him.

He quickened his pace, dodged a speeding car, reached the meridian, heard a honking horn, and jerked around. He caught sight of a gangly figure in a tattered raincoat waving at him, trying to flag him down. He pivoted back and hurried in front of cars going full tilt toward the clock tower. Glancing back again, he caught a glimpse of scraggly dark hair and a gaunt face barely a few yards away. As he reached the lane, he had no intention of running but hoped that by ignoring him the deadbeat would finally get the message.

But it was no-go. Despite all the honking and screeching brakes, the guy, who at first glance must be in his early twenties, kept coming after him. In no time he was almost upon him as Josh hurried past a wrought-iron railing fronting a squat brick office building halfway up the lane.

"Whoa," the deadbeat said, tapping Josh on the back and spinning in front of him, blocking his way. "No problem, man. You got the wrong idea."

Josh was about to say, "I doubt it," but thought better of it. All he had to do was strike up a conversation and he'd miss hooking up with J.J. Taking his cue from the guy's gasping and then suddenly bending over, Josh brushed by him, hoping this was the end of it.

But the deadbeat quickly recovered and began to gain ground, saying, "Hey, wait up. I seen you getting out of your car, looking around, looking lost as hell. So I says to myself, maybe I could be of service. Civic minded like. A kinda tit for tat."

Paying him no mind, Josh rushed ahead, but the deadbeat would have none of it.

"All you have to do is listen to my proposition, man," he said, his hoarse voice meshing with his gasping. "I mean, that way we both make out. 'Cause I know these streets backwards and forwards. I can steer you right, save you a helluva lot of time. Alls I would need is a little coin to get me some duds, get my hair cut maybe, and change gears, so to speak. Slip into a new line of work. That's the plan, you read me?"

Shaking his head, Josh passed the vestry close to the constant thrum of the traffic up ahead, heading east to the Green, when J.J.'s biker leathers emerged out of nowhere, mounted the front stone steps of the church, and yelled, "Beat it, Carmine! Knock it off! Get lost!"

"In your ear, J.J. This dude is mine."

Josh was only a few feet away now when J. J. added, "Go play in traffic, will ya? When we need you we'll rattle your cage."

Josh perched himself on the second stone step, J.J. above him and Carmine below on the sidewalk like a strange grouping for a photo shoot.

"I saw him first, I tell ya," Carmine hollered. "Bright and early I wake up, says to myself the signs call for a career change. Something's bound to turn up and here he is." Focusing directly on Josh he said "Come on, man. All I need is a little stake."

"Oh, that's rich," said J.J., hollering back. "What's the matter, the market on Quaaludes dry up? Having trouble meeting today's quota shaking down the tourists? If you don't split, jerko, I'm calling the cops."

"Yeah, right. Look who's talkin'. The world's number one juvie. They got her fingerprints on file, man. So tell her it's all a misunderstanding and you're cool with it and all."

"Forget it," Josh said, totally frustrated. "I barely have time to confer with J.J. thanks to you. So if you'd take your signs and proposition someplace else, I can get on with my business."

Like a hurt child, Carmine looked down and away and drew back.

"You heard him," J.J. said. "So move those feet."

Carmine took his time scuffling off. Halfway down the street, heading toward the Green, he called back. "You're gonna be sorry for this! You're gonna need me, man. Maybe not today but soon, real soon. 'Cause she is just a loser juvie and my signs never lie!"

There was a momentary lull until J.J. shrugged and said, "Okay, okay. You want to hear about it? I was sixteen and in love. I skipped school and played go-between. I knew he was hot-wiring late-model cars. I knew they were stolen, but I got off on the buzz. And it was a damn sight better than another stretch in the tenth grade. Will that do it for you?"

"So," Josh said, getting back to business, "a guy who happened to be linked to the FBI came along, pulled you out of your wayward ways, and turned your life around. Which has a lot to do with why you decided to show up here and give me the benefit of the doubt."

"Wrong-o. The only reason I'm standing here is 'cause Uncle Fredo is now taken to drink over losing his wholesale produce business, and I am totally bummed out seeing the markets I drummed up go down the tubes if something don't break. Even though I don't trust you as far as I can throw you, what with Uncle Fredo's moaning really getting to me, I went ahead and got hold of Mike."

"That's great."

"Not so fast, not so fast. What did you mean when you said you was in a bind yourself?"

"Let's say it's about an IOU that I never saw coming and leave it at that."

"Oh yeah? Well Mike Devlin ain't buying none of it unless."

"Unless what?"

"What are you, serious? Some deportee back in town don't exactly cut it. And no way, no how does a maybe-reporter who happens to know the muscle who broke Fredo's arm and is in tight with the hood who tossed me on my butt when I just wanted to know what gives. It all don't wash, no way, no how."

"Granted. But add the Vor."

"The what?"

"The Vor brotherhood and their recent activity in these parts, the deportee-kingpin's background and association with the Red Syndicate, plus the FBI's activities directly linked to his machinations."

"Bull. Don't try to snow me, pal, with all that doubletalk. I'm sayin' Mike wants names. The foreman hood on the loading dock who was giving me grief plus his license plate. He wants the skinny on what's going down in the warehouse they hijacked from us and a time-line. He wants proof you're on the inside under pressure, a way to check you out and like that before there's any sit-down between him and you or whatever. Otherwise it's all a crock, and me and Uncle Fredo have had it. So, I'll take a juicy handoff tomorrow, same time same station, or forget it."

Before she could take off, Josh reached out and grabbed her arm.

"Outta my way," she said, jerking her arm back. "In the meantime, I gotta come up with a plan B besides even thinking of throwing in with some iffy white-collar type like you."

"Look, I've got to call my editor by five. I need some corroboration to convince him."

J.J. scampered down the steps, turned back, and said, "Well, I guess that makes two of us you gotta convince." Before Josh could stop her, she rushed away from the church entrance, dissolving into a gaggle of passersby headed toward the Green.

Josh reached inside his jacket pocket for a pen and a notepad and jotted down the items required to appease Agent Mike Devlin. He then made his way down the steps, retraced his path by the vestry and the wrought-iron fence fronting the squat brick office building, crossed the two-way street, and hurried down the side of the library.

He tapped the remote on his keychain, unlatched the car door, slid behind the wheel, and was about to hit the ignition when his cell phone rang.

He glanced at his watch. He still had a few minutes before he was due at the loading dock, took the call just in case, only to be accosted by Ackerman's grating voice.

"Okay, Bartlet, what's going on here?"

Before he had a chance to tell Ackerman he was on a tight schedule and now was not a good time, Ackerman lit right into him.

"I left two messages on your cell but what do I get? Nada, zippo, zilch."

"I've been way too busy to check old calls."

"Terrific. I just now got hold of your editor and told him I don't appreciate my best illustration—telling the lady to ditch her control freak of a husband and get a life—cut from my profile. Not only that, you've flown the coop I'm told, and here I am holding the bag. So, like I said, what gives in this nutty backwater?"

As Ackerman continued to carry on, Josh reached for some way to cut him off.

"So," said Ackerman, his tone getting even more grating. "Now get this, will ya? He says he cut this sample of my brilliant instant insights because church ladies in these parts are devoted to their husbands and families, the outfit that owns the paper would not appreciate any aspersions on the sanctity of marriage, and the blowback would put a crimp on circulation. Can you beat it? Like I said, what the hell is going on here?"

Jumping in, Josh said, "Actually, it's only chance and the good ol' uncertainty principle while stuff keeps happening."

"What are you talking here, for Pete's sake?"

"Come on, Ackerman, get with it. What do you expect? Always stirring things up but never suffering the consequences? It's about time you caught on, don't you think?"

"Hey, what's gotten into you? Where are you anyways?"

"Not nestled in the Blue Ridge, that's for sure. Not naïve enough to go all that way to soothe my nervous condition and whine because my knack for disruption isn't appreciated."

"Oh yeah? Where do you come by this attitude all of a sudden? Since when do you start mouthing off?"

"Since I got dragooned. Since I had to walk the mean streets you ran away from."

"Now wait a second."

"No time. The long and short of it is, you used me to pitch your instant agitation method. In turn you provided Teddy Roosevelt. So I'd say we're even."

Not about to give Ackerman a second more of his time, he powered off the connection and noted that the quarks were really working overtime today.

CHAPTER TWENTY

Josh now had a second reason for arriving a few minutes early. If he could get to the warehouse before Sal pulled in, he could spot which car Sal was driving and note his preferred parking place. Then eventually slip by the idle box trucks and mark down his license plate, the first of Agent Devlin's prerequisites.

But as luck would have it, Sal was already perched on the loading dock, the triple-wide steel rolling door fully open behind him. As Josh pulled in farther, he saw that the cleaning crew had been replaced by a gangly guy on a ladder hanging trays of fluorescent lighting.

He parked in the spot closest to the busy street and decided to affect a nonchalant pose. He eased out of the car and ambled toward the dock as if he'd accepted his circumstances, was going along with Zharko's orders, and was simply heading back into the confines of the office. But he'd no sooner walked up the ramp and was about to brush by Sal's stocky form when Sal yanked him back.

"Not so fast, not so fast," Sal said. "I gotta know. I put it off and put it off and still don't get it. I can see if you was an accountant type with granny glasses, spent time in a low-security slammer in Danbury for embezzlement and such. Living in a dorm, like in a summer camp, easy visiting hours, on the phone, spending money on electronics and books and all. I'm saying, I could buy it if you got some mileage on you and been around the block a bunch of times and knew the ropes. But even that pain-in-the-butt J.J. took you for some kind of choir boy right off the bat and was yelling it out for all to hear."

"That's what comes of first impressions," Josh said, trying to get by him. "Looks can be deceiving."

"Don't give me that," Sal said, yanking him back again.

"Is this the way it's going to be?" Josh said, trying to make light of it. "We can't even have a civilized conversation?"

"Knock it off," Sal said, poking him in the chest. "I'm saying, it just don't figure. How'd you really manage to get that juvie, who was coming straight at me, who I know for a fact was still pissed over Vlad laying the wood to her uncle Fredo. How'd you get her to scramble back to her clunker of a jeep? What'd you say, 'cause she was gunning for me. I rousted you to take care of it, to see if you was up to it, which don't figure. Which Zharko must've known in the first place. And here you pulled it off."

"I reasoned with her, that's all. I'm good with words, which Zharko did figure on in the first place."

"Like hell. You don't reason with no juvie like her no matter what words you use."

"I told her you weren't the kind of guy to listen to anything she had to say. If she kept it up, things would only get worse."

"And so?"

"And so she pouted for a minute and gave in. Anyway, what difference does it make? I said I'd look into her plight when I got the chance and maybe come up with some way to reconcile things."

"Don't give me any of that crap. What do you take me for? I said I don't buy it, it don't figure, and that's what I meant."

Josh couldn't get over the fact that the more he tried to get with the program, the more dubious he appeared. He tried to pass this one off with a shrug, which got him nowhere.

"I got my eye on you, pal. Maybe you got some moves to square it with Zharko, but they sure as hell don't get by me. You report back to Zharko by phone 'cause he's gotta lay low. But I see you direct, out in the open, right in your face. So leave the door open to your cubbyhole. So's I can check in on you, keep my eye on the electric work today and such, and scope out any busted-up jeep turning in here figuring you're an easy mark. You follow?"

Sal poked him even harder. "And that goes double if ever anybody else comes poking around and gets chummy with you." That said, he shambled into the recesses of the warehouse.

Josh stood motionless on the loading dock. The overcast sky had shifted to a darker gunmetal gray, the cool dampness dropped a few degrees as a breeze kicked up. At the driveway entrance, the nearby traffic continued to zip by into the center of town or head in the opposite direction for the crisscrossing ramps south on Route 8 for Naugatuck and New Haven, or east on 84 for Hartford. All of it underscored the same old flux. Nothing could be counted on, none of it held still. Elements only now and then appeared to be in a holding pattern if you didn't know any better.

Adding to his awareness, he couldn't afford to underestimate guys like Sal. He'd never run into any one of Sal's ilk, and he'd simply have to watch his step.

Taking in the whole picture at this point, he could see that the stakes weren't merely confined to some big score like a typical heist movie. There was Zharko on the loose and what Vlad had done to J.J.'s uncle Fredo on Zharko's orders. There was the threat of repercussions, Zharko taking it out on Irina and Molly. There was always Zharko and his flashing blade and mercurial nature— no telling the collateral damage until Zharko was finally put out of commission. No matter how inept Josh was at this juggling act, continuing to get his hands on bits of compelling information in order to get someone to intervene was still the key. And the only conceivable someone was still J.J.'s contact, Agent Devlin.

He also reminded himself that compelling information also came into play to placate editor Paul, at his desk in Black

Mountain, in the next few hours. Placate him and keep his job at the paper, a prospect appearing more and more dubious. He'd jumped the gun before he left, plying Paul with all kinds of unsubstantiated leads that might appeal to a former investigative journalist from the gangland of Baltimore, a hook based on absolutely nothing but desperation at the spur of the moment. He'd have to go ahead with the call, but the more he thought about it, the more prospects vis-à-vis Paul and the *Black Mountain News* seemed a long shot.

Bypassing the workman up on the ladder, he worked his way to the cinderblock office and left the door only slightly ajar. To give himself a bit of cover from Sal's prying eyes as he manned the phone, worked the computer, and took notes.

The only recourse was to focus on what was doable. Which meant getting back to Sal's license plate. He came up with a simple plan and broke it down into four parts. First, he'd slip out, make sure Sal wasn't around, assume Sal was making good on his plan to watch out for J.J. by the street entrance. If the coast was clear, Josh would proceed past the loading dock down the near ramp, duck, and make an educated guess as to which of the parked cars was Sal's. Notepad in hand, he'd jot down the plate number, then make his way back before Sal or anyone else spotted him.

Finding Sal nowhere in sight, he drifted down the near wall, careful to avoid being noticed by the gangly workman in white coveralls perched high up on the ladder checking the fluorescent bulb connections. But all at once he heard yelling far over near the busy street. He peered out. It wasn't an old jeep that had pulled in, but an older model Cadillac—boxy, beige, and faded—stopped short at the start of the drive. A burly guy in a long black leather coat was standing by the hood of the car giving Sal a hard time.

Josh waited until he was sure the burly guy and Sal remained stationary. He couldn't hear what they were arguing about and assumed it would last at least another couple of minutes. He drifted down the ramp, hunkered down, and positioned himself at the edge of the second dumpster overflowing with debris.

Since, unlike Josh, the two other vehicles were backed into the parking spaces, all Josh had to do was take a quick look and scoot back up the side ramp, across the wall, and into the office. But before Josh had a chance to slip by the first dumpster, pass the electrician's van, and take down the license plate of the vintage maroon Lincoln sedan said to be favored by the local mafia back in the day, Sal began heading his way with the burly guy close on his heels.

Josh couldn't help recalling how familiar this was, taking him back to his first hide-and-seek behind the old wooden chair. As if what was out there was always strange and other, and he'd need a buffer between himself and the outside world. Like hiding behind his camera. His only hope in this instance hinged on the two guys stopping once more before they reached the trucks and staying put while Josh scooted forward, jotted down the number on the plates, and took off.

Oddly enough, when the two guys did pause, it was the gist of the argument that caught Josh's attention.

"Come on, will ya," the burly guy belted out. "My nephew was good enough to roust the box trucks for ya, drive them over here, but he ain't good enough to be cut in on the action?"

"That's not the point," Sal hollered back. "Get it through your head."

"Oh yeah? Then what is the point? You keep beatin' around the bush but somehow can't give it to me straight."

"Nobody local is the damn point. Nobody who in any way can be connected with the old outfit. Does that do it for ya? Have we finally struck brain?"

"You mean nobody who looks like you and me can take this load on the road."

"I didn't say that."

"But that's what you meant."

There was a lull before Sal mentioned something about being on the lookout for a juvie who was giving him trouble. The two of them drifted a few yards toward the street and stopped again by the faded Cadillac when the argument picked up as loudly as before.

"So you can't use none of us standup guys," the burly guy said. "No friends, or friends of ours who might want to get in on a little taste. So where you gonna get standup guys who don't look like us and are still teamsters, huh? Answer me that. My guess is Philly. You're gonna put the call out all the way to Philly. You're gonna go to all that to keep this under wraps and screw over the rest of us or any single wise guy from the old neighborhood."

"Will you shut up, Tulio?" Sal yelled at the top of his lungs. "A little louder and we'll dance to it!"

Tulio began grumbling something or other under his breath, kept grumbling, and so did Sal in response. As the sound of their voices grew dimmer and they meandered toward the street, Josh made a few cursory notes. He also jotted down the make and model of Sal's car but didn't want to risk getting any closer as he glanced up and noticed the gangly electrician atop the ladder directly in his line of vision. Not only that, but he seemed to have stopped work and was peering down, perhaps intent on getting a bead on what all the fuss was about.

It immediately registered that the longer Josh remained hunkered down, the greater the chance of being spotted. The only option was to bluff his way back. Move as quickly as possible while allaying any suspicions. It was clearly a matter of authority, as Josh recalled small or slightly built actors playing mob bosses in

old movies—actors like James Cagney or Edward G. Robinson who
got by on sheer bluster. Sal himself was a good four or five inches
shorter than Tulio. It was all a matter of attitude and swagger.

Josh stood, scurried up the ramp, careful not to draw Sal's
attention across the way, passed by the overhang, and accosted the
guy peering down on him as if Josh had just come from attending
to official business.

"What do you think you're doing?" Josh snapped, staring right
back up at the guy. "We're on a tight schedule here."

"Just making sure, is all."

"Of what?"

"The wiring, for one. Sal said it was old and crumbling.
Probably wouldn't pass code. He sure was right."

"Sal who?"

"Sal Scarola, who else? You don't believe me? He's right down
there."

"I know he's right down there. I've a good mind to take
your lollygagging up with him. If the wiring isn't up to code, do
something about it."

"All right already. Cool it down, will ya?"

Josh could have taken this remark as insubordination. But he
couldn't carry on with the charade. In fact, he was totally surprised
he went this far. He turned sharply and headed back to the office,
hoping that the tremor in his voice hadn't been a dead giveaway.

Back at his desk, his door slightly ajar to appease Sal, he
incorporated this new information into his evidence document.
He also added that apparently Zharko wanted to avoid any
connection with the Mafia, was keeping himself and even Vlad the
Enforcer (except when urgently needed dealing with J.J.'s uncle)
deep in the shadows, and put the word out that the heavy lifting
would be done primarily by non-ethnic types ostensibly from

Philadelphia. He folded this assessment, slid it into an envelope, and slipped the envelope into his attaché case.

A few minutes later, Sal reappeared, looking flustered. He covered this up by alluding to phase two, noting that cleaning up the mess of the produce operation left the hassle of bringing everything up to code. "How did that little guy Fredo get away with it all these years?" Sal asked, expecting no answer. As suddenly as he'd barged in, he was off again after giving Josh another one of those wary looks.

The good news was the fact that Sal had dropped his suspicions about J.J. and Josh being in league and was apparently no longer concerned about her return. But he still obviously harbored doubts about Josh's presence and function.

After Sal left, regardless of anything else Josh could have accomplished, he focused on appearing to be well qualified for this task and, in a sense, playing ball for both Sal's and Zharko's benefit. He proceeded to field a number of phone calls asking about routes, stopovers, and approximate dates when this operation would be up and running. To appease the callers, echoing Sal, he told them that, as indicated, they were going through a preliminary phase and were presently engaged in bringing the premises up to code. He took notes of his activities to hand back to Sal, often stalling callers when he wasn't getting away with the usual brushoff, replying he'd have to take it up with the operations chief and get back to them ASAP. And then there were the emails to reply to.

All this took up so much time, he soon lost track of his own agenda. Notably, the impending prospect of having to deal with Paul's impossible demands back at the paper. Couple that with deciphering a call from Raul and contending with another from Zharko and his mercurial moods and suspicions, by four p.m. Josh had reached the point where he couldn't take any more. The only solution was to call Paul this moment and try to buy some more time. Without further ado, he got out his cell and hit the speed-dial number.

But the second Paul picked up, he was off and running and Josh didn't stand a chance.

"All right," Paul said. "Let's have it. You did or didn't come to terms with your mother over an IOU. Yes or no?"

"Yes, in part. Except—"

"Except what?" Josh clearly made out the snap of a thick rubber band signaling Paul's growing impatience.

"Except," Josh said, "that's for openers. There's a lot more to it."

"Don't tell me. You're going to keep pushing the link with the Russian Mafia, which just happens to link up with the IOU and your mother, taking us south some 850 miles to a nefarious operation in Ashville close to my bailiwick. Good God, Josh, give me a break."

"If you'll give me a minute to explain, that happened to be exactly the ringleader's idea when he tracked me down. It's not so far-fetched. There are examples of all kinds of illicit trafficking emanating from the northeast. In addition, the ringleader happens to be the holder of the IOU, engaged in some offshoot of this very kind of trafficking, was subsequently deported, and is back from Russia or that vicinity."

"Oh, please. And you just happen to be in on it?"

"I am in on coded messages sent from a contact named Raul from the Caymans or Havana or somewhere where the Gulf Stream is warm and swift. If things work out, I also have a line on an FBI field agent who can step in."

"You know what this sounds like?"

"I don't care what it sounds like. The whole enterprise hinges on truck shipments, that's the link, and that's the trucking operation I am calling from."

More rubber band snapping until Paul said, "Shipments of what? What the hell are you talking about?"

"I don't know yet. But I'll get back to you as soon as I get a handle on it . . . I mean, as soon as I convince the special agent, get vetted, and he can relay it to—"

"Stop it. Don't you realize how lame this is? How totally convoluted? An introverted features writer who has seen far too many old flicks wants to extend his stay up in Connecticut by playing me for a goddamn fool."

Josh wanted to spell out what a bind he was in and his relationship with Zharko that brought him to this predicament. But there was no way to explain any of it the way Paul was hammering at him. Instead, he cut in and said, "If you would just give me the benefit of the doubt."

"Like hell. We are who we are, buddy. All of us laboring in the fields, no matter how much we'd like to make it more than it is. And no way are you going to con me into playing along. I will expect you back here first thing Monday morning. Failing that, I'll expect a certified fax from this phantom field agent of yours on my desk at the same time stating that your services are integral to a high-priority investigation vetted by the Bureau. One that will culminate in a covert raid in Asheville within the next few days."

"Oh, good grief, Paul."

"Good grief is right. In reality, there never has been nor ever will be any organized crime activity in Asheville among the naturopathic clinics, folk singers, trendy eateries, and tourists flocking to the grounds of the Biltmore Estate."

"I know. Don't you see? That's what makes it ideal."

"That's what makes it off the wall, chum. But you know who I blame? Guys like Ackerman who come down here and get hold of some impressionable sucker like you. Conning you with a load of bull like instant self-actualization. This is it, your last chance.

Either you get off it or what you're looking at is some severance pay and a place in a long unemployment line with the rest of the bozos who just got fired."

The click of the receiver left Josh with the feeling that no matter how he failed to justify it, by some twist of fate and the vagaries of chance, he'd been summoned. He couldn't sneak off to the same old stand in Black Mountain and get by. He could no longer hide out anywhere.

Unbidden, the line from that obscure poem crossed his mind once again: *Take the journey, find your way home.*

He opened his attaché case, got out a notepad, and added some notes for Agent Devlin:

Sal Scarola, the operations manager, drives a vintage maroon Lincoln Continental favored by Waterbury mobsters back in the day. Another mobster-type named Tulio wants a piece of the action. The ringleader hiding in the wings is a rogue gypsy in addition to being a deportee, dead set on transporting illicit goods across state lines . . . Raul is in on it, sending coded messages re: the Gulfstream probably from Havana. Given the ringleader's vengeful nature, there are dire consequences in the offing if anything comes between him and the big payoff.

He sat back, unable to stifle the notion he was failing miserably and actually getting ahead of the game.

CHAPTER TWENTY-ONE

A few minutes before the end of his shift, Josh received another call from Raul. Adding to the previous messages, this one noted that the weather continued to be balmy, the trade winds favorable, and "boating from the Malecon still a joy."

Checking Google, Josh learned that his overall hunch was right. The Malecon was a broad esplanade and seawall that stretched for eight kilometers from the mouth of Havana Harbor in Old Havana. Josh pictured smooth sailing once the product (whatever it was) left the Florida Keys on its way to destinations along the Gulf Stream—perhaps doubling back through New Orleans up into the Heartland, crisscrossing every which way with the Bahamas, not the Caymans on the other side of Cuba, as the much closer and more convenient site for a shell company to handle illicit transactions, launder proceeds, and so forth.

When Zharko called immediately afterwards, Josh relayed the message from Raul. At the same time, he reimagined a shipment of contraband to Asheville and the box trucks loaded from there. However, none of these notions had any verifiable merit.

When Zharko cut into his thoughts and asked what else he had to report, he spoke of the inquiries he'd been fielding and suggested that customers were getting antsy and maybe Zharko should think of speeding things up.

"Oh, you think?" Zharko barked right back. "Bright good boy who knows nothing of trucking business? Who imagines, like speaking of Irina and her depression of which he also knows nothing, who goes to college and writes many words and is now spinning wheels over what I should be doing."

"It only just crossed my mind."

"But why? For what cockamamie reason?"

This time it was Zharko's turn to pause and pull back. A suspended moment that made Josh wonder if Zharko had been in touch with Sal and Sal still wasn't buying Josh's act. And maybe the electrician on the ladder had conferred with Sal who'd passed it on, plus Sal's continuing suspicions about the incident with Josh and J.J.

"What is it?" Josh said. "Something amiss?"

"You tell me, bright good boy who knows better than to cross Zharko or even think of such a thing. You are telling me as one who is obedient for sure, like trained dog and goddamn better be."

"Of course, Zharko."

"What is of course? Say to me."

"Everything's fine. I know nothing about the trucking business. It's not my place to be making suggestions or giving out advice. I just do my job as proficiently as possible."

Another silence until Zharko said, "Not only *my* ears and eyes on the lookout, you are following me?"

"Absolutely. You've got eyes and ears everywhere. Like Sal."

"Eyes and ears on you who has big place on my list. Who absolutely must watch every step he is taking. I am signing off for now, bright good boy who is hanging by a thread."

As Zharko summarily ended the call, Josh would have given anything to get back in touch with Molly. Listen to a voice that was soft and nonthreatening. And during special moments, intimate, bordering on loving.

But a call to Molly indicating anything he was going through would only upset her unless he could pull off another offhand-Josh rendition and make it brief. Moreover, Molly's place was only a mile or so east of the dirt lane and gypsy camper where Zharko might very well be holed up back in the woods. As of now, Josh would always have to keep Zharko's close proximity in mind, which might very well add an edge to the exchange.

He made the call anyway from his cell phone. But her tone turned out to be a bit cool. As though she might have had second thoughts about his family secrets and how troublesome his situation was.

"Listen," Molly said after a tad more hemming and hawing. "As it happens, the gals from school and I have our monthly potluck supper tonight, and tomorrow we have an outing to take the kids on a field trip to the Bethlehem Fair. An all-day affair, as you may recall, that leaves me bushed by the time everything is finished and the kids are back with their parents."

"And you'll be content to settle in, watch a little TV, and get ready for bed."

"More or less."

"And I should have known better than assume you'd drop all your plans anytime I came busting into your life again, replete with a wacked-out new venture."

"That's not what I'm saying. Just a minute." Molly excused herself to attend to a beef stew for the potluck she said was simmering on the stove. There was a clattering of pans and sliding of kitchen drawers opening and shutting until she got back on her landline.

"Again," Molly said, sounding a bit more distraught than cool this time, "as it happens, I just got off the phone with George. He tried to sound sensible but managed to get around to admonishing me for many things."

"Including me."

"Now that you mention it, he did say it's not going to lead to anything. I'm just stalling and for everyone's sake I should keep my feet on the ground, tend to my work and thoughts of the future."

"Ah yes, good old practical George. After all, none of us are still young and foolish and simply can't afford to regress."

"You're not listening to me."

"I certainly am. That's my stock in trade. Listening. Taking everything into account. Fully aware of the distress that comes of any departure from the norm."

"Josh, let's face it. We all need a little time and space."

"Fine. I will keep a low profile and we'll let it ride."

"Are you mad?"

"Of course not. I told you, I have become very sensitive of late, listening closely, being understanding, and allowing things to play themselves out."

"Really?"

"Absolutely. Trying my best to take it all in."

This half-hearted attempt at smoothing things over was followed by bits of murmuring small talk until they said their goodbyes. He couldn't bring himself to tell her that the chances of his allowing things to simply play themselves out were just about nil.

He took his time driving back to the Litchfield Hills, well past the inn until he reached the Bantam Lake area. There he pulled into the parking lot across from the converted red barn movie theater where he spent hours as a child escaping into the world of foreign intrigue. He slipped into the twin red barn known as Woods Pit BBQ, found an empty rustic table in the far corner, and ordered a plate of ribs, corn bread, and all the fixings along with a bracing cup of hot mulled cider to ward off the lingering damp chill.

He almost succeeded in putting his skittering thoughts about

Molly and his abiding loneliness on hold for a while, warmed by the homey atmosphere and the cute little kids and their parents teasing each other in the tables by the front windows.

Soon, the FM country music piped in from the overhanging speakers segued to a folk singer with a deep, wistful voice. The lyrics of his song certainly weren't directed at Josh, but they struck a chord all the same:

> *Daddy, won't you take me wherever you travel,*
> *take me, oh take me wherever you roam*
> *I'll be your sidekick down the lost highway*
> *through the deep canyons wherever you go . . .*

In that moment, he began longing for the daddy he never knew. Soon, other songs came to mind he'd heard over the folk music station back in Asheville. Lyrics and melodies that filled him with the same sense of longing for something he never had. Other "take me back" or "take me to" songs, hopping a freight train, being a "ramblin' man," leaving him just short of getting all choked up.

He knew these songs were akin to the mythic noble quests, something to latch onto in the darkness of the silver screen as the stranger comes to town to take on the gunslingers and cattle rustlers so the good citizens can resume their peaceful lives. The stranger always takes on the struggle and, when it's all over, rides off into the sunset one more unsung hero. Josh knew all of it was a fantasy. Nevertheless, he let himself be carried away from his troubles.

And wished he could call Molly back and try to do better this time.

CHAPTER TWENTY-TWO

Realizing he still didn't have anything compelling to get Agent Devlin on board, Josh spent the next few hours on his laptop back in his room. Perhaps if he came up with a link to Gulfstream Transfer and Raul before turning in for the night, something that would jibe with the leads he had to offer, he'd be in a better position to get some help.

But after taking a few stabs at it, he came up empty. He found a reference to a branch of Gulfstream Transfer opening up in Waterbury in the near future. But that only accounted for the calls and e-mails he received at the warehouse and the standard services and routes he echoed, adding stock replies like "will be up and running in the very near future. Look for our ad in the *Waterbury Republican American* newspaper." All boilerplate responses that meant little after the trucks took off for Asheville with Josh still holding the fort as the front man until it all tapered off and the damage was done. The only significant discovery he made was the fact there was no listing for Gulfstream Transfer itself no matter how hard he looked.

He scoured the web for such things as the exact makeup of shell corporations and found out they existed only on paper as a vehicle for business transactions, just as he thought. Employed for tax evasion and money laundering, based in tax havens like the Caymans and, again, the Bahamas. The more he read about it, the later it got and the more he still found himself with no direct link to Zharko's trucking scheme, Asheville, the Florida Keys, Havana, and off to who knows where.

Checking up on someone by the name of Raul and/or the membership of a Teamsters Union in Philadelphia Tulio alluded to was a complete non-starter.

By the time midnight rolled around, he had given up on compelling additional information apart from the notes he had in hand.

—··—

Saturday morning arrived well before he was ready to meet the day having had only a few hours of tossing and turning. He wolfed down a little breakfast downstairs at the inn's short-order nook. The only positive sign was the occasional glints of sunlight through the cloud cover as he got set to contend once again with the traffic south on Route 8 heading back to the parking lot close to the dark-granite Episcopal church and the Waterbury Green. The cool dampness held steady, though, as he wondered if J.J. would give him a break and accept the few leads he'd stuffed into an envelope and hook up with Agent Devlin anyway. At least it was worth a try. The only thing, in fact, he had going for him.

Fighting off the drowsy fatigue, he slipped behind the wheel of the rental, carefully avoided the cars racing past him, and reached downtown Waterbury a good forty minutes before the half-day Saturday shift at the warehouse. Passing the entrance, he jockeyed by the Waterbury paper and the train station, hung a left, and managed to park in the same spot by the library.

With no sign of the deadbeat Carmine this time, he crossed the two-lane traffic and made his way up the narrow lane, passed the vestry, took the steps that fronted the looming stone church, and waited. While he stood there, remaining as inconspicuous as possible, he noted the scattering of passersby headed toward the Green, ostensibly on their way to their own half-day shifts. He watched the cars as well, cruising east toward the local college or possibly the mall. It was too early, cool, and damp for anyone to leisurely occupy the benches that dotted the fringes of the Green. For the moment at least, Josh had the sense that the quarks were not unduly agitated, and what passed for normal in this city was the order of the day.

But it didn't take long for him to realize that J.J. was late.

Then, unless his drowsy eyes were deceiving him, off in the distance to his right he could swear he caught a glimpse of Carmine at the far corner by the end of the Green coming his way, pointing in his direction. Whoever he was signaling to was impossible to tell as a city bus pulled up at a stop in front of the benches and obscured Josh's view.

Seconds later, J.J. appeared from around the church pillars sporting her biker's leathers as usual, looking harassed and expectant at the same time.

"Well," J.J. said, "you got the skinny or what?"

"I've got something that's maybe good enough."

"Something and maybe don't cut it, pal."

Despite himself, he couldn't help peering over into the distance again at the bus stop. The last thing he needed right now was another altercation between Carmine and J.J. while Carmine worked on Josh.

"Hey," J.J. said. "Snap out of it. What are you doing? I am going outta my way here and so far you ain't giving me nothing."

"Sorry. I thought I saw Carmine pointing in this direction, about to offer his services again."

"No surprise on that score. He's had the word out he's available as a gofer, dog walker, snitch, errand boy, or whatever. So, let it go and let's see what you got."

Josh reached into his blazer pocket and handed her the envelope.

She slipped out his notations, studied them for a minute, and shook her head. "What is this? You examine the plates. You got three names here and some maybe this and maybe that. You think feds deal in guessing games? You think Mike is gonna go get some Ouija board and call out, 'Sal Scarola . . . a Waterbury hood name of Tulio . . . Raul reporting from Havana who's in on it saying whether the coast is clear'? The deal was you gotta sell me. I myself am into sales, in case you forgot. I gotta sell restaurants on Fredo's fresh produce or there's nothing doing, and you gotta bowl me over before I lay it on Mike."

"I'm doing the best I can. But it is imminent, I'm telling you. It's going to be set in motion any time now and something has got to be done."

"Yeah, yeah, you got hauling something also writ here. Hauling what? What are we talking? Some gypsy you write here is the kingpin with no name. Some guy I didn't see no place around, he's behind it?"

Josh wasn't at all sure why he didn't divulge Zharko's name. Perhaps he didn't want to entangle his mother's dubious relationship and perhaps he didn't want word to get out and jeopardize what he was up to. "You see—" Josh started to say before J.J. cut him off.

"Hey, will you get with it? You gotta at least tell me what's going down that would get the feds to hop right on it. And if you can't do that, who is this deportee that would make anybody think he sure as hell was at it again? Because Mike's got no time or reason to go all the way down to headquarters in New Haven and look up the data files on some no-name joker. And then check you out 'cause that's *my* job. You getting my drift here or flaking out on me?"

"Look—"

"No, you look. If it wasn't for my Uncle Fredo worse by the minute, all beat-up and climbing the walls, I would drop you in a flash. You got one more try and that's it. I scoped it out and figure it's only a half day on Saturday for whatever Sal and the crew is doing at the loading dock. Then they break for the rest of the weekend like it's some normal operation. So that gives you the rest of the morning to knock me for a loop. But I'll give you till two to come through with something juicy or you and me is quits and I don't mean perhaps. This exact same spot, pal, and I ain't gonna wait a minute longer."

Josh checked his watch. He peered out again as another bus pulled out by the stop on the Green. He only got a glimpse, but he could swear Carmine was at it again, signaling someone. When he glanced back, J.J. was gone.

Leaving the church, he made his way back down the side lane, crossed the two-way street over to the library, looking every which way till he reached the rental car. He looked around a few more times before slipping behind the wheel and putting the car in gear. Driving west down the long block toward the looming granite clock tower, train station, and newspaper building with still over twenty-five minutes to spare, he crossed over and parked in the circular drive fronting the far edge of the brick newspaper building. It was a long shot, but appeasing his go-between J.J. was still his only chance.

He entered the building and walked straight to the receptionist counter behind the glass partition. The middle-aged lady in the thick bifocals told him only a skeleton crew was on today but Russ Cabot, the managing editor, should be in the newsroom up on the third floor by twelve thirty. Yes, Russ was friendly, grouchy but benign. Yes, he had immediate access to the digital files on the database on his computer, and yes, breaking local and state news including criminal activities and court proceedings from the past few years should be accessible. If, of course, Russ had any interest and time to spare. Then again, Josh might have to wait and come back Monday to find out what Russ came up with, if anything.

Josh thanked her and left, checked out the scene across the busy intersection up and down the sidewalks but failed to get a bead on anyone suspicious looking who Carmine may have contacted.

Back behind the wheel, he took a left at the adjacent traffic light, cruised under the overpass, hung another left into the warehouse drive, and pulled in by the idle box trucks. Another few seconds till he was up the ramp a good five minutes before Sal arrived, moved past a few workmen tidying up, and slipped into his office. He left the door open once more, set on killing enough time engaging in his duties until twelve twenty or so when he could get in the car, scoot back, and get managing editor Russ Cabot to give him a line on the modus operandi that got Zharko Vadja deported a year or two ago. Some compelling fact that would act as a springboard J.J. would readily pass on to Agent Devlin and get a strong countermeasure going. Depending on whether anything would come of this last-ditch effort by two p.m. when J.J. would presumably be waiting at the church counting the seconds.

Nothing of any import took place the rest of that morning unless you count the funny looks Sal kept giving him each time he appeared at the threshold, lingering for a moment. Once, he pointed a finger while Josh was reciting the same stock answers when fielding a call. The gesture could have meant any number of things, but Josh took it as "Better keep in line, buster, or else." Raul came through with one of his calls, mid-morning this time. It seems the trade winds were still balmy, the saltwater waves still gently splashing against the Malecon, shipping was running smoothly across the waters of the Gulf Stream.

In the meantime, Josh took a minute to scribble down Zharko's full name and a space for a court case ruling Devlin would no doubt require, handed off to J.J. by way of Russ Cabot, managing editor.

When it came time to wrap up, Josh paced himself so that Sal would have absolutely no reason to suspect he was up to anything. He left the premises just after twelve thirty, eased behind the wheel, drove off slowly, turned right instead of left back up to Route 8 and the Litchfield Hills, indicating at this leisurely pace he might well be off to the nearby mall to purchase a few necessities. He made a sharp right at the intersection and pulled into the circular drive by the far edge of the red-brick building that housed the newspaper, keeping the car more or less out of sight.

Getting out, he froze the moment he spotted Carmine in his rumpled garb across the street. Carmine didn't gesture to anyone this time. He stood stock still and then whipped out a cell phone. It was another opportunity for Josh to guess what this all meant, but he couldn't waste the time.

Disregarding whatever Carmine was doing, he hurried into the building, took the elevator up to the third floor, and took in the high ceilings and great expanse that dwarfed the antique clock with Roman numerals hovering over the sprinkling of reporters hunched over their computers. Judging by the cursory description the woman at the information counter had given him earlier, the slight figure on the phone in the far corner by an oversized window—the guy with the grizzled gray beard, suspenders, and yellow bow tie—surely belonged to managing editor Russ. He went over to him, stood by his oaken desk, and waited till he was off the phone. A glance up at the old railroad clock told him he had no more than forty minutes before he took the elevator down, rushed over to his car, drove over to the library parking lot, found a space, dodged the traffic, and hurried up the narrow lane to the front of the church in time to meet J.J. with a much more promising lead. In short, forty minutes to nail down the exploits of Zharko Vadja that caused his expulsion from this country and justify surveillance of his present activities leading to his imminent recapture. Thus potentially nipping a major criminal escapade in the bud.

It didn't at all help that Cabot, unlike Paul back at the *Black Mountain News*, was in no rush, acknowledged Josh's presence with a wink and a nod, but continued to respond to the caller in a lazy tone: "Uh-huh . . . oh yeah . . . right, right, I know what you mean . . ." His nonchalance was further underscored by a wry smile on his thin lips and a glint in his eyes, in direct contrast with Josh's bleary eyes and the growing anxiety overtaking his easygoing act back at the warehouse.

A minute or so later, Cabot hung up, leaned back, fumbled with his loose bow tie and said, "So, what's on your mind, fella? Something I can do for you?"

Giving him no chance to keep the small talk going, Josh showed him his press card and told him he was originally from Litchfield way back when, was up here caught in a bind, and was opting on the feds intervening. But it all hinged on coming up with a lead on a rogue gypsy's modus operandi as soon as possible.

"Hold it," Cabot said, giving up on straightening his bow tie. "Run that by me again. Real slow this time."

"The thing of it is, I'm in kind of a rush and would be greatly indebted if you could check your newspaper's database for any information on someone by the name of Zharko Vadja. To be more precise, his deportation at a court hearing in this state not more than two years ago."

"You're serious?"

"Yes sir, you bet."

"And even if I wanted to," said Cabot, sitting up, "even if I had nothing better to do, why would I humor a perfect stranger who, from the looks of you, would be better off getting a good night's sleep? Then much, much later, going back to the drawing board and coming up with a normal approach like anyone else."

"But I can't. I just plain have no other alternative. I need some hard evidence to get this thing moving. Or else, given a window of only a couple of days, any chance for intervention is shot!"

There was a pause, heightened by the insistent tick-tock of the railroad clock overhead.

Cabot leaned back again, curled his fingers together like a wise old counselor and said, "Pardon me if I still don't get it. Your press card says features reporter. Every features reporter we have, and every one I know of, covers mild human interest stories. I've got two homebody-type gals out there right now covering the Bethlehem Fair. All the attractions, why folks keep coming back year after year with their kids. Topics that make people forget their cares and woes, not some impending high-profile crime."

"I know, I know. All of that is as opposite from my situation as can be."

"Then tell me, what are you doing? And what does your editor back in Carolina think of your running around up here looking for trouble?"

"He thinks I've gone off half-cocked. He told me to drop it. He's as much as written me off."

"So?"

"So that's not the point. My back's against the wall for reasons I won't go into and I only want somebody whose jurisdiction it is to step in before it's too late. It so happens it's emanating from here, this very location, proceeding south down across state lines. And this is my only opportunity to do a handoff so that something can be done."

When Cabot still didn't respond, Josh said, "For God's sake, all I ask is a few minutes of your time, what can you lose? I've Googled all I can Google. I've dug up all I can dig up. All I need is a solid reference to a deportation hearing that must have taken place a relatively short while ago and a disposition on the charges. That's all. One lousy source, one lousy news item, and I'm out of here, out of your hair."

The ticking clock seemed even more insistent as Josh reached inside his jacket pocket for his notation underscoring the name Zharko Vadja and placed it smack dab on Cabot's blotter.

Ever so slowly, Cabot examined the note, looked at Josh, looked down again, sighed, and tapped the keyboard of his PC. This was followed by more tapping and sighing and not the slightest communication with Josh as Josh drifted back and sat down in a chair by the wall.

Once, Cabot stopped tapping on the keyboard, stared at the computer screen, started to jot something down, and then thought better of it. Josh sprang up and said, "Listen, I'll take anything you've got."

"Not on my watch, you won't. Who is this Zharko guy? What's he done? What more damage could he do? Why bother? The only reason I can see on my end is if he's local. Plus the fact that there hasn't been any crime scene to speak of in these parts for quite some time. In short, if it's maybe starting up again, I could be interested."

Josh sat back down, got so antsy after another few minutes that he rose up again and went over to a water fountain at the far end of the room. A young woman wearing oversized glasses with pink frames looked up from her desk and said, "He only seems to be indifferent. But once he's on it, he's like a terrier digging for a bone. I wouldn't push it if I were you."

Josh nodded, took some sips from the water fountain, returned, and sat back down again.

After another ten minutes or so, Cabot finally stopped tapping on the keyboard, glared at the computer screen for a while, and ran off two copies. "One for me, one for you," Cabot said. "In case anything ever comes of this."

Cabot folded the printouts. Josh jumped up again, but instead of handing over a copy, Cabot hung on to it and said, "Fella, in truth, if I were you, I'd think twice about all this. If things aren't working out down in Carolina, it so happens they're starting up the old *Lakeville Journal*. Think about it. Up in the rolling hills in the northwest corner close to the Berkshires, nestled among quaint Connecticut towns like Sharon and Salisbury. Perfect for a features guy who has no business getting discombobulated over a long shot like this. Take it from me, fella. Let it ride."

"I'll take it under advisement," Josh said, snatching up the printout. Without bothering to read it, he stuck it in the inside pocket of his jacket. "I really appreciate this," he called over his shoulder as he hurried off. "If things work out, I'll be in touch."

"Just don't push it," Cabot called back. "And watch your step."

"You bet."

Ignoring the handful of reporters looking up from their desks, he rushed over to the elevator, anxiously waited for the elevator light to come on, felt woozy as the elevator descended, exited the premises, and stopped short as he saw Carmine nervously leaning on Josh's rental car.

There was no way he was going to deal with Carmine again and lose even a few seconds of precious time. But as another wave of fatigue came over him, he shuffled over to the corner edge of the building and closed his eyes. Just then, he sensed something coming his way.

The next thing he knew, Vlad's thickset form came upon him, his massive fists clutched the lapels of Josh's blazer dragging him down the alley, and smashed him against the brick wall.

"What you doing in newspaper building?" asked Vlad.

Stunned, at first Josh didn't reply. Then he said, "Nothing really," as he tried to pull himself away. "Look, I really must go."

Tugging harder against Vlad's grip, Josh spotted Carmine again no more than a few yards away with a sheepish look on his face.

"You will explain," said Vlad, yanking him back against the wall. "Two times this Carmine says you are with girl who has uncle—little man I must convince to stay quiet."

"Sorry. Can we talk about this later?" Josh lurched with all his might.

Vlad flung him back again yelling, "No!" Suddenly there was an excruciating pain in Josh's midsection and ribs as Vlad's sharp jabs slammed into his body, sending him sliding down to the gravel, knocking the wind out of him. There was nothing but pain and gasping now as Vlad stood over him.

"This is wakeup call for good-behaved boy, Zharko says, who go behind our back. Who make us drag back here to play front, but what really he is playing at?"

Josh barely knew what was happening as Vlad bent over, jerked on his jacket, and patted him down yelling, "Where is cell phone? Where?" Another twisting jerk until Vlad came up with it out of Josh's blazer side pocket. "Contacts on phone tell who else you talk to. Newspaper people, maybe police, maybe little uncle, maybe other people. Will see what cell phone tells us. Will see what more lessons good-behaved boy need."

Vlad rose, kicked Josh's ribs with his boot so hard that Josh screamed.

"Maybe you sleep in alley tonight," Vlad said, hovering over him. "Maybe you crawl back to Zharko. I am finished here."

Vlad shambled off. The pain in his midsection was piercing as Carmine soon reappeared.

"Listen, man," Carmine said, "Word was out they wanted a spotter. I was still mad at the way you and J.J. treated me whilst I was just looking for a stake, so's I pitched in. But didn't know they was gonna lean on you. Hey, talk to me, what can I do?"

"Catch J.J. at the church. Run. Tell her, tell her."

"What? That's it?"

"Yes! Run, dammit, run!"

As Carmine shrugged and rushed off, it was all Josh could do to check his watch and try to get to his feet. The only chance of Carmine catching J.J. was the possibility she might wait a couple of minutes after two even though she said she wouldn't. At any rate, he couldn't just lie there.

But the stabbing, radiating pain in his rib cage made trying to get up that much more excruciating. Each time he tried to rise, bracing himself against the brick wall, the worse it got, each intake of breath cutting right through him. After one more attempt, which only led to enervating whimpers, he remained propped against the wall. If no one showed up, he could try calling out. But who would hear him above the traffic noises below the alleyway? Who would come out to the edge of the car park and peer down? Nobody.

More time went by until, out of nowhere, J.J. and Carmine rushed toward him. Josh could barely speak, wincing and moaning as they hoisted him and struggled to get him up the alley into the passenger side of J.J.'s awaiting jeep.

Somehow, J.J. convinced Carmine to take Josh's car to her uncle's place a mile south in the Town Plot section. Josh didn't question this, didn't question anything. It was all he could do to hang on as J.J. jockeyed the jeep around to the main drag heading west for the ER of the Waterbury Hospital. All the while, she shouted over the grinding motor that it was okay. She and Carmine had grown up in the very same Town Plot section where he was taking Josh's car. Carmine was always getting into trouble, going to confession, swearing he was going to do right but not right now. She carried on some more, yelling louder over the throbbing of the old jeep motor as if getting beaten up by Vlad had earned Josh combat points. There was something else about Carmine introducing her to her ex who, likewise, first got her into trouble. And back again to convincing stashing Josh's car rental out of sight as a good move so Sal or whoever would figure Josh drove himself to the ER and would be out of commission for a spell. By this point, Josh couldn't take any more of her blabbing as he tried to hang on for dear life, worried sick his ribs might be fractured.

The next hours were a complete blur as he waited his turn, with J.J. yammering away, detailing her fights and scrapes over the years to gloss over any concern she might have over Josh's condition. She did so while they were surrounded by a growing number of sufferers of motorcycle accidents, deep gashes, viruses and high fevers, and an endless array of other ailments. Eventually, Josh was seen, taped up, given shots that made him even more woozy, and was told he had a combination of bruised ribs, stress, and sleep deprivation.

By now he was in such pain that the ER doctor offered to pre-scribe Percocet to tide him over, but Josh would have none of it. He wasn't about to swallow opioids under any conditions. The ER doctor nodded, prescribed rest and Tylenol with codeine instead, and told him not to overdo it for at least the next couple of days. A short time later, armed with a vial of pills, he was discharged into the care of J.J., who claimed to be his first cousin. Josh's United Health card took care of any expenses.

As twilight came on, another bumpy ride in the jeep took him to J.J.'s uncle Fredo's house. He was so out of it by then he couldn't think straight, let alone raise any objection. He could only hope the radiating pain would subside, even for a little while.

CHAPTER TWENTY-THREE

hortly after, fighting through the aches and grogginess, it all came back to him. He tried to get through to J.J., to tell her Vlad had swiped his cell phone and there was no way to contact Molly, whose phone number he didn't know by heart. He said things like "What if they try the M anyway?" His fuzzy attempt at communicating failed to reveal who M as in Molly was, and his protests were eclipsed when he was plunked down in a spare bedroom surrounded by religious icons, the white-clapboard house he found himself in redolent with the baked-in aroma of sauces and pasta dishes over the years.

Moments later, as J.J. reappeared, another concern over Molly's safety caused him to blurt out the name of the village and house number of the sublet, plus the fact she taught little kids and couldn't handle any rough treatment. But that fear was met with J.J.'s, "Cool it already. Haven't you had enough for one day?"

"But you don't understand."

"Hey, back off will ya? About this Molly chick, I'm sure it will keep. Nobody is going to lose any sleep over an M on a swiped cell. So, I'll get back to you about my weekend out-of-town personal messenger rates if and when I decide I can use some coin. I'm talking tomorrow, wasting a perfectly good Sunday morning. Until then, do me a favor, huh? Spare us any more agony for a little while."

With his thoughts still swirling, Josh vaguely recalled getting a glimpse of Uncle Fredo's wisps of white hair, red-rimmed eyes, hound-dog expression on his wrinkled face, and his left arm in a sling. Slumped over a desk in a tiny parlor as J.J. was helping Josh shamble through the house to this spare room. Fredo seemed to have been going over his ledgers, a shot glass close by along with a bottle of whiskey. Even more vague was a recollection of J.J.'s aunt's weary face, saying things like, "It isn't fair, is it? You work hard all your life, try to do the right thing, and look what happens."

"I know, I know" was all Josh had been able to mutter.

All the while, with the aunt half talking to herself, there was more of the same. But he hadn't replied to any of her worrisome concerns. No more able to offer any answers than continue to protest about Molly.

Time passed. He hadn't noticed when J.J. left the house or when this slight, gentle little woman pulled a blanket over him and turned off the light. Everything at last culminating in a senseless slumber that carried him well past dawn until the ringing of bells.

And it was on that following morning, not long after the uncle and aunt left for church, that J.J. burst back onto the scene, plopped a breakfast tray of French toast, bacon, and coffee the aunt had made across his lap, and accosted him with a proposition.

"Okay, pal, you awake? Here's the deal. Starting with your lame directions, getting on MapQuest, figuring on forty minutes to get there, tossing in a little spiel—hey, are you getting this?"

A bit less aching and groggy, Josh did his best to sit up, took a few sips of coffee, and said, "Before noon, you mean . . . well before the chartered bus to the Bethlehem Fair. Have to know if she's set to go off with the kids or she's in bad shape. Have to know if she's okay. Have to know."

"Yeah, yeah, whatever. Listen, I've never been up in that neck of the woods, which makes the trip that much more of a pain in the butt. But, lucky for you, what with the cash-flow problem I've been having after those goons shut my meal ticket down, and with nothing better to do, you're on. So, where was I?"

"About to take off," Josh said, heartened, sitting up straighter. "Arriving at the sublet close to the Litchfield Green even though you're not keen on the idea."

"Yeah, yeah, right, catching up to her in time. So, what we got here is a little do-si-do before she decides whether or not to give me the boot, having never run into my type before with no notice. Maybe we get past that and I make my spiel pussyfooting around you getting mugged and the creep swiping your cell phone. Plus you'll be in touch soon as you come around 'cause you ain't in no shape to carry on no relationship at the present moment. But you can start up again so long as nothing else bad comes your way."

"Don't say that."

"Don't say what? Hey, you give it a shot. It goes the way it goes, like everything else."

Before Josh could come up with a much better message for Molly, J.J. dropped her invoice on the nightstand and said, "This is for openers. I'll hit you with the final tab after I'm done." She left the room and came right back. "Say, just for kicks, what would you do if that goon Vlad didn't swipe your cell? Would you call her from here and set her straight?"

Josh had no answer for that one.

"Cripes, you white-collar types. Me and my ex let each other have it. We didn't mess around with formalities. We'd clear the air right off the bat and let the chips fall where they may. That's the difference. Later, man."

Before Josh had a chance to stop her and go over the message, she bolted out of the room. Within seconds, there was a slam of the front door, the throbbing of the old jeep engine and, in short order, Josh was left in complete silence.

Some time later, well after he picked at his breakfast and just sat there propped up against the headboard, J.J.'s uncle Fredo and aunt returned from church. As far as Josh could tell, Fredo went straight back to struggling with his ledgers in the parlor and slowly draining the bottle of whiskey. At the same time, the aunt, dressed in a dark blue dress that clung to her slight frame, poked her weary face into the bedroom and offered to take his breakfast tray. He nodded, she traipsed in, took the tray off his lap, and lingered by the doorway.

"May I ask you something?" she said. "You being a college man, J.J. said, and hurt by the same rough person like my Fredo."

Josh could only give her a nod as a wave of fatigue came over him. He did notice that she must have been very pretty at one time, her long gray hair with tints of auburn, her hazel eyes once aglow, her wan face free of lines and wrinkles. Only her soft voice had retained a certain dreamy quality.

"Well you see," she said, "at this morning's service, the priest's sermon was about Jonah and the whale. He was telling the congregation about Jonah running off, getting on a ship, and being tossed overboard . . . I'm not sure if I'm telling it right, but the point was that landing in the belly of the whale was the same as hitting bottom. But right afterwards, Fredo was even more upset because he himself hadn't done any such thing, hadn't run away. He'd stayed with it through thick and thin and now look at him. He's at rock bottom too."

"I understand," Josh said, trying to be accommodating.

"The thing of it is, Jonah complained and then saw his way clear, as if once you've reached the bottom there's no way but up. For the life of him, however, Fredo can't see any way out. He's got all these bills to pay. His crew, who's been with him all these years, are out of work as a result and—can you possibly help me here?

What can I say about all this? How should Fredo look at it? And what are you yourself going to do?"

Josh thought for a moment and said, "Well, I guess we both got blindsided." But he knew that was no answer. Having no clue about Jonah or how the parable ended, he said, "Sorry. I'm not good for much right now, let alone deciphering morals . . . guess I'm just all tapped out."

She tried to hide her disappointment, turned away, lingered for a few more seconds, and drifted off.

His despair grew worse when he thought about Molly once more. Even if she were okay, even if there was no way Zharko could locate or contact her, what would she make of how hapless he'd become? Mugged on the mean streets, hanging out with J.J. No matter what he'd gotten himself into, a life with stodgy George was far preferable than on-again, off-again feckless Josh. Come to think of it, an encounter with J.J. right now was probably the last straw.

— · —

Roughly around this same time, J.J. was gunning the motor of the old jeep, climbing steep Route 118 to the Litchfield Green high above. The jeep as reluctant as J.J. to reach what she'd been told was a WASPy world stretching out to the Litchfield Hills and the gateway north to the nooks and valleys of the Berkshires of Massachusetts. Pricey inns and B&Bs and tea shops she'd heard had no use for some ex-juvie peddling wholesale produce. She wouldn't know how to dress and act among those types even if she wanted to and had the opportunity. She'd tell it like it was and queer the whole deal.

The more she thought about being caught up there with the WASPs, the more itchy she got, half wishing the gearshift would strip, forcing her to make a U-turn and hightail it back to the kind of street people she knew. Straining its guts out, the jeep did make it to the village center. From there it took her a minute to get her bearings.

Like it was staged or something, sunlight streamed through the low-hanging cloud cover and held tight. To J.J.'s mind, all that was missing were a bunch of guys in tuxedos, sawing away on their violins, playing some drippy classical music. Gone was any hint of factories, gray granite, and a melting pot of ethnic types. Or Town Plot, for that matter, with Mafia memories still talked about or kept under wraps. Instead, oversized white-frame houses lined both sides of the street, glistening in the sunlight, plaques by the front doors with names like Silas, Ezra, and Caleb. Plus dates like 1761, so you'd swear you'd stumbled onto a museum or colonial theme park. Except for a couple of well-dressed ladies walking their pedigree dogs and some shiny expensive cars tooling around, you could swear there were no living people around either. If she got lost, it was the last place she'd find another J.J. like herself to help out. No Jolandas with a stepfather named Sid Janus. No mom named Angie who, when Sid dumped them, wound up on the night shift of a bottle plant in Terryville to make ends meet.

Deciding she'd stalled long enough as the shafts of sunlight decided to play it quits, she cruised up North Street with even more humongous white-frame houses on both sides and glitzier cars parked on extra-wide gravel drives. Soon she veered off the main drag and pulled onto the side street like Josh said while he was barely coming out of it. By now she'd just about had it with this *Better Homes & Gardens*–type setup and forgot exactly what she was going to say. She was even hoping this M-for-Molly had split so she could leave one of her "Sorry I missed you" produce cards and beat it the hell out of there.

But no such luck. There was the number on the fancy cast-iron mailbox. The dollhouse past the picket fence was an overdose of the cutes. Perfect digs for a perfect teacher who taught perfect little WASPy kids.

J.J. shrugged off the squeal of her brakes, hoped no neighbors beyond the neat hedges would come out and give her grief for ruining the atmosphere. She parked on the grassy swale at the side of the road and hopped out. The squeal of the brakes and the sight of her clunker of a jeep must have done the trick because there she was behind the glass storm door, peeking out at her. As far as J.J. could tell, she had one of those standard trim figures, was wearing a trendy pale blue windbreaker over a pair of matching slacks, and was about to go on what types like her call an outing like Josh said. As J.J. got out, unlatched the gate, and moved up the cobblestone walkway, the short honey-blonde hair and set of the chick's blue eyes was a dead giveaway.

J.J. shook her head and took a deep breath. She was an unwanted townie, which damn well suited her fine. She didn't want to be there any more than this M-for-Molly wanted her there. The sooner she could get herself back where she belonged wasn't soon enough.

She stepped onto the front porch, and before she had a chance to open her mouth, this Molly person opened the door partway and said in the nicest way, "May I help you?"

The nice tone and politeness completely threw J.J. Now she'd have to back off a notch and adjust her spiel. What was the use of shooting from the hip when they weren't out to get you?

When Molly tried a little harder and said, "Are you lost? Do you need directions?" J.J. smirked, took a beat, and said, "No, lady, I'm only delivering a message. I see you're all set to split so, to make it short, your boyfriend Josh—"

"Excuse me. He's not exactly my boyfriend."

"Great, whatever. So, here's the message."

"Message? I don't understand. Why couldn't he simply call me? He knows I'd be heading to the Bethlehem Fair right about now and could have reached me earlier if there was something pressing."

"Good point, right on the nose. You're heading out and I'm dropping off this little bit of news and heading back 'cause he's not able to reach you. 'Cause the long and short of it is, he ran into a little trouble, got banged up, and lost his cell phone while he was at it."

"Oh?" Molly said, taken aback. "Is he hurt? Was it an accident? Tell me."

"Sort of but not exactly. You see, there he was, minding his own business, close to an alleyway in Waterbury—"

"But why? He's always avoided Waterbury, let alone alleyways. And his only contact there, supposedly, is a lawyer in regard to a promissory note."

"Well, hey, what can I tell you? Some goon clipped him yesterday and, like I said, swiped his cell phone. So's I wind up hauling him over to the ER and like that."

"The ER? Was he badly hurt? And how did you get involved? This is all so strange."

"I can see that. But the kicker is, right now he's over at my aunt and uncle's place sleeping it off. They themselves ain't strange, believe me. They're the best, which can be a real pain if you get my drift, all the time harping on right and wrong, good and bad. So, since you're not exactly listed in the contacts on his cell, only listed as M, he don't know your number by heart and maybe or maybe not you're doing okay. Which makes it all up for grabs in his woozy head and why he sent me and why he's kinda worried sick to make sure you, at least, are okay."

Molly paused for the longest time, looking past J.J. and then finally right at her. "You're telling me that somehow he ran into you, or has run into you before in his dealings in Waterbury. In any event, you came along after this unfortunate incident, took him to the ER and then to your uncle and aunt's place. He's in bad shape, yet he's worried about me."

"No, no, not in real bad shape, only worn out and kinda banged up, like I said. Anyways, you ain't got the time and I ain't got the time and was never any good at explanations or sticking my nose into domestic affairs and like that. Maybe he'll fill you in better soon as he's up and about. I got no call to deal with this any longer. Just put it down as some cut-rate messenger service from Waterbury. He'll be okay, you're okay, I gotta go."

J.J. started to leave the porch, realized she still hadn't gotten the answer, and turned back. "So, you *are* okay, right? Nobody's been bothering you or nothing? No lowlifes or wise guys and such?"

"Why would that happen?"

"No reason. None. Great. I'll take that as a no."

"But I still don't know what to think."

"Don't. Put it outta your brain and have yourself a nice little time at the fair."

J.J. hurried back down the cobblestones, swung open the gate, slid back behind the wheel, hit the ignition and took off. Still unsure how to put it to Josh as to how this Molly took it. Maybe come up with something like, "No worries, pal. She's doing swell and no more than a tiny bit worried about you. When you get the chance, you could fill her in, make up something fine and dandy she'd go for."

But that wasn't the half of it, as far as she was concerned. Except from looking forward to a little coin from Josh that would get her through the week, prospects were lousy. She had nothing going for her, after telling her mom she'd be out of her hair 'cause things were going so good on the sales front she'd have her own place. In fact, Fredo and her aunt were down the tubes unless Sal and his crew suddenly decided all bets were off. And even if—which had as much chance as a snowball in hell—you can't run a produce supply operation and set up new customers to keep it going and then have the chain yanked out from beneath. Fredo was right now flopped over his books, hitting the bottle, going over losses that he couldn't cut. And this Josh, this pencil-pusher choir boy she hardly knew, was all part of it, dropping somewheres in the middle of this mess that had no way out.

—··—

Actually, by now Josh was moored in a restless funk. The words of the obscure poem—*Take the journey, find your way home*—seemed so remote. So did any semblance of a hero's journey or Teddy Roosevelt's credo about picking yourself up and daring bravely. Paul called it a wake-up call when you're resigned to the fact that you are who you are and you're not fooling anybody.

But despite the aches and pains, he couldn't continue to remain motionless. Couldn't bring himself to ask the aunt to keep tending to him, fetch the vial of Tylenol capsules with codeine from the ER and a glass of water as though he were totally incapacitated. He could, at the very least, try to get up. After all, the doctor said his ribs were bruised, not fractured. All he had to do was get a good night's sleep and take it easy for a couple of days. He was not an invalid.

Wincing, he turned to his side and gazed out the window, past the lace curtains, beyond the rooftops of other weathered clapboard houses across the street. The stretch of sky seemed to be mocking him: now overcast, then roiling a bit, then giving way to shafts of sunlight turning the sky into lighter shades of pearl gray. Moments later, the cloud cover settled once more into hanging folds of gunmetal gray, too inert to amount to anything more.

More hung up than ever, he thought if he dozed off again, his head might clear and he might come out of it and come to terms. But after closing his eyes for a few minutes, he was still in limbo. Even if a glass of water and the vial of Tylenol were close at hand, the codeine would only give him a splitting headache and resolve nothing.

Still and all, he longed for Molly. His longing soon evoked those old folk songs about hopping a freight train to somewhere or someone. As usual, all the longing in the world wouldn't change a thing. There was nothing for it but to sit tight, wait for J.J. to return and give him the news.

Instead, his eyes trained on the rumpled blazer hanging on the back of the ladderback chair by the window. The one that held the printout from managing editor Russ Cabot folded in the inside pocket.

Wincing like crazy, he sat up straight as can be and said, "Right. Aren't you forgetting something? You didn't exactly come up empty, now did you?"

As though answering his call, the aunt appeared in the doorway. "Something wrong?" she asked as she took a few steps toward him. "Is there something I can do?"

"It's okay, ma'am," Josh said. "Just yelling at myself." He wanted to say he was pulling a Teddy Roosevelt, but she wouldn't understand any more than he understood the lesson of Jonah and the whale.

"By the way," he said, trying to tone things down, "what is your name? I can't keep calling you ma'am."

"Sophie," she said. "And yours?"

"Josh, just make it Josh. So . . . look, Sophie, the thing of it is, I don't know how far I'll get and how I'm ever going to repay you. But as soon as I hear from J.J. and if a certain young woman is all right—"

"Oh, please. I only wish we could get to know one another better before you even think of trying to get out of bed. You see, J.J. never fills us in. She's always so offhand and in such a rush. And here you were last night . . . and Carmine pulling in earlier driving your rental car, and me wondering whatever is to become of us."

"I know. I'm sorry about all of it. I have to at least try to get cracking for everyone's sake."

He made an attempt to position himself to get up, but she rushed over to stop him.

"Now don't agitate yourself. You sit back, I'll plump up the pillows, and we'll talk this whole thing over."

"No, no, please," Josh said, poised at the edge of the bed. "I just can't lie back anymore. If you'll give me a minute, I'll get ready for J.J.'s report and we'll take it from there."

"But she didn't say where she was going. Is there more trouble in store?" Clasping her tiny hands, she said, "Oh, dear, don't tell me. But what can be done? Carmine reminded me what happens when you go to the police. You see, Carmine is from this neighborhood . . . has been mixed up in lots of trouble himself. He should know. He says you're just asking for it."

"No worries, Sophie. It's only a personal matter. You're not listed on my stolen phone. Nothing to do with you or what you and Fredo have already been through, I promise."

"Truly?"

"Truly. Cross my heart."

Gradually getting used to the strain on his rib cage, he eased himself off the bed. Sophie backed away, saying, "Now don't you do anything foolish. Oh, it's all such a muddle, isn't it?" She hesitated, let it go at that, turned away, and closed the door.

He found his loafers, managed to slip them on, and began to walk around the room. He paused at the ladderback chair by the window and then gingerly carried on. He went into the adjacent bathroom, washed his face, disregarded his haggard reflection, and ran his fingers through his hair. There was nothing he could do about his rumpled button-down shirt and trousers, so he went back into the bedroom and paused at the rumbling sound of the jeep pulling into the drive and, soon after, the clunk of the screen door.

Bracing himself by the chair, he got set for the news.

In no time, there was a knock and then J.J. barged into the room. "Hey, what gives?"

"Never mind. Tell me what happened."

J.J. brushed by him, went over to the nightstand, studied her invoice, got out a ballpoint pen, and began making corrections.

"What are you doing?" Josh asked. "Talk to me."

"I am taking into account not only the added expense on a Sunday but the hassle of dealing with a chick you obviously haven't leveled with. So, give me a minute now I see you're up and ready to join the living."

"I want to know if she's okay. Has she been threatened? How much did you tell her? What was her response?"

"What is this, some soap opera?" J.J. said, adding in some more figures, folding her makeshift invoice, striding right over to him, and sticking it into his shirt pocket. "Let's not go off the rails here. Anyways, she's safe and snug in her WASPy little world and not all screwed up like you and me. So, you cool it down for a sec while I go check on Sophie and Fredo, see what's what. I tell ya, something's gotta give around here. I mean it."

CHAPTER TWENTY-FOUR

J osh took the printout from Russ Cabot out of the inside pocket of his blazer, studied it for a moment, and murmured, "I knew it, I knew it." Seconds later, he overheard J.J. yelling at Sophie, saying, "Enough with the Sunday school crap. Give me a break, will ya?" Josh slipped the printout back into his blazer and had no choice but to go out there and force the issue. After all, J.J. just told him something had to give and she was absolutely right.

He shuffled down the hallway and into the parlor in time to spot Fredo at his desk, surreptitiously reaching for a half-full bottle of whiskey. His account ledgers were in such disarray and his eyes so red-rimmed, he made no pretext at being busy at work. Though they'd never really encountered each other, he poured himself a shot, raised his glass with his good arm, and said, "Ah, and here's another of the walking wounded throwing in the towel."

Josh could have kept looking for J.J. but felt he should at least say something.

"I know it looks that way," Josh said, leaning on an armchair, "but it's not over yet. Not by a long shot."

"Oh, you think so, do you?" Fredo said, throwing his head back, downing the shot of whiskey. "Been around a long time, son. Seen a lot. Seen things come and go. Now it's my turn. Should have known better."

"It's not your fault, believe me."

Fredo's careworn face twitched in apparent puzzlement. He ran his mottled hands through the wisps of grayish-white hair and said, "Not my fault, he says. Tell me another one. Always thought the produce business was one thing the hoods wouldn't touch. They hadn't ever before. Why bother with fruits and vegetables? No percentage in that. Not like the bars and restaurants and whatnot with steady customers and lots of cash moving in and out."

He held onto the desk to steady himself. "Right, the mob boys, what a piece of work. Grabbing the best tables, showing off the women they'd picked up. Saw a bunch of them once at Aldo's on the west end taking over the banquets. Flashy rings, gold chains, yelling at waiters. Floozies with big hair and silk dresses. Fooled myself, thought that was all over by now. But what can you do? What can the little guy do?"

Sophie came out of the kitchen and tried to remove the whiskey bottle, but he slid it back so it stood prominently out of her reach. "You promised," she said. "It's Sunday, Fredo."

"That's right," Fredo said. "Sins of omission, sins of commission."

Sophie looked up at Josh and said, "You have to forgive him. He's not usually this way. He rests on Sunday after running around all week. Of course, all that has changed. But, like I was saying to you, maybe we can all think it over together." She looked down at Fredo and then back up again at Josh. "If you'll hold on . . . You see, I never want to give up hope. Do you understand?"

She gave him another of those imploring looks and padded back into the kitchen.

Fredo reached for the bottle and knocked some business cards onto the braided rug. Fixated by the cards, he went off on another reverie. "Those are for special customers with my home phone on it. Getting ready every spring for select fruit and vegetable orders . . . looking forward to the coming season, you see. Fancy restaurants up on the lake in New Preston. Plump asparagus and buttery lettuce . . . tasty berries for special desserts . . . juicy, ripe nectarines, not like those hard as a rock ones you get in the grocery stores . . ."

Josh reached down, pocketed one of the cards, replaced the others on the desk, and promised to call him as soon as anything broke. He turned away and left him alone. Not because he wanted to but because he really had nothing to else to offer, and getting hold of J.J. was more pressing.

He slipped through the back door and looked around until he spotted her sitting outside on a wooden picnic table bench, her back to the house. She was facing a stretch of blackened chimneys below in the distance, like rows of pipes jutting up to the sky from the endless stretch of roofs of an abandoned rolling brass mill dating back, it was said, to the Second World War. Abandonment being a theme in his own life if he wasn't so sick and tired of feeling sorry for himself.

He worked his way past the faded brick patio, still wincing but minding it a bit less, and plunked himself down on the bench next to J.J. She took a deep drag from the stub of her cigarette and said, "Don't start with me, pal. I'm warning you. I'm in no mood."

Streams of early afternoon sunlight broke through the haze continuing its game of hide-and-seek when Josh said, "That's too bad, missy. But we have to finish this."

"Finish, yeah, you said it. You and me are finished. We're all finished. All the hoping crap is finished. For a minute you think you got something going and along it comes outta nowheres and knocks you back on your ass. Talk to Uncle Fredo, you seen him, and he won't stop moaning about it. As if I hadn't tried. Him and Sophie with her bleeding-heart routine drove me right out here for some goddamn peace and quiet. And the last thing I need is you starting in on me."

J.J. flipped the cigarette stub out into the weeds, reached inside her bomber jacket for a crushed pack, and was about to pluck out another when Josh grabbed her hand and rose up.

"Hey, what are you doing?"

"You said something's got to give, as in finish this mess."

Shielding her eyes from another burst of sunshine, J.J. looked up at him and said, "Give as in give up. I've had it. It's over."

"No, it isn't. Think back. We got interrupted, remember? I was supposed to meet you at two o'clock but got hammered by Vlad thanks to your good ol' neighborly snitch Carmine."

"It was your play, man. It didn't work out so good, but that's the way it goes. So, forget about it, will ya? You and me are quits. Ta-dum!"

"It's not about me or you or Fredo or Sophie. It's about a helluva lot more suffering beyond our little problems." Josh reached inside his blazer and waved the folded printout. "So, multiply it a hundredfold soon as our kingpin sits up there on his throne somewhere in the Gulf or God-knows-where."

Rising up as well, staring Josh right in the face, she said, "Boy, that goon Vlad must've done a lot more than whacking you in the ribs. He must've done a job on your head while he was at it. Slammed it good and hard against that brick wall."

"Get off it, J.J. We had a deal. I have to go back there, which is hard enough. But I've got to know there's a chance there'll be some backup. Your guy Devlin wanted something tangible, right? You said you'd hand it to him if I actually came across." Waving the printout again, he said, "Well, here it is. Got it from a bona fide source via the managing editor of the Waterbury paper. You found me there right up against the building, right?"

"So?"

"So, what do you think I was doing there? You are either going to complete the deal or keep dragging your feet. But if you do keep dragging your feet, it'll be too late and the fallout will be on your head."

"Can we drop this conscience bull? Aunt Sophie is always pulling that day and night. It really gets to you, you know? Besides, speaking of stalling, I just ran an errand for you, and I'm not counting hauling your butt to the ER and all, which I done gratis 'cause it reminded me of the old days. You not ratting on Carmine, I mean, or even that Russian goon Vlad who laid the wood to you like he done to Fredo, telling the doc in the ER you were mugged by some dude in an alley you never laid eyes on. That's all well and good and I give you points and drag you here to mend your bones. But I ain't seen no compensation yet for all the hassle of dealing with your nice but uppity chick."

Josh reached into his pants pocket, drew out some bills, and slapped them into J.J.'s hand. "Here, hope this covers it and it wasn't too painful for you." Then he slapped the printout into J.J.'s hands as well. "The least you can do is read about the charges against Zharko Vadja in one particular recent case resulting, according to this court case ruling itemized in the *Hartford Courant*, in his deportation. Add that to the fact, if I don't miss my guess, he's hiring three drivers from Philly, all Scandinavian, non-Mafia types, to man those three box trucks parked in front of the warehouse, set to roll in the next day or two with a stopover at a hub in Asheville. And again, from what I gather, soon as those trucks are fully loaded and hit the Gulf, Zharko will be free and clear and set up forever."

"Says who?"

"Says me as the result of keeping my eyes and ears open and picking up clues everywhere I look. I will either get a pass for having the grit to drag my carcass back to the warehouse tomorrow or they'll be on to me. Either way, I'll call from the inn first thing tomorrow morning whether I'm still on it or have been muzzled or God knows what."

"What inn and how you gonna call?"

"The Litchfield Inn. I've got one of your uncle's business cards, will use the landline in my room to get in touch. Sophie or Fredo will relay the message to you, and you'll put me in the loop with Devlin. On the other hand, if anything's amiss there'll be no call because Zharko'll have me under wraps."

Not about to wait for J.J.'s response or carry on any longer, he turned and scuffled back into the house.

Calling behind his back, J.J. said, "Great exit lines, pal. I'll bet you don't make it to the car. Or at least ain't able to drive outta here and wind up right back in bed!"

Ignoring her, Josh made his way into the kitchen and patted Sophie gently on the shoulder. "J.J. is laying odds. Don't listen to her."

"Wait," Sophie said with that same plaintive look in her eyes. "Where are you going? You mustn't hurt yourself."

"Not if I play it at a safe remove. That's what I'm good at."

Wincing with every step, he turned toward Fredo, who was neither slumped over working on his ledgers nor hitting the bottle this time. Just running on empty, more or less waiting it out.

Josh held up Fredo's business card to make sure he noticed and said, "Got your number and promise to try a lot harder."

He hoped the words might register and cause a little sparkle in his eyes. But with no reply forthcoming, he let it go, returned to the spare room, grabbed the car keys off the top of the dresser along with the pharmacy bag from the hospital. He kept moving, down the hallway and out the front door. Reaching the car, he squirmed behind the wheel, fighting through the twinges of pain, hit the ignition, and proceeded through the maze of unfamiliar streets looking for a junction north onto Route 8.

Luckily the traffic was light this Sunday. J.J.'s bet he would never make it this far coupled with the open road spurred him on.

—··—

Back at the inn, it took him the longest time to shave, shower, change the bandage wrap, put on some clean clothes, and arrange for expedited valet service for his blazer, rumpled pants, dress shirt, and tie.

As late afternoon faded into evening, he noticed a red light on the phone on the sideboard next to the TV. He went over, thought better of it, ordered a hearty early supper, and took his time digesting it. By the time the dishes were cleared by the room service attendant, the wear and tear on his ribs began to get to him again. The pain was somewhat alleviated by another round of Tylenol with codeine, but the medicine made him as groggy as ever.

As night came on, though he'd managed to put aside thoughts of J.J., Sophie, Fredo, and Zharko for the moment, thoughts of Molly still lingered. Especially what she might have thought when confronted with J.J. right before she was bound for a fun day at the fair as the weather started to clear up. The way J.J. put it, Molly was only slightly thrown. But J.J. was prone to sloughing things off in her hurry to drop in and get out as quickly as possible, and Molly would never show her true feelings to a street-tough stranger like J.J.

He went over to the narrow desk with the Formica top, glanced past the TV, saw that the red light was still on by the telephone, and shrugged it off again. He got out a first-class Forever stamp from the attaché case, sat at the desk, took out a sheet of inn stationery, retrieved his fountain pen, and began drafting a note about his experiences during the past two days. Leveling with Molly in his offhand way but not touching on anything that would cause her any concern.

But an apt lead sentence eluded him. So did some way to gloss over the recent events. How in the world could a person leave a newspaper building, wander over to the corner of an alley, get pummeled by a thug who was after his cell phone, be rescued by a street girl in a jeep who took him to the ER, and wind up at her aunt and uncle's place while a neighborly deadbeat parked his car?

After tossing each attempt into the wastebasket, he reached a point when he couldn't keep his eyes open no matter how much he wanted to stay in touch.

Soon he found himself daydreaming of those sunny days before the Christmas incident and mayhem. Back to that spring when he first began to walk Molly Hunter home from school. Buttercups and daffodils had sprung up next to the sidewalks, the fingers of his left hand brushed against her right hand, and little by little their fingers would intertwine until they were holding hands. When they crossed over into the lane that took them to her house near the top of the rise, she would lower her eyes and let go of his hand as if they were secret sweethearts and must part before her mother waved to her from the veranda.

The daydream faded, replaced by a firm resolve to write to Molly when he wasn't fighting off the effects of codeine and twinges of pain. He got into his pajamas and settled for a good night's sleep, telling himself that Molly had mentioned they both needed some time and space and was predisposed to let things ride for a while until he sorted things out. Not including, that is, his mishap in the alley, which he'd tackle once again at the earliest opportunity.

Before turning off the light, he forced himself to at least deal with the lit bulb on the landline phone. He dialed the front desk and was told that the caller had inquired about his whereabouts several times these last two days but left no name or message. Josh hung up, not at all sure about getting a good night's sleep no matter how many points he allotted himself for making it this far.

In the interim, it didn't take much to imagine which anonymous character might have been anxious to locate him and nail him down.

CHAPTER TWENTY-FIVE

A few hours before, Zharko quit calling the inn on his disposable cell phone and stormed out of the gypsy camper into the woods. They call it "fit to be tied" in this country, and that was so true for him now. How many times had he hung out in this camper thinking of times when you must sit back and what happens? You lose out. Winners and losers, always winners and losers and nothing between.

Like when old Uncle Groffo shipped him over here. For his own good, Groffo had said. And Novac got him a job at riding stables. So, who comes along in nice bus with nice-behaved girls? Son of headmaster with blond hair and blue eyes, maybe ten years older than pretty girl Irina. This son, always looking at her, always after her like she was more special than light-haired gadzo girls. Son's name sounding like Hugh maybe. Short, fuzzy gadzo name like so many others here, like Ken, Phil, and Bob. Names with no heart, no fire, no soul. Songs you hear are likewise, with no chance to feel catch in your throat as balalaikas pick up steam and you are dancing wild, maybe leaping on tables. Nothing close like that here. People living side by side or by little hills and streams with nowhere big to cross like Caucasus peaks and steppes; no gorges or frozen Volga down to Caspian Sea. No space for gypsies of old to roam and hold horse races. This gadzo Hugh with blond hair and blue eyes knows nothing of this, treats you like dirty stable boy, leaves Irina with child and is gone. Betrayal. Everywhere you look, always betrayal with no outlets for revenge.

And now Irina, who speaks brusque like short gadzo names,

like one who betrays her, who once looked up to you because you are older, like wise brother. But now she and maybe Novac, too, are up to something, under the table, around the corner or what have you got.

But even worse, waiting, speaking only through throwaway cell phones. Worrying, thinking, all the time thinking. Pressure building with no way to vent with loose ends that keep mounting up.

And so many out to get you if you do not watch out, setting you off. And much worse still, old Waterbury Mafia types like goddamn Tulio, closing in, sniffing around like hungry dogs.

So irritated now, so beside himself, he paced off twelve yards through pine needles like old days in carnival outside Bucharest. He drew a line with his boot through soft earth, hurried inside camper, and grabbed cardboard target he had made in shape of a head, neck, and shoulders, plus thumb tacks. He went back outside, marched same twelve yards and tacked this cutout against pine tree oozing with sap. He marched back to line in dirt and stood stock still.

Everything was reminding him of things while hanging back in woods these days. Something was very much off-kilter and always, day by day, hour by hour, growing worse.

Staring at the cutout brought memories of Nadia, who cheated on him with carnival barker. That time when he first learned of betrayal when he was barely twenty. And that night, during their act, blade nicked side of her neck. He had thrown it hard. Not to cause great harm. Only enough to make her flinch with fear in her eyes as he pulled out blade and wiped off trickle of blood. Enough to make her think twice next time and to for sure pay her back.

And so, in shadows of looming pines in this clearing, with dull afternoon light fading, he faced target like that very night at carnival time. He'd practiced here, getting better and better to vent and keep in shape. Vent so much churning inside because you never know when knife with razor-sharp Hoffritz blade for sure would be needed.

He stared hard at the target. He slipped the switchblade out of the sheath by his back pocket. Holding it by his hip, he touched the trigger and shot the blade out with a sharp click. He loved the click like the cock of a gun. He loved holding still, showing no signs on his face. Blank, only waiting for signal for someone to call it. Or catching signs like a squirm, shudder or movement of a finger from one standing opposite him.

His hand shot forward with the swivel of his hip as the blade hit the target quivering. He stepped toward the target of remembered outline of Nadia's neck and saw he had only missed by a sliver. He yanked the blade out, folded the knife and slipped it back in the sheath by his hip. Each day he had gotten better, quick and clean. Each day he had gotten more hungry for this wet work as his pulse quickened and his blood was up.

He went back inside, made some hot, thick coffee from the old country, and began to brood over some satisfactory way to release this pent-up hunger for real. To leave his mark and keep things from unraveling. But first he needed absolute proof.

He hit the speed dial number for Sal on his burner cell phone. Sal picked up almost immediately with no hesitation. By now Sal knew damn well of Zharko's concerns.

"Hey, I told you," Sal said before Zharko even asked.

"You tell me once again."

Sal sighed and went into the same song and dance trying to calm Zharko down, only adding a few different words like "Hey Jeez, it's Sunday, Zharko," "Maybe not," "We'll see," and "As for this Josh character you saddled us with—"

"Forget this Josh for now," Zharko cut in. "I am telling you I want to know about Tulio."

"Yeah, but come to think of it, this Josh character might've heard the whole thing. The electrician saw him crouching by the dumpsters."

"I tell you later I deal with this Josh. Time is running short if this Tulio has other ideas. So you will tell me again for sure now."

During the short delay while Sal thought it over, Zharko recalled Sal once worked for Tulio, was part of the old Waterbury mob, had talked Zharko into giving Tulio's nephew a piece of the action in rounding up three box trucks that were clean and certified. Zharko also remembered taking a chance taking Sal on board in the first place even though he'd used him once before.

"Okay," Sal said, cutting into Zharko's thoughts, "this is exactly how it went down. In a nutshell, Tulio didn't exactly like the fact his nephew couldn't horn in on the action. And you were putting the word out for some talent all the way over to Philly who were WASP-like or Scandinavian and such, and not at all from the old days. Hinting maybe you was prejudiced and like that while his crew was primed and ready. I mean, he's saying what is your problem? This don't call for some whack job or nothing."

"So, finally you come out with what I know all this time."

"Because why complicate it?"

Zharko ended the call yelling, "To keep a close eye, that is why! I will be getting back to you."

Just short of cursing at the top of his lungs, Zharko poured himself another steaming cup of dark, bitter brew and pondered once again. *Whack job.* Always some special language in this country. Politicians when caught red-handed say is all a hoax as they try to squirm out. People all the time saying, "How's it going?" which is way of telling, "I am too busy and don't want to know." And "whack job" is one more as mob is hiding real meanings. "I've been sent for," meaning I am going to "get whacked" meaning

"I screwed up" meaning I botched the job and "ratted" on you, meaning I betrayed, got caught, and will get executed. Then there is "a friend of mine," which is not same as "a friend of ours," and on it goes, round and round.

Which all comes down to only message people always get loud and clear is violence. Even when is so simple like now. So what is keeping Vlad? How long it takes to walk up to main road and over to hardware store to buy little tube of nail glue?

Calming himself down, he opened the cabinet under the camper sink and got out the pipe for a bomb. Someone made it for him down in Town Plot section of Waterbury a while back but he didn't remember who made it or who he had in mind for a target. Only that he had suspicions and these people were working for Tulio. It blew over when he, Zharko, got deported but was starting up again and must be stopped quick.

He put the pipe on the sink counter and reached under the cabinet again and studied what bomb maker wrote on the index card. Short section of pipe was closed at both ends with brass caps. Filled with aluminum powder and carbon tetrachloride, firecracker sparkler sticking out of hole was the fuse. All he must do was seal it with liquid nail glue and he was in business. Ready to make sure Tulio knew how things stood before trucks roll very soon. Knowing he covered all bases like they are saying. Because everything was riding on Gulfstream Transfer and nothing would stand in his way.

—··—

When it was pitch dark, he and Vlad were ready to go. It was best opportunity. No traffic, nothing moving this time of night deep in east end of Waterbury below the main drag. Maybe someone walking a dog but nothing more. Mostly people getting ready for bed and good night's sleep for big start of work week. It was also good to try all fixed-up gypsy camper out because tomorrow people would be talking, not only about blast and fire. But maybe many would say—those walking dogs or looking out the window— many would swear they saw gypsy flag on passing camper or one parked by Marta's restaurant before it happened or seconds after. And Tulio would for sure hear with everyone talking. And Tulio would know what happened to his restaurant. Tulio would be warned for sure never to what they call "horn in."

So off they went, Zharko driving, Vlad in passenger seat by his side as they joined Route 8 heading south by Waterville exit. To pass the time, Zharko asked, "You hit Sonny, who calls himself Josh now, hard but not too hard, yes?"

"Short punches for first warning like always. Plus good hard kick."

"And he puts up no fight?"

"Crumples like straw."

"A coward, you could say, since he was little, hiding behind chairs. Spooked is good word for it, you agree?"

"Yes, for sure."

"So he goes to hospital but how he gets there? In car, which you say was gone when you go to check but doesn't come back to the inn? So, where he is holed up maybe?"

"I do not know."

Still cruising along, a few minutes later it was Vlad's turn to speak. "About cell phone, what you find out?"

Zharko had nothing to report. "New but not many contacts."

"But names of contacts?"

"No names. Only letters when is new and you have little time, or for shorthand in case you lose cell phone and want nobody to know. Letters like CVS, UPS, DMV, NA."

"NA?"

"I try in case. Man with nasty voice answers by name of Noah Ackerman. Gives me hard time like I am salesman and says he has no time for 'lowlifes hawking products'."

"So, no police letters on cell phone, no one to report me."

"Nothing."

Another few minutes of silence and Vlad was at it again. "Why we doing this?"

"Why you ask? Why we get deported? We let guard down. Someone fingers me, wants in on smuggling racket. Is so long ago you forget? Not yet two years so long is out of your mind?"

"No."

"Then don't ask."

With that settled, they spent the next twenty minutes or so in silence.

Zharko did, however, keep Josh's whereabouts in the forefront of his list of loose ends as he turned past the deserted Waterbury Green and eased into the east end of town with its closed shops and old abandoned movie theaters. It took a few wrong turns down streets of dilapidated buildings before he found the side street he was looking for, judging from what he recalled from the old days. Soon, he caught sight of Marta's restaurant at the crest of the next turn and stopped across the street.

Seen from this angle, peering left and right, it struck him how everything had changed since he last was here. To his right, directly across from Marta's, he spotted what used to be a Lincoln dealership that serviced the local politicians and mob bosses and lieutenants displaying glossy new limos and town cars with a bustling service department next door. But it had given way to a used car lot with a bunch of old models they didn't make any more like Pontiacs and Oldsmobiles plus a run-down repair shop. Across the street to his left, next to the pitted drive and parking lot, was a seedy Italian bakery that may or may not be closed down. The same went for the liquor store on the other side.

With no cars approaching from either side, he made a U-turn, backed into the pitted drive next to the restaurant, shut off the motor, got out, and took it all in again.

He figured he might have had to park the camper on a vacant lot a few blocks away and sneak around on foot. But standing here, he saw there was no point. He had pictured the firebombing would make a big splash, what with some mobsters and politicians still around, dining out at Marta's as always, picking up pastry afterwards and stocking up on liquor. Then tomorrow, being in shock over what they found, police cars and a fire engine still on the scene, passersby gawking, Tulio scratching his head, all upset. He had pictured a big to-do. But no big to-do was in the offing. That whole world was gone, and it was no wonder Tulio was itching for a big score to make him whole again.

Zharko cursed loud enough for anyone to hear. Wishing Tulio's henchmen would come by so he could let them have it, he got out the pipe bomb and a small crowbar. Vlad, who seemed disappointed as well, asked, "This is big deal? This is what you go to all this trouble for?"

"Never mind. You will sit in driver's seat and honk horn in case, yes?"

Vlad got out of the camper, peered up and down the street, stared at Marta's smudged plate-glass front window, shook his head, scuffed back, and got behind the wheel.

Zharko drifted down the faded-yellow clapboarded side of the building and laughed when he came upon a backyard that had been supplanted by a sprawling junkyard. Determined to go ahead with it anyway, to at least send a message, he spotted a ventilation shaft under the eaves of the low-slung kitchen roof.

He flung the crowbar aside, which wasn't needed to bust into a warped back door barely on its hinges, and let out another scornful laugh at the clang of the crow bar against the asphalt, a sound no one would hear. He pulled over a plastic milk crate, stood on top, jammed the pipe all the way into the ventilation shaft with only the bent sparkler fuse showing, lit the fuse, hopped off the crate, and watched the sparkles.

He'd planned to light the fuse and run as fast as he could to the awaiting camper, tell Vlad to gun the motor and pass by the blasts, smoke, and flames curling up behind the restaurant as they sped away pretending to be shaken onlookers. But now he only stepped back until he tripped over a rusty car radiator.

Cursing yet again, it crossed his mind that Sal told him Tulio had pulled into the warehouse driving an old Cadillac that had seen better days. One Tulio probably picked up for a song, as they say, no doubt from the used car lot across the street from his broken-down restaurant. To make matters worse, this arson was doing Tulio a favor and he would file an insurance claim. And while he was waiting to collect, with no restaurant or means of support, he would need to horn in on Zharko's big score more than ever. Failing that, he could put in for a "whack job" on Zharko as Sal had mentioned sloughing off the possibility. But now there was no way to slough it off. Now everything was twice as bad for Zharko to deal with, to worry about.

Crazy with rage, Zharko rushed over, picked up the crowbar, shielding his eyes from the billowing smoke as the rear of the building caught fire, and ran past the camper. Before Vlad could stop him, he hurled the crowbar with all his might, shattering and splintering the smudged plate-glass front window. Vlad grabbed him from behind and tugged at him, but Zharko pushed him away, intent on at least enjoying the damage he'd done. Yelling over the crackling flames that had reached the roof, Vlad told him he was leaving himself open, he'd get caught, wind up in jail, ruining everything.

Too upset to even think about driving, Zharko threw up his hands, rushed back to the camper, got into the passenger seat, and let Vlad start the engine and get them out of there. But Vlad had no sooner turned out of the drive trying to get his bearings when a grizzled old man in a dented green Chevy pickup coming from the opposite direction pulled alongside and asked, "Say, what the hell happened?"

Hitting the brakes, Vlad shook his head.

Just then, sirens wailed somewhere in the distance, closing in.

"Damn," the old man said, "better beat it. Next thing it'll be cop cars. I tell ya, this section of town is going to hell in a handbag."

The old man spun his truck around, cut in front of them, and waved out his window as if leading two lost souls in a gypsy camper to safety.

CHAPTER TWENTY-SIX

The following Monday over breakfast at the inn, Josh kept telling himself to look at the present state of affairs objectively. The anonymous phone calls to his room were perfectly natural. It made sense for Zharko or one of his cronies to check up on him, to see whether he made it back okay. They might have even tried to get hold of Carmine, the snitch, who might have known if Josh had some acquaintance who provided him with a place to hole up for a short while until he was on the mend. As for his cell phone, he'd discounted any fallout the second he learned that M-for-Molly elicited no repercussions and was as vague as Esq.

In any case, the sooner he reported back to the warehouse, the sooner he could dispel any misgivings on their part. Maybe even earn a commendation for taking his beating like a man, a notion he picked up from old noir movies. The point was, the sooner he got back into Teddy Roosevelt's arena, the better.

Except for the inability to move quickly, he'd aroused no notice on the part of his fellow suits holding forth around him. He was more or less dressed as neatly as before, wolfing down his bacon, eggs, toast, and coffee as they did in this busy breakfast nook, preoccupied with getting on with the business at hand like the rest, which would take them swiftly away to urban hubs south, east, and west in the next few minutes.

The only sticking point was getting his story straight so it wouldn't be obvious he was faking it. He had been getting adept at it lately, warding Zharko off before the run-in with Vlad. And, through J.J., offering Molly more bits and pieces while leaving out the harrowing details. And now here he was about to downplay his recuperation, which was a far cry from what he was used to: reporting as accurately as possible. In a sense, he had to become an actor reciting his lines without a hitch if he was going to pull this off and resume his place at the listening post.

With that ploy settled, in no time he was part of the scramble to the shiny-new rental cars awaiting in the inn's parking lot and only a tad behind the fray as they all took off on their appointed rounds.

Taking his sweet time cruising down 118 and then slipping south onto Route 8, he used the contest of cars racing and passing one another to steady his mind, focus solely on his driving while holding steady in the right-hand lane.

Some thirty-five minutes later, he eased into the warehouse drive. His aim was to be at his desk, fielding calls and taking care of business as usual. Behaving in such a way that any concerns would fade away with a few casual remarks, meaning that whatever punishment had been dealt out was par for the course and it was simply time to move on.

But almost immediately he began to have second thoughts. Sal's vintage maroon sedan was already sitting there in the usual spot ahead of the three box trucks at the loading dock. The steel rolling door was fully raised and Sal's burly form stood there, arms crossed, holding a clipboard as though this confrontation was his first order of business.

Thoughts of Carmine divulging everything, even to the tune of parking Josh's car in front of J.J.'s aunt and uncle's house, crossed Josh's mind, and who knew what else Sal hadn't figured on.

Grimacing, attaché case in hand, Josh made his way carefully up the side ramp. Sal said not a word and lagged a few feet behind as Josh continued on his way by the near wall. For the first time there was no activity at all within the confines of the hanger-like space, which made the silence, save for Sal's scuffing boots, that much more unnerving.

Josh opened the door, sat himself down at the desk, booted up the computer, and flipped open the latches of the attaché case. Sal moved in and slammed the case lid down so hard Josh barely jerked his hands back.

"Okay, smartass," Sal said, hovering over Josh's shoulder, holding up his clipboard and retractable pen as if he were about to conduct a survey. "Let's start at the top. What were you doing sneaking in and out of the newspaper building? What did you tell them, what did they tell you, and what message did you get back to your paper down in the boonies?"

Hesitating, realizing that trying to wedge in his canned speech would only make him sound guilty, he decided to toss in snippets of truth. "As it happens," Josh said, "I have no job down in Carolina anymore. My editor didn't buy my lame excuse for taking off and since I'm originally from here—"

"Way back when, Zharko says you was from these parts." Nudging Josh's shoulder, Sal pressed harder. "Come on, out with it. Zharko says talking to you over the phone don't cut it no more. You'd keep lying in your teeth and he'd have no way to tell 'cause you are good with words. Which, as far as I can see, is as far as what little use I got for you goes."

"Exactly," Josh countered. "They're thinking of reviving the old *Lakeville Journal* up in the northwest corner. With nothing else going for me and counting on the fact this trucking stint is only slated to last a short while longer, I thought I'd look into it."

"This ain't Lakeville, it's Waterbury."

"I was only looking for a lead, any opportunity with a small paper in the hills or the Berkshires. That's the way the business works, through the grapevine. I go in, ask the managing editor if I could leave off a resume or get the name of a helpful contact. Otherwise, I've got nothing going for me and I'll wind up in the cold."

"How do we know this? How do we know any of what you were up to if we didn't put the word out and Carmine don't tip us off? Carmine we can trust 'cause he's hungry and knows what happens if he stiffs us. Not green like you and boneheaded enough to hook up with that brat-juvie J.J. in broad daylight who you said you got rid of. And she ain't the kind to be put off by some suit she ain't never seen and then meet up. Which makes no sense!"

For emphasis, he whacked Josh hard across the back with the clipboard. Reflexively, Josh twisted away and clutched his ribs.

"Now the way you grabbed your ribs, that I believe and is all I believe. So, let's move on to where you been holing up. Take it from the time Vlad clocked you."

Resorting to his canned speech, Josh said, "Well, I couldn't just lie there, now could I? Couldn't wait the rest of the afternoon in pain for someone to come by and, for no reason, peer down the alley and decide to play the good Samaritan."

"So you done what?"

"I crawled over to my car, which happened to be parked at the edge of the circular drive, so close I could see the front grill."

"A scrawny guy like you?"

"A scrawny guy like me who was deathly afraid Vlad had fractured my ribs."

"Get outta here," Sal said, shoving Josh's shoulder. "If he'd have clipped you that hard, the pain would've torn through each move you made and you would've gotten nowheres."

"Okay," Josh said, straightening up, "I wasn't thinking clearly. I only wanted to get out of there, check into the ER, and get attended to."

Sal walked away, came right back, and said, "So even then, even if you crawled over, hoisted yourself up from the front grill to the hood, slid over to the driver's side without tearing your guts out, even if you drove outta there, we checked Saint Mary's Hospital, which was only a couple of blocks away, and they ain't got no record of you."

Josh was more than ready for this one. "Maybe if I was thinking straight, if I had a better knowledge of this area. But all I knew about was the Waterbury Hospital. So I went past the overpass to the west side of town, pulled into the emergency entrance, a paramedic lifted me out and so forth. The upshot is, the ribs were badly bruised, killing me every time I took a deep breath. They plied me with pain pills, kept me overnight for observation, and I didn't get back to the inn until late yesterday afternoon."

Sal didn't reply, scribbled down some things on his clipboard, and shook his head.

"And if you don't believe me," Josh said, calling Sal's bluff, "check admissions and discharge. They've got my United Health card on file."

Sal started to jot that down as well and then thought better of it. "Since when do you mouth off like this? I figured you for the mousey, polite kind."

"Pain, codeine, and getting clobbered does a job on you. And then getting interrogated. Makes you a bit testy."

Sal glowered at him. "And while we're at it, what do you know about a little firebombing at Marta's last night a little before midnight?"

Josh sat up and said, "Okay, I'll bite. What is Marta's and what are you trying to pin on me now?"

This time Sal slammed the clipboard on the desk. "All right, let's go back aways. What were you doing the other day squatting down by the dumpsters? And don't give me no cock and bull. The electrician seen you and caught you cold."

This time Josh was totally thrown off guard. He booted up the computer. "Just a minute, I've got to answer a pressing query. I promised I'd get right back to them first thing Monday morning."

Turning the monitor away from him, Sal said, "Don't hand me that crap. I want answers."

"Right," Josh said, gathering his thoughts. "When I heard all the yelling out there on the drive, I left my post, spotted the old Caddy and the big guy in the leather coat and the way the two of you were so chummy . . ."

"Yeah, yeah, go on."

"Well, I had to find out how far this thing goes. It's bad enough being forced to act as a front. But if it's also going to involve unsavory characters, mobsters in point of fact . . ."

"That does it. Don't go nowheres, don't do nothing funny, don't even think about it." With that, Sal barged off as briskly as he'd barged in.

For a time, Josh just stared at the blank wall. A part of him had actually counted on Teddy Roosevelt's dictum. That credit was due to those who pick themselves up and carry on. Even J.J. was impressed and told him so. He did tough it out and came crawling back here having more or less paid his dues. But Sal didn't see it that way no matter how hard he'd tried to fend him off. He'd gone from suspicion to putting Josh on notice, which was the last thing Josh needed at this point as the erratic quarks and the uncertainty principle gained the upper hand.

CHAPTER TWENTY-SEVEN

Josh spent the rest of that Monday morning going through the motions, waiting for the axe to fall. The only thing of note was Raul's recorded call, which sounded a bit more urgent: *The Gulfstream waters are navigable, the trade winds balmy, the seawall—the Malecon—beckoning you now.*

Then it happened. A few minutes after noon, Sal burst in and said, "You ain't going out for lunch today."

Josh looked up from the computer screen. "What do you mean?"

"You ain't slipping into no Waterbury newspaper, signaling nobody, nothing like that. And no more giving me lip about how innocent you are, twisting your story so's it sounds okay."

"I don't get it. What are you saying?"

"I'm saying things are gonna change around here. For starters, what do you want to eat? I'll add it to my order. So? Speak up."

Unable to get his mind around what was going on, Josh said, "A BLT, French fries, and a coke would be fine."

"You got it."

Sal started to leave. Josh stopped him. "Wait a minute. How far does this new regimen go?"

"Let's just say, after I put Zharko wise, we got new orders from him. So, the regimen—or whatever you want to call it—is changing for you real good."

Giving Josh no chance to prolong the discussion, Sal walked out.

Again Josh found himself staring at the blank wall. He'd read that people who blunder into situations over their heads are called fish out of water. Aside from watching movies like *Out of the Past* with mobsters catching up to Robert Mitchum, Josh had no idea how things worked in the world of crime, especially for complete novices. Mitchum's character knew exactly what was in store for him. Totally unprepared, Josh had been trying to come to terms, safeguard Molly, pass the baton somehow to Devlin, and step out of the way. But he might have realized the second Carmine blew the whistle, everything was up for grabs and nothing would be the same.

He spent the rest of the afternoon scarcely going through the motions this time. Wondering what exactly he was in for.

—··—

At quitting time, having accomplished virtually nothing and noting there was no activity in the warehouse, nothing to report even if he had the opportunity, the moment he was about to walk down the ramp to his car, Sal came over and hit him with the latest.

"Enjoy the ride. It'll be the last one on your own."

"And what is that supposed to mean?"

Sal broke into a smile, ended the exchange with "You'll find out soon enough," and walked away.

Still wincing every time he tried to move quickly, Josh made his way down the ramp, got behind the wheel, and waited after he started the engine, wondering if Sal had been ordered to tail him. But Sal merely pulled out, slowed at the end of the drive, turned, and meshed with the traffic heading into the city.

Josh proceeded in the opposite direction. Soon he was heading north up Route 8, hugging the right lane as usual, his mind in a fog. Driving almost by rote, he barely noticed passing East Litchfield as he took the steep climb up 118. The colonial ambiance of the

Litchfield Green, Molly's school on his left, and the lane leading down to the woods and his mother's cabin barely registered.

He pulled into the inn, parked as close as he could to the entrance, made his way past the desk clerk without saying a word, even when the desk clerk seemed to be trying to get his attention. He took the elevator to the third floor still in a partial daze, ambled down the pristine white corridor, got out his pass key, opened the door and froze. There, waiting for him by the picture windows overlooking the circular drive, was none other than Zharko.

Dressed in his signature denims and rose-red blouse, the twitch of his high cheekbones set in his chiseled features gave away the fact that now Josh was really in for it.

"Ah, a room attendant must have let you in," Josh said, trying to disarm the situation. "The receptionist just tried to give me a heads-up, but I was too preoccupied to respond."

When Zharko didn't fall for this fake pleasantry, Josh added, "Can I get you anything? I could call for room service. There's also a little fridge with soft drinks and tiny bottles of booze, I think, although I haven't touched it. And there's a coffee maker."

"You will sit," Zharko said in a chilly tone far different from any Josh had encountered.

"Yes, I will sit. I can only stay on my feet for so long, as you can well imagine. I mean, your sidekick Vlad sure can punch, got to hand it to him. Very efficient. Wastes no time mincing words, lands his blows just right."

Josh hated the way he was babbling. But it was second nature in order to bypass any authority figure who was dissatisfied with something he'd done or failed to do.

"You will also shut your mouth while we are having it out. Good expression, no? Having it out while person in catbird seat makes plain to good boy who is always obedient what can of worms he has fallen into."

Zharko suddenly sprang forward, ripped the landline from the wall, and tossed it in the wastebasket. "So there is no interruptions or calls made outside to who knows, and loose ends will be much less loose."

He returned to the picture window and pulled the blinds, dimming the ambient light cast by the late afternoon.

Josh rose up, pulled the flimsy padded club chair a few feet back and over to one side so there was as much space as possible between the two of them, and sat back down. The door to the room was only a few yards to his right in case he had to spring up and hightail it out of there despite his sore ribs. But, after repositioning himself, he noticed Zharko glancing at his laptop lying open on the nightstand next to the TV, right across from the window. He had no idea if Zharko was at all computer savvy. If he was, what would stop him from booting it up and logging onto Josh's file on Zharko's activities and all the conjectures Josh had made vis-à-vis Zharko's master plan? Not a damn thing.

"So," Josh said, to distract him, "would you mind telling me what this is all about? As it happens, I've never suddenly encountered an unannounced visitor in my hotel room. Even back in Black Mountain, I couldn't see you and Vlad approaching, didn't have time to prepare, but at least I was on home ground and had ample time to get my bearings. But here you are, bearing down on me, giving me no time to think."

Waiting for a response, Josh felt a shudder run through him. He was really trapped this time, and all his efforts to avoid this moment had been for naught. It was always out there, biding its time, and his babbling was worth zilch.

Zharko's gaze drifted up to the ceiling as his eyes darted left and right. "Is true what they are saying," he said. "You should know what goes around comes around and get this into your brain. So you are scared and behave like scared little boy hiding behind chairs while watching and hearing what you should not be watching and hearing. So now reminders are needed to show what exactly is coming around if you are not playing your cards right. To make certain you damn well see plain as day!"

As Zharko's eyes darted around again, it struck Josh that Zharko was not just volatile and mercurial. He was unhinged, possibly barking mad. Josh held perfectly still as Zharko segued into his act.

"And so," Zharko said, "in cold winter day under pine trees would be best if was twelve paces between me and cockamamie embezzler Gregor like strict duel. Like finding proof who is real man, like old days in carnival outside Bucharest as people watching, holding their breath while I make cheating sweetheart pay. Her eyes open wide. She confesses one second before blade nicks her neck. People clap. Is drill like everyone knows. Is perfect. Is good."

Zharko lingered, his hand dangling by his right hip. Then, before Josh knew what was happening, there was a click and Zharko's hand shot forward, a blade hurtled past Josh's face and slammed into the door.

"But no," Zharko said, rushing over, tugging and retracting the blade. He walked back to the window and replaced the switchblade in its sheath by his hip. "In cold winter day under pine trees Gregor is crowding me. Has pistol under ski jacket and reaching for it. So, with no time, no other way . . ." Moving in slow motion as if caught in a daydream, his hand pushed outward as if parting a heavy curtain, glided behind his hip, and released the blade once more . . . reached high up and plunged the blade straight down, again and again. The next time he raised his hand he left it suspended and then finally snapped out of it. All the while, Josh held his breath and tried to stifle the shiver running up his spine to no avail. It was only when Zharko retracted the switchblade and returned it to its sheath by his back pocket that Josh was able to breathe.

Staring directly at Josh, Zharko said, "You see now, yes, tell me true, circles within circles? Bailing Irina from gadzo people who leave her in lurch to have little bastard Sonny. Later, little bastard Sonny hears screaming in woods and watches Gregor screaming last time for good. How? Because sometimes there is goddamn cockamamie glitch, which is part of betrayal, which many times comes around. When back is turned, smuggling goods on waterways, someone tells, so I am deported. Again betrayal comes around. This time, maybe you while back is turned, poking around. But always Zharko has his eye out. Has eye out night and day so to get him before he gets you!"

Switching gears yet again, a smirk stretched across Zharko's thin lips and his dark beady eyes opened wide. "So this is upshot. You can refuse, this is free country. But this is also what I am holding over your head. Girl you are sweet on, girl Irina tells me you still in touch with, girl I can track down because you know I am good at tracking down. This girl no longer safe, my hand to whatever American god you like, unless you stay what they call under house arrest, what Sal is coming to tell you soon with knock on this door. We keep you on short leash whole time, every minute, until big score is finished with no more talk from you with words you twist and polish bright, and things you do behind my back. Is enough already!"

Zharko eyed the laptop once more, lifted the lid, peered at the screen, and shoved it onto the rug. Giving Josh no chance to say another word, he brushed by him, jerked open the door, and slammed it shut behind him.

In the whirl of his mind, Josh recalled the cell phone they took from him looking for contacts. And now Zharko eyed the laptop before shoving it onto the rug, having already underscored Josh's possible betrayal.

He got up, went over, gingerly bent down, grabbed the laptop, placed it on the nightstand, and opened the lid. He had to boot it up, open Documents, scroll down to the file on Zharko—facts, suppositions, new developments—and delete it while there was still time. But he no sooner opened the recent entries when there was a knock on the door.

He highlighted the text and called out, "Just a minute!" The knocking got louder as Josh hit the delete button and tried to exit. But a bulletin came up asking if he wanted to save the changes he'd made. The knocking turned into pounding as he hit *save.* The problem was, though the pages were now blank, the name of the file still existed. With nothing else for it, he exited Word, got back onto the home page and news of the day, hurried over to the door, and opened it only to be confronted by Sal.

Barging by him as Josh closed the door, Sal said, "Okay, wise ass, what were you doing?"

"Well, as you doubtless know, Zharko was lurking in my room, waiting. Then immediately began laying into me, wouldn't let me get a word in edgewise and—"

"Never mind." Sal glanced around, plucked the phone out of the wastebasket, examined the ripped chord, dropped it and gazed at the open lid of the laptop, the homepage shining in the dim light with the shades still drawn. "You checking out the news and sports? That's why you kept me waiting? Come on, don't hand me that."

"Okay," Josh said, winging it. "I was rattled after his litany of threats, ripping out the phone, and tossing my laptop onto the floor. Naturally, I wanted to make sure it was still working. It's the latest model. I am a reporter, might have to hand in a sample of my work. I told you about visiting the Waterbury paper, looking for openings around here after losing my job back in Carolina."

"You are some piece of work, you know that? Got an answer for everything. So, what we got here is your writing, plus access to your e-mail, plus who knows what." Closing the lid and sticking the laptop under his arm, he went on. "We'll just add this to the cell phone and make sure you got no access to outside calls while we're at it. And also while we're at it, here's the skinny on how we keep you under lock and key. You're gonna pack, come down and follow me in your rental to the Holiday Inn just down the block from the warehouse. We're gonna turn in the rental for you at the local Enterprise outfit. To make it short, your movements are gonna be restricted till we hit the road Thursday and all the way through to the payoff."

"All the way through?"

"Yeah. If you make it that long, we'll see."

"But in terms of my debt—I mean, Zharko said I only had to play at being a front man at the warehouse."

"That was before you started screwing around. That was when Zharko said you knew nothing and wouldn't even think of makin' no waves. That is all over. So move it and pack, I don't got all day. Unless you want to do this the hard way."

Josh shook his head. "But Zharko acknowledged this is a free country. Which means there are always options."

Sal stopped at the door and glanced back. "Right. Your option right now is to toe the line or else. Hey, you gonna pack or what?"

— ·· —

Later on, still completely thrown, Josh took in his new sur-roundings. As far as he could tell, this Holiday Inn was barely functional, an old property badly in need of renovation. In its heyday, it probably served sales reps and the like when Waterbury was a thriving factory town. Since that was no longer the case, at best it served those who needed a quick stopover off Route 84 on their way to Hartford to the east or New Haven to the south. He wouldn't be at all surprised if this place was soon converted to an inner-city apartment building.

As for his room on the second floor where he seemed to be the sole guest on this Monday evening (except for Sal who was ensconced somewhere down from the lobby), it too was on its last legs. Shabbily furnished, the few furniture pieces were old and dark, and the TV was a model that hadn't been made in years. Apart from dialing for room service, the landline next to the TV was of no use. Sal informed him that dialing 9 for an outside line would be tabulated, and since Sal was footing the bill for Josh's brief stay, any number he dialed would be reported. To top it all off, a faint musky odor permeated every inch of space, especially near the stained linen drapes and the lumpy queen-sized bed opposite the windows. The windows looked out onto dumpsters in the alley to complete the picture.

By the time eight p.m. rolled around and room service had provided him with a light supper, he was totally dejected. He couldn't count on anything and had no way to get in touch with anyone without getting caught. Still and all, he couldn't help hoping by sheer chance something was out there working in his favor.

CHAPTER TWENTY-EIGHT

A t first glance, it was just another early Tuesday morning and Mike Devlin was just another guy sitting on a bench on the Waterbury Green enjoying the first balmy day in recent memory. There was nothing special about a barrel-chested, square-faced man about six foot three who had probably played football in his teens for the local Catholic high school. Moreover, he was a fixture on that winning team whose starting line was typically made up of brawny youngsters of Irish decent. Nowadays this guy could easily be taken as a coach or a fitness trainer with a little leisurely time on his hands were it not for his silver-flecked, close-cropped hair and the lines in his face accenting a decidedly worried look. And it was this worried look that was closer to the truth in terms of what was actually going on.

For starters, sooner rather than later Mike Devlin would be pushing fifty, the age FBI agents retire. The age those in good standing go on to maintain a semi-retired status, still performing investigative assignments. But at this rate, his prospects were up in the air. As a matter of fact, that's why he got here early, to think things over and take stock for the umpteenth time before making a firm decision. What did he actually have going for him? Wife— none. Family—none. Relationships or even chances for any at present—none. Career? That again was his immediate problem stemming from his last assignment which he completely botched.

It all stemmed from the fact that the FBI was able to function as a money-laundering facilitator. And so, working undercover, Devlin made friends with a mobster with ties to a savings and loan outfit out of nearby Naugatuck. The objective was to get this known mobster to launder FBI funds (known as reverse money laundering) through a legitimate financial institution. In effect, Devlin needed an SCA (specific criminal activity) to make a case.

One night, at a noisy strip club on the banks of the Naugatuck River, Devlin had had it with pussyfooting around. Champing at the bit, sick and tired of humoring this guy who was a real pain in the butt and bragging all the time about his sex life. Besides, at this point Devlin had had a few too many doubles of John Jameson Irish whiskey on the rocks. So he made an "awkward jab" instead of waiting for the prescribed opportune time. He came right out with it and let on he'd accumulated tons of cash he needed cleaned. Somehow—maybe because he was pushing it so hard, maybe because he hadn't checked back with his supervisor exactly how much Bureau money he'd need to reroute, or even the source of the dirty money in his possession—the whole sting operation fell apart when he started talking in circles. The mobbed-up guy gave him a funny look and said, "Oh, yeah? I'll catch you later, man." Afterwards he no longer answered Devlin's phone calls.

As a direct result, Devlin had been put on the shelf, placed on "special projects," which was another way of keeping him occupied with Mickey Mouse surveillance here and there around the Naugatuck Valley. With all this spare time on his hands, he made do with working out at the gym, staying in touch with J.J. as her Big Brother–like mentor, keeping her on the straight and narrow. Why? He couldn't exactly say except there was something more to her than met the eye and he needed something to feel good about that made a difference in his sorry life.

As far as J.J.'s current situation and her relationship with some altar-boy-reporter-type named Josh was concerned, Devlin was caught between the old rock and a hard place. If he didn't stick his neck out, he wouldn't further jeopardize his standing with the Bureau, which was the same as spinning his wheels. On the other hand, as dubious as it seemed, it was a way to make amends and salvage any chance for investigative assignments beyond retirement age. Plus avoiding winding up as a night watchman or security guard if, in point of fact, this iffy escapade actually had any legs.

He spent another few minutes mulling all of this over while watching people who, unlike him, were functioning: catching a bus, hailing a cab, rushing to and fro to the nearby shops and office buildings across the way. He did this until J.J. finally showed up all out of breath.

"Okay," J.J. said, standing over him. "Here's the skinny. He was supposed to call Aunt Sophie first thing this morning. No call. So I called the inn."

"Hold it. Wait a minute," Devlin said. "What inn? What are you talking about? And what's so important that couldn't wait?"

"The Litchfield Inn is the damn inn, Mike. Josh let it slip that's where he's been holing up. Except I call and guess what? Early last night some rough character checked him out and elbowed him to his rental car and followed close behind as they both took off. For my money that character was Sal, the honcho I told you about who tossed me out of the warehouse. Don't you see, don't you get it?"

"No, I don't see and I don't get it. Simmer down and take it from the top. Logical, remember? Professional. You never go off half-cocked."

"Oh yeah, easy for you to say."

"Not so easy for me to say. So get hold of yourself. You're not seventeen anymore."

"And you're not my mother."

"Fine. Make the case why this go-round is so urgent. Can you do that?"

J.J. turned away and reached into her leather jacket for a pack of cigarettes. She plucked one out along with a plastic lighter, took a couple of deep drags, noted him glaring at her and said, "I know, I know. I quit till lately when everything fell apart on me. So okay, I'm chilling. I'm cooling it, see?"

She stubbed out the cigarette on the grass with her biker boot as a pink-haired woman scuffled by and wagged a finger at her. "Okay, okay," J.J. said, ignoring the little old lady. "Take it all together. The printout I gave you yesterday, a matter of record straight from the paper's database or whatever. Plus all the rest of it and you making handoffs all along and getting the ball rolling, right?"

"Uh-huh." Devlin didn't have the heart to tell her that his old partner Ray Hernandez down in the field office in New Haven was dragging his heels looking into it.

"All right," J.J. said. "Try this on for size and keep filling in the blanks. Last I heard from Josh, long-haul truckers are gonna roll to some other warehouse down in Asheville, Carolina. I'm talking maybe tomorrow or the next day. Only they ain't using local talent, whoever they are besides Sal. They put the word out and they're importing guys all the way from Philly. And that ain't all. No ethnic types, which especially means no Italian or Russian Mafia or any of the guys you've kept tabs on. Only Scandinavian or whiter than white bozos with licenses and stuff, set to go at a moment's notice."

"And you're so hot to trot this morning because why?"

"'Cause my uncle Fredo is coming unglued, Aunt Sophie has gone all Sunday school on me, and my mother'll be pulling her hair out if I have to shack up at her place again all broke and jobless. And that's for openers. Plus, and get this, seems that bastard Sal has got the screws on Josh and will not let him out of his sight, and Josh has got no phone, no way out, else he would've called."

"So now you're worried about him."

"'Cause what we got here is a Boy Scout type, in over his head, who turned out to be a standup guy even after this joker Vlad laid the wood to him, and he's now got his back against the wall. 'Cause we can't just leave him hanging out to dry."

J.J. lit another cigarette. Neither one spoke for a moment.

Presently, they both spotted Carmine sauntering onto the far end of the Green as if he hadn't a care in the world. From this distance, on this balmy, sunny day, he almost looked civilized: his straggly hair cut short, his tattered coat replaced by a shiny yellow windbreaker. Apart from his new appearance, the notion that he might actually come in handy right about now was beginning to occur to them both.

—··—

In the meantime, Josh now knew what it felt like to be a captive. His movements were so curtailed that after having Enterprise pick up his rental car, Sal drove him to the warehouse and right back to the seedy Holiday Inn. Josh assumed this arrangement would go on for a day or so until he was hauled onto one of the trucks heading south. This notion was amplified by little digs Sal kept tossing at him, like "I wouldn't trust you as far as I could throw you" and "Zharko has got you on a short leash, bozo. Get it through your head. You ain't never gonna be left on your own, no way, no how."

Other signals underscored the fact things were rapidly proceeding. A huge moving van pulled into the loading dock and workmen hastily went about unloading wooden crates that, doubtless, would be placed inside the three box trucks once the order for a trio of purely Caucasian-looking drivers was filled forthwith.

Another signal was the switch in Raul's daily message. This time it seemed the trade winds were still favorable, not only for departure from the Malecon sailing for the Florida Keys but also for smooth sailing in a southerly direction down the eastern seaboard, across to the mountains and beyond. To take advantage of this fair weather pattern, travelers and boatmen should head out given a target date encompassing this coming weekend. There was no mistaking that all systems were go.

But the most curious signal came around noon, once the moving van left the premises and right before Sal was due to ask Josh about his takeout preference for lunch. In fact, the hollering was so loud, it drew Josh from the office to a spot a few yards from the near ramp. At first, Josh couldn't tell who it was that Sal was dickering with by the side of his car. It took Josh a moment to make out the fact that the clean-shaven, neatly dressed object of Sal's wrath was none other than Carmine. As for the issue, Sal finally hollered, "Will you goddamn forget about it? No pizza and no kinda presents tomorrow or the next day 'cause he won't be here and it makes no difference how bad you feel about rattin' on him!"

"Okay, okay," Carmine said, spotting Josh. "At least let me shake his hand and say no hard feelings. I tell ya, I can't sleep knowing what that Russian done to him and me making out from it with lots of cash in my pockets and these new duds and all."

Before Sal could stop him, Carmine went bounding up the ramp, pumped Josh's hand while handing him something at the same time. "Jeez, man," Carmine said. "Like I just told Sal, I thought they was just gonna lean on you a little. But hey, if you need anything or something comes to mind . . ."

But that was all Carmine could say as Sal grabbed the collar of his windbreaker, spun him around, and sent him tripping back down the ramp. Undaunted, Carmine looked up, waved, said, "See ya around, man," and ran off.

"Enough already," Sal said, motioning Josh to get back to work.

Josh kept his fist clenched as he went back to the office, sat down, and stared at the book of matches embossed with the name of a local pizzeria. Still at a loss, he flipped it open and stared at the writing on the blank inside cover:

Hang in there, this from Mike. 203-758-9501
Later, man.

J.J.

CHAPTER TWENTY-NINE

L ater that afternoon, Mike Devlin was seated in the far corner of Atticus Books and Tea Shoppe on Chapel Street across from the Yale campus. Even on this balmy day with the Yalies on reading days in preparation for final exams and the place almost empty, Devlin felt conspicuous as always traveling down to New Haven. Apart from being close to the field office while still in the doghouse, he was also out of place here at Atticus with the walls lined with oversized intellectual paperback books from top to bottom and end to end, including the philosophy section hovering above him whose titles alone were beyond his comprehension.

Now add the prospect of his old partner Ray Hernandez barging in and carrying on about aspects of cognitive psychology before they got down to business. Punctuated by Devlin always the one to say, "Come on, Ray, enough with the academics, let's get down to it." And Ray countering with, "Okay. But let's talk about it first, Mike, and make absolutely sure you appreciate the realities." Devlin's only hope was that this time Ray wouldn't jump on him, reminding him if only he'd spent a little time reviewing the racketeer's profile, he would have realized the guy was covering up an inferiority complex. He should have let him carry on, eased into it so the guy wouldn't have been exposed. Lured him instead of flat-out calling his bluff.

Luckily, it turned out that Ray was on a tight schedule as he came in and had no time to hash over failed assignments. But it still meant Devlin would have to play it by ear and not get Ray off on another lecture.

Ray plopped himself down at the little round table and ordered a cappuccino and a chocolate croissant while Devlin continued to nurse his ginger tea and cinnamon toast. Devlin couldn't help notice that no matter the time of day, Ray always looked like the FBI poster boy—short black hair neatly coiffed, dark blue suit and light blue tie, freshly shaven, non-descript eyes, nose, and a thin line for a mouth, Mount Blanc fountain pen and small leather-bound notepad at the ready.

Glancing at his notes, Ray started right in. "So, coupled with the last bit you added this morning, it looks like we may have an overall pattern here. The first inklings involve counterfeit passports, visas, and green cards our boy Zharko was providing Russian émigrés and others infiltrating from Eastern Europe. He was also exporting stolen gems to brokers in Moscow and receiving a kickback. All very sketchy, mind you, flitting overseas and turning up again. There's some note about doing away with a confederate by the name of Gregor who served as a facilitator but, again, nothing solid. Gregor seems to have disappeared from the scene about twenty years back. There was also some real estate wheeling and dealing on Zharko's part in the Litchfield Hills over the last few years, but yet again nothing to go on, no solid case. In a nutshell, we're talking about a slippery character, back at it with no certainty what *it* is, sans any apparent affiliation or regard for boundaries and the law."

"Fine," Devlin said. "But can we just cut to the chase?"

At that moment, the cappuccino arrived along with the croissant. Ray nodded to the waitress, gave Devlin a long-suffering look, and took a sip of cappuccino. "Listen to this guy, will you. I've fit this into my spare time, not to mention you said there was no rush. Just look into it, you said. Check the databases, do a little cross-referencing. 'You never know, Ray. What have you got to lose, something could pan out.' Then, first thing this morning, what happens? All of a sudden, it's a rush job."

"That's right. But if we could bring it up to date. Latest developments, something to go on, impending right now."

After a bite of his croissant and a few more sips of cappuccino, Ray riffled through his notes. "All right. So here is where we pick up the most recent MO. It seems Zharko was in on a freeze-dried seafood operation from Cape Cod smuggling kilos of cocaine down the eastern seaboard. For his part, Zharko muscled in on certain large seafood distributors utilizing a Russian strongman to ease the way. And that's when they both got deported, as noted in the printout you faxed, a little less than two years ago. And now you say he's back and active, on his own operation via a long-haul operation out of Waterbury with a pipeline heading south. So I pushed it, went through channels, pulled a few strings."

At this point Ray stopped talking. Devlin waited him out, watching him nibbling, sipping and crossing things out with his pen. Then, when he couldn't stand it any longer, Devlin said, "The fair-haired drivers, Ray. A window of about forty-eight hours or much less till they start rolling. A greenhorn ex-reporter who stumbled into this, winds up under the gun, shanghaied. A guy who set out to blow the whistle but needs some help. He's got my burner cell number good for only a couple days and, as far as I know, has no access to a phone and is under close watch and lock and key."

Ray put away his pen. "All I can tell you, given this extremely short notice, is a vague connection I ran across. There's a fly-by-night outfit one of our own could still be on board and then again not. Maybe some way to contact him. I mean, we are talking a total crapshoot here. I wish you'd filled me in on what this Boy Scout was up to a week ago instead of just lollygagging around the periphery."

"I didn't know a week ago. I just found out early this morning about the truckers and all. So give me a break, will you? Listen, if something does pan out—you and me together—I get some credit, right? Get out of special projects, Mickey Mouse errands, and hooked up again with the area supervisory special agent. Then, continuing to do good, in line for some yearly extensions when the time comes. I'm saying I'm right to push it now and there's way more to this after the smoke clears, right?"

Shaking his head, his pencil-thin lips stretched wide in a smirk, Ray said, "That's it. Good ol' Mike, jumping the gun, champing at the bit now that he's hot to trot. Hyping it up, playing the result before things barely got started."

Leaning forward, Devlin said, "Okay, then look at it this way. This Zharko character was only partly in on some cocaine caper. But now he's sneaked back here, in the catbird seat, raring to hit and run. What could he be hauling or got his hands on that's worth the risk? If you could pull some more strings and hook us up, wouldn't *that* be something for the both of us? Can't you see that? Come on, Ray, you're in the loop. Get on the stick and call me soon as it starts paying off."

In the silence that followed, Ray had that look in his eyes. As usual, it didn't mean yes and it didn't mean no. But it could mean he was thinking about it signaling a maybe for sure.

—··—

For Josh's part that day, he overheard Sal on his cell phone indicating the arrival of the three truckers: "The drivers, who else? . . . Well, when can I expect them? . . . Hell, you must have some idea by now. What route did they take?" Josh tried to imagine what some outfit from the Philadelphia area would consider a non-mobster type to placate Zharko. Moreover, was there a pool from which to choose or could guys volunteer for the job? Given Zharko's paranoia regarding betrayal among the criminal types he'd dealt with, all Josh could come up with was three "gadzo" drivers who were not wholly unlike Josh in appearance. Caucasian, more or less regular guys, and Josh could only leave it at that.

As the day wore on, with still no sign of the chosen three, Raul's message was just as pressing. After Josh's chores were completed and Sal had carted him back to the scruffy motel, Josh was getting even more anxious. And it wasn't only that he wanted this house-arrest stint to end. It was his role in all this going forward. He had no idea how to parlay Mike Devlin's cell number with the arrival of three anonymous truckers about to get cracking, hauling him back to Carolina and beyond. His notion of paying off his so-called debt, avoiding becoming an accomplice while handing over a nefarious scheme to J.J.'s FBI contact seemed so naïve at this point. It came down to surreptitiously making a phone call based on an imminent criminal escapade he knew nothing about.

Be that as it may, the three drivers finally did show up in the empty Holiday Inn lobby around seven p.m. that evening. Josh took the elevator down to the lobby and deposited some change in the adjacent soda and bottled water dispenser as a ploy to at least try to check things out. Soon Sal spotted him standing there and ushered him over. Clutching a bottle of spring water, Josh nodded as Sal introduced him as "our white-collar front, office manager, and that sorta thing." Josh noticed that all three wore rustic warm-up jackets over their cargo pants. The tall, rawboned one with a shock of blond hair and a lantern jaw was introduced as the Swede. The heavyset one with trimmed red hair and beard was called Rusty. And the short, muscular one with the receding hairline and round, stubbly face was called Dutch. All three barely responded to their introductions and looked to Sal for the next move. Taking the hint, Sal dismissed Josh, brushing him off with a simple excuse.

"Okay, sport, I'm sure you can go back up and watch TV or something. These guys here ran into heavy traffic and are hours late. I gotta fill them in and get them settled a couple of doors down from me with no time to waste. You copy?"

Josh nodded once more and took the elevator back up to his room. He decided that while Sal was getting the drivers oriented, he'd dash off the letter to Molly he'd been struggling with, slip out to the post office—only a block away next to the library—drop the letter in the outdoor mailbox, and hurry back. All told, it wouldn't take more than four or five minutes. He certainly couldn't hand the letter to anyone at the front desk who was in cahoots with Sal. And the way things were going, this was his only chance. He couldn't stand not being in touch, not at least conveying the message running through his mind all the while. And so he reached into the attaché case, sat at the rickety desk, pen in hand, envelope and one of the last of his stamps at the ready, and dashed off the note as fast as he could while attempting to be as forthcoming as possible:

Molly,

I'm writing because, first of all, I want you to know I never meant to keep anything from you. Not ever. But I was caught between my shaky beginnings, my mother's deep dark secrets, my fears and my desire to protect you—I mean, it's not as if no one ever knew where to find you. So I sent J.J. to make sure you were okay and there were no repercussions from what just happened to me.

You see, I always tried to tap dance around it hoping something would change. You must have noticed I was a lot more chipper a year or so ago. I'd just gotten word my old nemesis had been deported and, after all, America is the land of the second chance, you can change your name, etc. Still, I didn't want to say anything until I was absolutely sure he was gone for good. Turns out I was right to wait because he came back. Not only that, he forced me to come up here hanging some iffy IOU over my head. And that's why I've been so flustered now.

In short, he's more volatile than ever, completely paranoid and lashes out with no warning. If they hadn't clobbered me and taken my cell phone, hadn't pinned me down, I wouldn't be writing this. But still, I thought if I could hand the ball over, step aside while someone or something took over, took charge . . .

There I go again, rambling like crazy. I'm saying if I ever get free, I'll explain everything. In the meantime, whatever you decide to do, and heaven knows you deserve a happy, uncomplicated life, I wish you every happiness.

Yours always,

Josh

Josh folded the note, stuck it in the small envelope, affixed the stamp, and crammed it in the inside pocket of his old windbreaker. He took the elevator to the main floor, looked down the hallway, and barely made out the muffled sound of Sal's voice carrying on with the truckers. He glanced past the glass doors to the front desk, spotted no one on duty who'd tell on him, and slipped outside. No rain, partly cloudy, slightly cool, the streets virtually empty. He looked around, glanced at his watch, and timed himself. He figured it took thirty seconds to go to the corner, wait until the light changed, and cross the street. It took another minute to rush straight down the sidewalk, another few seconds to turn the corner, cross over and deposit the letter, which should be picked up first thing tomorrow, Wednesday. All set, he tried to sprint but because of his sore ribs could only hurry, gasping, slowing the pace and then picking it up again. In this awkward, sporadic way, thankful at least no one was on the street to stop him and offer assistance, he covered the distance, including waiting for the light to change, going and returning almost three minutes over schedule.

As he scurried back from the corner as best he could and approached the front glass doors, there they were on the top steps standing side by side like a trio of gunslingers in an old Western. Grimacing, catching his breath, he looked up at the three truckers and said, "Hi, fellas. Guess I've been cooped up too long and just had to get some fresh air. But I'm so out of shape."

They didn't respond. As he scuffed forward and hoped they'd let him pass, he also hoped they'd take him at his word after his intro as an erstwhile pencil pusher. And perhaps they, too, needed a breath of fresh air after all their traveling, were only taking in the lay of the land and wouldn't report him to Sal. After all, it wasn't much to hope for and, given the quarks and the vagaries of chance, you can't lose them all.

CHAPTER THIRTY

N obody apparently told on him, as there seemed to be no repercussions from his trip to the mailbox and back. At the same time, there didn't seem to be any specific agenda for the next day, at least at the outset. What's more, the three truck drivers apparently didn't know one another, continuing to make do with an occasional nod or cool exchange. It reminded Josh of those old heist movies where the operatives who had distinctive roles to play were total strangers. So that anyone who got caught couldn't squeal on anyone else because nobody was known other than by their nicknames like Rusty, Dutch, and the Swede. How they got here also remained a mystery—perhaps individually picked up at different locales and dropped off by some driver at this rendezvous point. By the same token, it wouldn't surprise Josh if none of them knew that the ringleader was Zharko, his enforcer was a stocky Russian called Vlad, or when and where they both might show up. What the three of them were promised was anyone's guess. All anyone knew was that for now Sal was calling the shots. All of this, as far as Josh was concerned, only added to the gaps in this escalating caper.

As for this Wednesday's activities at the warehouse, the truckers began by spending time getting used to their assigned box trucks and checking out the vehicle mechanically at some designated garage in the vicinity. Sometime later, they loaded up the empty crates that had been dropped off the day before and took off in staggered intervals. Josh could only guess that Sal wanted to make sure they weren't being tailed and were getting used to the terrain and how their individual vehicle handled.

The message Josh deciphered today from Raul regarding boating conditions, etc., was still basically positive and pressing. Josh's other so-called duties were the same with the office door left partly ajar so that Sal could occasionally keep tabs and drop in from time to time to adjust the manifest log on the wall, including mileage in case some caller, for whatever reason, wanted to be apprised of the trial run to various fictitious locales.

As the day wore on, even if by some miracle Josh managed to slip out, find a phone, and call Devlin, he still had nothing significant to report. He was in possession of no ultimate destination or the interim shipping address in Asheville some 850 miles southwest, nor the nature of the cargo to intercept before it continued on its way along a trajectory to Key West. And even that was pure conjecture.

There were, however, two items of note. By late afternoon, the answering machine was set to inform future callers that this branch of Gulfstream Transfer would be on hiatus until further notice. Which meant there was no way Josh was going to be left behind to play the front man. No way Josh was going to be free on his own.

The second item was heralded by Sal as he came bursting into the office and said, "What's with you and the drivers?"

"What do you mean?"

"I asked for a volunteer for you to ride shotgun tomorrow. Two guys said no right off the bat and the Swede walked away, shaking his head as if I asked if he'd like to catch the flu. So I picked him 'cause I figure there is no way you're gonna get chummy and try to take off. Besides, I offered him a bonus if he kept you under wraps and delivered you in one piece starting with the first waystation. So, for openers, you're going on a little trial run."

Josh had no rebuttal.

A few minutes later, he found himself in the cab of the Swede's truck rumbling toward a diesel truck stop, the Swede not saying a word. After filling the gas tank, on the way back the Swede was apparently so frustrated being saddled with Josh, he pulled into a vacant lot, shut off the motor, reached inside his thick jacket, and pulled out a small handgun. Like a man of few words with the requisite cool, dry tone, he said, "You see this? It's a 9mm Glock 19 semi-automatic. Short grip and barrel, compact and easy to conceal. Even so, the magazine holds a fifteen-round clip."

"Why are you telling me this?" Josh asked, tensing up, shifting closer to the door handle.

"Because the last time out on one of these rush jobs, bullets were flying. My truck was hijacked, cargo taken, me left freezing out in the cold in the middle of the night. This time around I can fire a quick hail of rounds and end it right there." That said, he put the Glock back inside his jacket and just sat there staring straight ahead.

Unable to take the silence, Josh said, "Okay, I get it. This is your way to scare me so I won't bail, right? Because you figure I'm some relative or flunky wet behind the ears who has no business tagging along and Sal said I might get some funny ideas."

When the Swede still didn't respond, Josh said, "Well I've got news. I'm in a bind and would just as soon have nothing to do with this. I'm saying I've been coerced. I've got no choice."

Reaching for the ignition, the Swede said, "Okay, stuck with you for the short haul. But, in the meantime, I don't want any small talk. Couldn't care less what you're in it for or why. I don't want to know you. Clear?"

"Crystal."

As they drove away, Josh still had no clue what he was in for except that the Glock 19 underscored potential jeopardy. In fact, it caused a lasting concern which prompted him later that night to fiddle with the TV remote at the Holiday Inn to try and gloss over his runaway thoughts. Any recourse to enable him to get a few hours of dreamless sleep before the trucks began to roll.

By ten p.m. he was all set, sitting up in bed, old-fashioned oversized remote in his hand. It turned out that the channels were limited to what was on offer from the local cable company. In effect, there was a weather channel, local news, a number of game shows, and an endless lineup of mindless reruns like *The Beverly Hillbillies, Gilligan's Island*, and *McHale's Navy*. There were also a few tabloid exposés and a recent documentary that caught Josh's attention and caused him to stop flipping the dial.

A ragged young girl, who looked a lot like J.J., sat cross-legged on the grass in a park in Ohio, her boyfriend unconscious by a tree nearby, a police woman giving him an injection. Glassy eyed, clutching her short-cropped hair, the girl kept moaning, "I don't know, man . . . I tell ya, I just don't know" as the cameraman moved in on her.

Soon she started to make a little more sense. "I mean, first off the OxyContin wasn't cutting it. Maybe in the beginning, way back when, but no more. Wasn't taking you away . . . wasn't tripping either of us out, you know?"

The girl hesitated, waited the longest time for approval. Getting nothing from the cameraman, she tried harder. "The stuff is impossible to come by, know what I'm sayin'? And even if you come across a couple of blisters, what do you get? A hundred micrograms. Stick it in your cheek, wait maybe twenty-five minutes when you stick it in the other cheek till the damn tablet dissolves. Now you got four hours tripping out. But you only can pop another lousy hundred. What kinda deal is that? If there was something stronger, lasting a good long while, now you're talkin'."

Still getting nothing from the cameraman, she swiveled her

head and called over to the policewoman, "Hey, lady, he coming out of it or what? Somebody gonna talk to me? What the hell's goin' on?"

Unable to take any more of this, Josh shut the TV off. Now his sleep time was cut even shorter as he sat up straighter and stared out the window at the streetlights, reluctant to switch off the porcelain lamp on the nightstand, which would leave only the shadows of the soiled drapes. Not unlike the shadows during the storm back in the Blue Ridge that were a precursor to his plight from the very beginning.

CHAPTER THIRTY-ONE

That Thursday, Josh assumed they'd get a jump on the highway traffic first thing, covering the 840 miles or so at a steady clip. But, once again, Sal was playing it cagey. The first truck, which turned out to be Rusty's, had taken off at the crack of dawn. Every now and then Sal would get on his Cobra CB two-way radio to check on Rusty's run and didn't back off for the first hundred miles. And even then, he wouldn't let Dutch take off next until another thirty minutes went by and, for all intents and purposes, Rusty was free and clear. All of which reminded Josh of the Swede's concern about hijackers, which didn't make any sense when you consider all three were only hauling the same empty crates loaded up the day before. Anyway, he and the Swede didn't get the all-clear until close to ten a.m. Taking into account the sea of tractor-trailer eighteen-wheel rigs by mid-morning, traffic jams and whatnot, plus pulling into a truck stop for a bite to eat, he and the Swede wouldn't be barreling into some Asheville destination until a good twelve hours later, perhaps close to eleven p.m. By then they'd most likely call it a night and carry on the next day when surely Sal would arrive and take it from there.

And so, the whole drive down and true to form, when he wasn't on the CB talking to Sal in that clipped way of his, the Swede only spoke to Josh when absolutely necessary, saying things like "You hungry yet?" and "Maybe we'll pull in for a bit when we get past this stretch."

At the same time, there was the rough ride and endless rumble and roar of the hell-bent diesel trucks in the passing lanes, occasional twinges of pain in Josh's ribs, and sheets of rain pattering on the hood of the cab as they hit a bottleneck at Harrisburg, Pennsylvania.

But, most of all, the farther they got, the greater his anxiety. It wasn't just the fact that his presence in the passenger seat underscored his complicity whether it was true or not. Most of all, the farther they went, the greater the distance from Molly and his dream of being with her living a sweet, normal life as he finally got his act together. All of it creating an apprehension concerning his ultimate fate which, coupled with the trip itself, put him in a groggy, restless state. His whole situation reminded him of the uncertainty principle: the willy-nilly quarks colliding and breaking apart. One moment they're particles, the next they're waves, constantly in flux with nothing you can count on, nothing you can control.

The relentless drive south would carry them across the Pennsylvania line, past West Virginia, a smidge of Virginia, skirting Knoxville in the Appalachians, heading smack dab into the Western Carolina Smokies, eventually landing full circle less than an hour's drive from his lost Black Mountain haven in the Blue Ridge.

But then, in regard to Knoxville, something crossed his mind. It was no accident that Zharko had him shipped off to these Tennessee mountains far from the activities of the Red Mafia back east. By the same token, it was no fluke that he recently tracked Josh down hiding out in this same region but further south and only some thirty miles or so east of Asheville—a locale he already had in mind, a town as Paul had pointed out was the last place to find a hub of any kind of Mafia activity. A spot Zharko must have decided would be ideal for a setup far from the beaten path and the fed's prying eyes. All told, it was conceivable that Asheville was not just a stopover. It very well could be Josh's last chance to get off this treadmill, blow the whistle, and prevent being permanently caught in Zharko's clutches—enveloped somewhere in the Gulf, his abiding dream forever dashed.

He considered taking in the lay of the land immediately when they arrived late that evening. Zharko was reliant on Raul's reports, which suggested that Zharko and Vlad fortunately would be well out of the way, waiting somewhere down in the Florida Keys, especially if you add Vlad's fixation on getting a sailing boat as his payoff. The Keys then were apparently the distribution outlet, from this point around the Gulf and up through New Orleans and Corpus Christi all the way to the Heartland. Distribution of whatever it happened to be, filling the empty crates—the kicker and the proverbial bottom line.

Keeping this whole scenario in the back of his mind, Josh's first order of business after getting his bearings would be to see whether there was any access to a phone. When the time came, assuming he hadn't just been spinning his wheels and if he actually uncovered the goods in time, Devlin's contact number would enable him to nip it all in the bud.

As the trip stretched on, he finally gave himself a break from all this pondering. He settled for dozing off now and then and reached into his windbreaker for a pain killer during a rest stop when he couldn't stand the on-again, off-again ache around his rib cage despite the resultant codeine headaches.

Hours later, at last they pulled into a hazy area on the northern outskirts of Asheville as the rain gave way to an overcast sky blotting out any traces of the moon and stars. While the Swede was busy parking the truck down a dusty track adjacent to a large, dilapidated storehouse, Josh got out and stretched his legs, as wobbly, tired, and groggy as could be.

In the darkness, looking down the dirt track, he saw that all three trucks were now adjacent to one another, their cargo doors in line with the side of the building and a small loading dock. Far to his right, given the faint sound of rippling water past the tree line was, doubtless, the ever-flowing French Broad River. Glancing to his left, he took in the narrow lane now leading off from the way they came in. As far as he could make out in the haze, it was some four or five blocks long, linking to streets heading south to the downtown hub. Gazing directly across from the dilapidated storehouse, he found a scattering of abandoned single-wide trailers perched on cinder blocks, separated by thickets of overgrown vegetation. Turning completely around, he determined that the only doable avenue of escape was a possible road, far from traffic, running alongside the river for miles until it hopefully met up with the River Arts District hooking up with nearby downtown Asheville. Once there, getting to a phone in case there was none to be had at the storehouse and reporting to Devlin all he'd gleaned, surely Devlin could then hook up with a possible field office in Asheville. If he were truly lucky, that is, the quarks were obliging and he was definitely on to something.

His fleeting thoughts of escape were cut short the second Rusty drifted out of the front of the storehouse and headed toward him. The scruffy redness of his hair and beard aside, it was the smirk that told Josh at least one of the truckers was halfway friendly. Dutch was still an enigma, like a wary, balding ex-wrestler who hadn't yet come to terms with this stint but was going along anyway. The Swede had made his attitude clear at the outset.

"Okay, fella," Rusty said, steering Josh back toward the front of the building. "According to Sal, after the Swede served his sentence, now it's me and then Dutch's turn. Let me show you where to sack out so's you can plainly see trying to take off in the middle of the night is a bad idea."

"What do you mean?"

"I mean there is no way you are any kinda front. A hostage or something more like. Am I right or am I right?"

"Whatever," Josh said. "Sacking out is the only option for me right now."

"Sacking out and watching your step. 'Cause none of us is in any mood to babysit."

Josh shrugged and followed suit as they wandered over to the entrance and navigated up the warped steps. Once inside, Josh held back for a second to take it all in. The place was illuminated only by the dim light of a dented overhead fixture hanging from the ceiling. A quick look told Josh this was a musty once-upon-a-time wholesale furniture outlet. Scattered all about the spacious main floor was an array of mismatched couches, armchairs, dining room sets, floor lamps, and what have you. To his immediate left was an office and another room that might have served as a customer lounge. Doubtless this was a perfect out-of-the-way location for whatever Zharko had in mind.

Presently, a tall man with a gaunt face, close-set eyes, and a crop of salt-and-pepper hair that looked as if it had been cut with pruning shears came toward them wearing a checkered flannel shirt and gray cargo work pants.

"This here is Ivan," Rusty said. "As I understand it, he's the caretaker while us truckers are holed up here."

"Yeah," Ivan said, as taciturn as the Swede. "That'll do it. I'm the caretaker." And that was it for Josh's first encounter with Ivan as he walked off down an aisle past the shabby lounge, turned and headed to the rear of the building.

Taking a deeper survey, Josh looked over to his right and noted that the interior extended out at least thirty yards past a number of rugs to the overhead loading door in a direct line with the parked trucks. A glimpse above him took him to a stairwell leading to a set of adjoining rooms separated by a bathroom. Turning back, he tried to peer beyond the rear of the aisle to where Ivan disappeared but to no avail. It was the only hidden area so far.

Out of nowhere, Dutch's short, muscular form appeared by Rusty's side, blocking Josh's view, clutching Josh's overnight bag. Shoving the bag at him, Dutch said, "Here you go, buddy. I say we all turn in at the same time. And here's the deal we worked out with Ivan."

Dutch hesitated, as if speaking out of turn, and looked to Rusty for approval. Rusty nodded. "Right," Dutch said as the Swede walked in, gave Josh that same disparaging look, and stood back, keeping his distance as usual.

Pointing at Josh, Dutch said, "You go up the stairs, all the way to the end past the bathroom, park yourself in that last room, and sack out on the cot. We'll be covering the exit down the staircase."

"Fine," Josh said.

"You sure?" Rusty chimed in. "I'll be next to the bathroom on the other side from you, Dutch in the room closest to the stairs. And the Swede here . . ."

"Downstairs in the little nook past the office just before the beds and mattresses," the Swede said. "But still close enough to cut you off before you reach the front door."

"In other words," Rusty added, "like I said. In case you get any ideas, we're a stopgap, me on the other side of the bathroom, Dutch next and the Swede close enough down there. Plus either Dutch or me having to nab you and toss you over the railing would keep us from getting a good night's sleep. Not to mention kinda messy." This tagline was delivered with a wink.

Predictably, the Swede drifted off, wanting no more to do with this.

Rusty and Dutch stayed put while Josh climbed the stairs. He sensed them still watching as he passed by the two rooms and the bathroom, opened the last door, tossed the overnight bag aside, and flopped down on the cot, too exhausted to even think about changing into his pajamas.

The way things were going, he assumed before tomorrow was over something had to give. Otherwise, why carefully park the trucks with the cargo doors in line with the loading dock? And why go to all the trouble to make sure Josh was carefully hemmed in?

He shut off the copper floor lamp next to the cot and waited until all the sounds of movement by the landing and below had ceased. A short time later, in the stillness somewhere past the reaches of the river, he thought he heard the plaintive sound of a harmonica or what mountain folks call a blues harp. Gradually, he picked out the melody line of that old prisoner ballad "Freight Train" and even recalled some of the lyrics:

Watch those old smoky mountains climb and they won't know where I've gone.

CHAPTER THIRTY-TWO

On that fateful Friday, everyone slept in late. Ivan, the caretaker, took off in his RV and brought back Josh and the crew some breakfast from a nearby fast-food restaurant. Things got cracking again when Sal pulled in looking the worse for wear after locking up the warehouse back in Waterbury and driving straight through to this backwater location. Despite his bloodshot eyes and the way he shambled around, by mid-morning he was back in harness playing the chief honcho and issuing orders left and right.

Oblivious to whether Josh heard or not, he commenced by calling everyone together in front of the dingy office next to the front entrance and announced they'd be using the same ploy to make sure all systems were go. The truckers would take off in staggered intervals at noon starting with the Swede, this time by his lonesome. As usual, Sal would be in touch on his walkie-talkie as each drove away down the narrow two-lane, hooked up with the main arteries, and turned onto 240 South for about thirty minutes, watching out for sudden off-ramps "that'll take you to hell and gone." If they were still on track, they were to go west on 40 for another thirty minutes to get used to the steep mountainous climbs and to make doubly sure no one was following, pulling them over, or creating any hassles whatsoever.

At this point, Rusty chimed in. "Hold it, Sal. Just thought you should know, us long-haul guys aren't used to this hide-and-seek game you keep playing. How far you going to take it?"

"As far as necessary."

"Meaning?"

"Meaning that's my lookout."

"Just saying is all, Sal. Just saying."

By the same token, Josh himself kept wondering about these tactics. Since the only cargo inside the trucks at present was the same load of empty crates, Josh figured if the trial run went without a hitch, the next time they all took off it would be for real. Which could very well be any time and the crates would be full. If that were the case, it would make some hidden part of this old furniture outlet a storage unit for the mysterious goods, a cargo that was always in question and the place itself more than a handy stopover on the way to the Keys. Which then underscored Sal's cautionary moves.

Moving on after his opening remarks, Sal hinted that when they took off for real, they'd have to bunch up. Something about bottlenecks and speed traps south of Charleston and "rubber-necking tourists" and "crazy drivers from Jersey." And something else that sounded like "can't let any one of you slip away."

Next, Sal took Ivan aside, still oblivious of the fact that Josh was hanging around by the staircase, and blurted out, "Listen, he's been pegged as a front so make like that's what he is. And make like you're the owner of this furniture outfit. I mean, you never know who might come by and you can't never be too careful."

When Ivan didn't respond, Sal added, "You're supposed to be useful, right? So keep it up. It won't kill you."

Ivan, who continued to be hard to figure out, came right back with, "Look, I'm tired of being jerked around. First thing I'm a go-fer bringing back breakfast. Now you want me to play some fake manager? Is this thing taking off or what?"

Raising his voice even louder, Sal said, "Give me a break. What if somebody spots trucks coming in here last night and then out of here today and coming back again? What are they gonna think?"

"Way back here? Anyways, I signed up for setting things up, getting hold of some cots and keeping an eye out. That's it."

"And now you're setting things up so it looks like it's operational with a legitimate reason for the trucks."

"But who's gonna know? Who's gonna come traipsing in and inquire?"

"Never mind. Straighten the goddamn furniture and all. Clean up with lots of space in between. Make like a guy who's gonna have a clearance sale and like that. Just do it!"

Disregarding the fact that Ivan still wasn't buying it, Sal rubbed his eyes and said, "Okay. I'm gonna set up shop right here next to the office. I'm the one now who keeps a sharp eye out on whatever might be coming in. You got a recliner in there, right, so's I can get a little shut-eye? Plus a TV that works, a nightstand for my walkie-talkie and like that? You done that like I asked?"

Ivan only squinted and watched Sal enter what probably once passed for a customer lounge. Once Sal closed the door, Ivan motioned for Josh to step into the adjoining office by the front door. Grumbling, he began ransacking the file cabinets in the corner while Josh sat on a swivel chair by a scarred wooden desk. In short order, Ivan came up with a bunch of blank tags with strings attached and scoured around until he located a handful of magic markers to boot.

While scanning the area for a phone and coming up empty, Josh thought of asking Ivan if he was the one who'd left the airline tickets in his mailbox back in Black Mountain over a week ago. But, then again, what difference would it make? The only thing that mattered now was locating a hidden storage room. If he located one, he'd have to look for a way to uncover the goods, which had to be on site. And find some way to contact Devlin either before the trucks took off or shortly after.

On the other hand, if it turned out he was completely mistaken and was caught poking around, things would be ten times worse. He'd be under constant surveillance. Any chance of coming to the aid of J.J., Uncle Fredo, and Aunt Sophie would be gone. Ensuring Molly's safety and getting back in touch would be a lost cause as well. Something told him that before the sun set today it was all or nothing. Even his rib cage, which had hardly bothered him lately, made him aware he could move freely anytime he sensed an opportunity. Either way, there was no excuse. There was only the sense of the kicker to the whole escapade hanging over him.

What kept him going over the next few hours were a few pointers. As he went through the motions with Ivan—sweeping up, dusting and polishing, affixing sale tags to the furniture and such—Ivan insisted on leaving a wide swath that ran all the way from the overhead door adjacent to the alley where the trucks were parked, past the rugs and dining room furniture to the mattress and box spring section, then all the way down to a latched door at the rear of the building (the very spot that was masked in darkness the night before). The door itself was warped, entry afforded by lifting a cast-iron gate-bar latch. In seeing to this cleared aisle and arriving at the latched door at the rear, he came across a large empty storage space to the left. When Ivan caught him loitering there, glancing at the gate-bar latch to the hidden door and back again over to the empty storage space, he jerked Josh away "What the hell you doing?"

"Nothing," Josh said, moving sharply back up the side aisle toward the front of the building. "Just wondering when this charade is going to end."

"What's that supposed to mean?"

"You know. Tagging, arranging the furniture, making a wide clean aisle from stem to stern. Pretending this is a revival of an actual wholesale furniture outlet."

"Not your damn business. Don't know what you're doing here

in the first place. Don't know anything about you except Sal wants to keep it that way long as you and the guys are here. So we done like Sal wanted. There's an end to it and shut up about it, okay?"

"Okay. I was just wondering, that's all."

"Well don't. Just go along. You get it now?"

"I get it." But Josh got a lot more out of this aisle clearing maneuver. No matter how much Ivan protested, he must've realized it wasn't all busywork or to fake a going concern. It was not for nothing there was now a clear path from the overhead door straight across and down all the way to a locked door and empty storage space. A huge gap just crying out to be filled by something well worth concealing on the other side.

As if on cue, this conjecture was interrupted by a banging outside the overhead door. Ivan went over, hoisted the door, and proceeded to help the Swede carry the empty crates from his truck all the way across and down to the latched door and deposit them at the back end of the storage space. This went on for a time until the Swede's truck was empty. Josh couldn't help linking the empty crates loaded up from Waterbury, a hidden trove behind the latched door, and a subsequent trip by three "bunched up" trucks all the way to the Keys.

Yet another pointer struck Josh a short time later when the Swede, obviously bone-tired by now, shuffled up the stairs, surreptitiously listening to his cell phone. Then he stopped short. He pocketed the cell, peered down, spotted Josh and shook his head, giving him another one of those long-suffering looks. Josh could only guess the Swede had just received some unexpected news and wanted to protest, saying something akin to "You have got to be kidding." Perhaps Josh was slated to ride shotgun again under the Swede's watchful eye. Shaking his head again, the Swede hurried down the stairs and made straight across for his digs above the space where the bedding was kept and slammed the door.

Regardless, while Josh waited for Ivan to reappear, the empty crate maneuvers continued with Rusty's arrival about thirty minutes later. His crates soon joined the Swede's in the storage space. When finished with his chore, Rusty came over in that same playful but wary way and asked Josh if he was behaving himself. When Josh nodded, Rusty made his way up to the landing and retired. About twenty minutes after that, the pattern repeated itself one last time with muscular Dutch, who predictably didn't interact with Josh at all, finished hauling the crates from his truck and yelled over to Ivan who slipped out of his room below the bedding section. He let Ivan know he'd be upstairs catching a little shut-eye like the other two guys, went up the landing and departed as well.

By six o'clock, after Ivan and Josh dusted off and rearranged the mattress and box springs section, Sal emerged from his quarters at the front of the building, called everybody together once more, and announced plans for supper.

Still looking the worse for wear, bleary-eyed and decidedly slower on the uptake, he suggested they all could use a good meal before "things got rolling." Since Ivan had mentioned a good Italian restaurant not more than fifteen minutes down the lane, Ivan would drive the truck drivers in his RV and Sal would remain and watch a few innings of a New York Yankees opening-day ball game while keeping Josh in check, plus watching out for any possible intruders. By seven or so, Ivan would bring Josh and Sal back something like linguine with clam sauce with lots of carbs to fortify them for "the big push."

Sick and tired of playing caretaker and mother hen, Ivan gave Sal a withering look which Sal didn't pick up on. Yawning, rubbing his eyes, Sal added, "I'm saying the pencil pusher here stays put. I don't want him anywheres near a phone."

The truckers and Ivan trickled off. Sal hesitated by the lounge door and looked back over at Josh. "Me, I'm watching a ball game like I said and keeping my eyes peeled out the window. What're you gonna do?"

Josh meandered over to the front door and said, "I need some fresh air after all this dusting, tagging, and shoving stuff around. Plus, I could use some time and space to think this all over."

"You got nothing to think over. As far as you're concerned, it's cut and dried."

Sal waited for Josh's reply, but Josh didn't want to waste any precious time arguing. The impasse was punctuated by the sound of Ivan's RV revving up outside the building.

"Hold it," Sal said as Josh started to ease out the door. "Don't you try to pull nothing."

"Like what?"

"Who knows with you."

"Look, I came crawling back, didn't I? Even after Vlad sent me to the ER, I came back. And I've caused you no grief ever since and even played furniture mover and floor sweeper. I just can't take being cooped up any longer."

As the sound of the RV began to trail off, Sal glanced around at the display and sparkling aisles. "Yeah, all right, good job. Nice and neat. Maybe you did earn a little break." Thinking it over some more, Sal said, "Right, you outta my hair for a few minutes, outta the way. I like it."

He walked straight over to Josh and poked his chest, "But swear you're gonna stick around. I don't want to have to go looking for you. You sure as hell don't want me to go looking for you, believe me." Another poke and Sal said, "You read me? Fifteen, twenty minutes tops."

"I read you. I get it. I'll be close by."

"Damn straight." With that, Sal went back to his quarters and closed the door.

Josh waited a minute until he heard the faint sound of a sportscaster's voice and crowd noise emanating from a TV and stepped outside. The air felt heavy and moist, the clouds thickening under the darkening sky, the tangy smell of the river close by.

He walked over to the dirt track, turned past the empty trucks and Sal's vintage maroon sedan at the side of the building, and paused. A mile or so away he heard the faint sound of brakes screeching and then honking. Perhaps some vehicle blocking the narrow lane while Ivan, as irritable as ever, was trying to get by.

Perhaps Sal heard the sounds, too, after opening a window and turning down the volume. Josh waited a moment longer as the noise of a ball game resumed and faded as Sal closed his window. There were no more sounds, his stalling was getting him nowhere, and he moved on.

Reaching the rear of the building, he cut across the tamped-down weeds until he came to what had to be the outer door of the latched room adjacent to the storage space. Almost immediately he saw things appeared to be set to go, the shackle of a keyed padlock pulled out above the hasp, the key still inserted. The same was true of the toolshed opposite. Whatever tools were needed were sitting there waiting, the shackle of the shed padlock swung freely open as well.

Hurrying back to the outer door, he grabbed the handle and hesitated when, yet again, he thought he heard something. Not driving down the lane toward the building but closer by, maybe back around the corner in the vicinity of the parked trucks and Sal's sedan. He held still a few seconds more and, once again, sloughed it off. If he kept this up, he'd lose his nerve and ruin this perfect opportunity. He settled for identifying what was stored inside as quickly as possible and getting out of there. If there truly was a big reveal, he'd contact Devlin as soon as he could get to a phone like he planned. If nothing came of this, he'd just scamper back and chalk it off.

He jerked open the outer door, slipped in, pulled the door closed, and spotted rows of cardboard boxes, enough to conceivably fill all the empty crates stacked in the storage space on the other side of the latched door. The whole scene was illuminated only by shafts of waning daylight seeping through a small overhead window, causing flickering shadows across the boxes and the concrete floor. The boxes were sealed by a single strip of clear packaging tape, a remaining roll hanging from a peg by the outer door. He looked over at the interior latched door and listened for approaching footsteps. Or, worst of all, the latch on the other side slipping open, forcing him to make a run for it. Yet again he waited and yet again there was nothing. Sal was apparently still ensconced at the front of the building watching the ball game, intermittently keeping an eye out his window for any vehicle drawing near. The only thing for it was to go outside, hope there was a box cutter in the tool shed, return, cut through the tape on the closest box, examine the contents, reseal it and leave.

He rushed out, rummaged around the shed, found what he was looking for, rushed back in, left the outer door ajar only a smidge, sliced open the box and put the cutter atop the box next to it. He pulled the cardboard flaps apart and peered inside. On top were oversized rolls of paper towels. He flipped a bunch of the rolls onto the concrete floor, reached deeper and came upon it.

There were countless little boxes containing vials of white tablets labeled *Acetylfentanyl*, ranging in strength from a hundred micrograms up to a thousand. Instantly, he recalled the documentary on cable TV: the glassy-eyed girl who looked like J.J. back in Ohio, moaning and wailing, her boyfriend OD'd and sprawled under a tree getting an injection from a policewoman. A hundred micrograms not enough, she said, waiting for it to disintegrate in your cheeks. But if there was a higher dose "that would last a long while . . ." And here it was—a distribution center in Key West as Raul sets sail from Havana, an offshore shell company already set up in the Grand Bahamas . . . Zharko hawking higher grades of synthetic heroin . . . venders coming from far and wide, the money pouring in, Vlad getting his boat . . . goods moving up through New Orleans into the Heartland, to Ohio and all over this land and God knows where else.

He reached for the rolls of paper towels and the packaging tape, fully intent on sealing up the box and clearing out when, suddenly, the outer door flew open.

He dropped everything, sprang up, and backed away through the boxes until he hit the rough wooden wall. And there confronting him was the chiseled face and piercing eyes that belonged to Zharko Vadja.

"Is betrayal," Zharko said. "Everywhere you look is betrayal. Irina sells out through Novac, runs off. Again is betrayal. Now you, because always to trust is big mistake. Generosity is big mistake. Like I goddamn know it all the time!"

Zharko grabbed the box cutter and flung it, just missing Josh's cheek as it ricocheted off the wall and clattered onto the concrete floor.

"Runs everywhere," Zharko said. "Runs in family for sure. In weak blood from father who sells out, then Irina, and now little bastard Sonny who grows up but is all the same."

There was a metallic taste in Josh's mouth as he broke into a cold sweat and reflexively glanced over his right shoulder at the thick interior door.

"No use," Zharko said. "Vlad is blocking road in gypsy camper so no stranger gets by. And Sal watching loud ball game out front will never hear."

"Don't be so sure," Josh said, glancing again at the interior door and holding up his watch. "Time's up, see? He gave me a reprieve of fifteen minutes and swore he'd come after me if I didn't show. So you'd better pull back and think of the fallout."

"Think of goddamn stories, you mean!" Zharko said, shoving the open box aside. "That is what you are good for. Which is why I turn around from coast road. Too easy to follow tourists to Sunshine State. Too easy without my eyes on you so you not dare. Stories only good when I am not looking all this time. You tell Sal you get into car and drive back to hospital. But Vlad tell me he hits you so good you collapse like rag doll. No way you get up, no way you drive anywhere. So, someone like brat J.J. pick you up, yes? And take you to hospital. You say no problem with Irina after you talk but, next thing I am knowing, she is gone. With Novac in cahoots is for sure. And all stories from you is same as lies!"

"You're seeing this all wrong," Josh said, raising his voice, hoping someone, anyone on the other side of the inner door would hear.

"I see good, dammit. I think good. I see Sonny who hides behind new name, hides away, hides when Tulio comes by warehouse and, at same time, is partners with brat-juvie J.J. I see she has old boyfriend who is cousin to Tulio and cousin to Sal who gets trucks from nephew to Tulio. Now comes brat J.J. after Vlad breaks uncle's arm and uncle wanting revenge. So, here is drill—quick, fast, one-two-three. No more stories and talk and playing goddamn games!"

Glancing back yet again, Josh could swear he heard the release of the latch on the other side of the door. Raising his voice even louder this time, Josh said, "You don't want to do this, Zharko, believe me. Speaking of betrayal, how are you going to explain why you showed up here traipsing back on foot? Do you really think Ivan would honk, put up with Vlad's lame excuse for blocking the road—Vlad who can barely speak English? Do you really suppose Ivan and the guys went along with this charade and drove on la-di-da to some chintzy restaurant?"

Fixated on Zharko's hand now, Josh said louder still, "I'm saying, when they burst in here, what are you going to do? What are you going tell them?"

"No one burst in. No one is explaining. Is only moment of truth. I warn you, show you how is done in hotel room. First with cheating sweetheart in carnival till she confess. Then you see out in cold woods what happens but was sloppy. Must be like old ways, like this. By count of three is too late, blade already at your throat. On count of one, you beg. By two, you talk. Who put you up? Start at bottom with J.J. for revenge for little uncle and work up to Tulio. Give to me plain as daytime."

Josh heard no more sounds from the other side of the door but shook his head anyway. Despite the chill running up his spine and the cold sweat, despite everything, he was not about to sacrifice J.J. or anyone else. "No," Josh said.

"What?" Zharko shouted.

"I said no." In the stillness, Josh refused to close his eyes, refused to beg, and remained rooted to the spot.

"Then you freaking asking for it!" Zharko said, peering outside to make sure. "On count of three, I goddamn say. Last chance. One . . ."

There was the snap of the switchblade by his side, his arm coiled back.

"Two . . ." His hand at the ready for the release.

On the count of "Three!" the inner door flew open with a burst of gunfire . . . the smell of cordite as the blade quivered in the wall by Josh's neck . . . the sight of Zharko's body twitching . . . then a look of utter amazement on his face as he crumpled to the floor.

Just as quickly, the Swede dropped his handgun, gripped Josh's arm, dragged him past the boxes and Zharko's prone body, and shoved him through the open door onto the weeds "Get out!" he yelled. "Get the hell out of here!"

Totally shaken, Josh picked himself up and lurched forward into the darkening night, passing the maroon sedan and box trucks, sprinting for the river. At the bend, he turned sharply, the faint wail of a blues harp somewhere high up in the ridges leading him on.

CHAPTER THIRTY-THREE

"**I** told you, I told you," Devlin blurted out over the landline. "Zharko bought it. By the time the field agents reached that spot in the boonies, that's what they found."

"That's it?" Josh asked.

"Except for an old maroon Lincoln parked on the side of the building."

"Except for Sal Scarola, three truckers, Ivan, and Vlad the enforcer. Except for a gypsy camper and three box trucks loaded to the gills with advance formula opioids. Except all the while, Gulfstream Transfer probably stood for this advanced synthetic heroin transferred to the Florida Keys and distributed to ports around the Gulf and to hell and gone. And maybe, just maybe, Sal is part of a takeover. That's why he stayed back waiting for Tulio just like Zharko said. As for the Swede—"

"Hey, hold it, will you? Simmer down. I'm telling you that's all my old partner could confirm. What do you expect anyway?"

It was well past ten that same evening. Somehow, Josh managed to hitch a ride with a guy in a battered pickup who dropped him off downtown at the Haywood Park Hotel. A desk clerk let him use a phone to call Devlin back in Connecticut and relay the details, who, in turn, told him to call back in a couple of hours and he'd see what he could find out. In the meantime, Josh took a cab some thirty minutes east to his cottage in Black Mountain. And now here he was, prodding Devlin long distance on his landline while Devlin kept fending him off.

"Look," Josh said, pressing on. "Just hear me out, will you?

Your old partner must have gotten a line on somebody who called it in. That accounts for the Swede peering down on me on the landing, shaking his head while on his cell phone. Which means he must have been talking to his handler who had gotten the word I was in a bind. After Vlad blocked the road, the Swede—who's from Philly, by the way—and the others doubled back. The Swede heard Zharko threatening me, unlatched the door and—"

"Oh, come on, give it a rest will you? You are totally over-loading the circuit."

"But I'm telling you it all fits."

"And I'm telling you to let it ride. Just for openers, if this Swede character was really undercover, he had to blend in, not give himself away like I once did and blow the whole thing. As for Zharko, according to the Bureau's file he could have moved on from smuggled cocaine from Canada under freeze-dried seafood to his own operation. But it's late, kid, and I can't get my mind around all you're throwing at me, including Tulio from the old Waterbury mob, Zharko who's been iced, shipments of advanced opioids on the loose, and I don't know what all. And you sure as hell are in no shape to even begin to understand procedure. So call it a night, okay? And thank God you're still in one piece."

"Call it a night? That's all you've got to offer while the trucks are rumbling south crossing state lines?"

"Theoretically. Maybe and a million other maybes."

There was a long delay until Devlin said, "All right, all right, tell you what. You sit tight, get some rest. I'll look into it some more tomorrow, see if I can get a bead on what's actually going down. Plus a line on some Swede from Philly's possible handler. Plus maybe even put in for an APB for three box trucks with Connecticut plates rolling south. How does that grab you?"

Josh didn't answer and continued to wait him out.

Then Devlin went on. "One hand washes the other, right? I

hear you write for a paper. In the meantime, tomorrow while you're getting back on your feet, you fill in the blanks, write me a story so I can file a preliminary report. One that makes some kind of sense and don't ramble all over the place so's I can connect the dots and get back in harness. And while you're at it, give J.J. a call. If she hadn't kept pestering me, we wouldn't be having this conversation and you'd still be up the kazoo."

"I'll do better than that," Josh said, cutting in. "I'll thank her in person. I have to get back to Waterbury anyways and get hold of this lawyer while there's time."

"All right, even better, back here in my bailiwick. Now about this Swede, if he's in cahoots with Tulio and wanted Zharko out of the way, that's another angle. Who knows? You see what I mean? Like I tell J.J., logic is key along with certifiable facts. Anything else is just shooting the breeze."

Josh thought about it and finally said, "Fine. In the meantime, you'll keep me up to date, let J.J. know I'm coming back?"

"And you will fill me in, chapter and verse, at the latest first thing Monday?"

"I guess."

"All right then, you're on." With that, Devlin abruptly ended the call.

Josh took his time and gathered his thoughts, keeping all the unfinished business in mind. Then went straight over to his closet, dug out Fredo's calling card from his rumpled blazer, returned to the kitchen, sat down and took another sip of strong tea. Reaching once more for his landline, he dialed the number, anxious to tell Aunt Sophie the news while careful to leave out any allusion to Zharko's violent end, leaving out practically everything.

The second Sophie picked up, he said, "Sophie, it's me, Josh. I know it's late but I'm down in Carolina and had to give you the news."

"Carolina? All the way down there? Oh, heavens, are you all right?"

"I'm fine. Everything's just fine."

"That is so good. Can't tell you how worried we were since we hadn't heard from you. Even J.J. was concerned, though she tries to hide it. Walking out, gazing at the stars."

"That's nice, I appreciate everyone's concern. Tell her I'll be dropping by. But I just wanted you to know that the warehouse has been abandoned. It's unoccupied."

"Fredo's warehouse?"

"Yes."

"All of a sudden? But how did that happen?"

"It's a long story. The upshot is the perpetrators are under investigation. There are no more trucks there, the place is empty, and Gulfstream Transfer has closed up shop. Which means Fredo can pick up where he left off and J.J. can go back to booking customers."

"You mean it? You really mean it?"

"Cross my heart. I just couldn't wait to tell you."

"Oh, Fredo, Fredo, wait till you hear!"

In her excitement, she dropped the handset, cutting off the connection, which was just as well, and left the other pressing issues. There was Irina. She'd let down her guard during that confrontation in her cabin and actually talked to him. Moreover, her tone became wistful and soft for the very first time. She couldn't have gone far, and Novac would know how to get in touch. With Zharko out of the picture, there could be a new beginning. After all, they were flesh and blood, the ties that bind and eventually—who knew—they might even celebrate Christmas. He could go and see Novac at his home early Monday morning before he left for his court dates. They could talk freely now and set up a reconciliation between mother and son. That was the best way to go about it. Surely it didn't have to end this way.

Josh considered the remaining items on his to-do list and systematically put his itinerary in order. He placed Molly a close second right after touching base with J.J. Not only because he didn't have Molly's number. He couldn't take being brushed off over the phone no matter how gently she put it. It was true that after all this she might very well have taken the note he mailed as a green light freeing her engagement with George. After all, like he wrote, who could blame her? She hadn't heard from him and she certainly deserved to get on with her life. But even so, he had to see her. Had to at least have one more encounter.

That settled, he went out to the potting shed, grabbed a beat-up gym bag, and began packing a few basics. He got back on the phone and booked a late morning short hop to the airport in Charlotte and a coach seat on a non-stop to Bradley airport north of Hartford.

— ·· —

Early the next morning, in keeping with everything else, the weather was unsettled. The banks of grayish-white clouds meandered across the sky as if trying to decide whether the day was going to be partly sunny, cloudy with afternoon thunderstorms, or a washout.

After getting dressed and fixing himself a quick breakfast, he glanced out the window just in time to catch a glance of perky Amanda wearing a tomboy outfit hopping into her mom's beige Chevy. Then he remembered—a dress rehearsal before the Saturday matinee at the community school down the road.

He scurried around, taking care of some last-minute details like booking a car rental from Enterprise at Bradley. He locked up, tossed the gym bag in the trunk of his old Subaru wagon, started the engine, and let it run for a few minutes after sitting all this time. He checked his watch, making sure to give himself ample time to get to the regional airport down in Fletcher, drove off, and almost immediately pulled into the private school parking lot in front of the rehearsal hall.

He went inside, careful not to draw any attention to himself, and slipped into the wings in time to catch a glimpse of Amanda leaping and twirling in front of the chorus of other kids on stage as the adult musicians in the pit amplified the beat. He wasn't at all sure what cut-down version of a Broadway musical she was in. Barefoot, dressed in a gingham shirt and overalls, she could have been playing the Artful Dodger in *Oliver* for all he knew. He was simply struck by the effortless way she strutted, whirled, and threw in a few somersaults for good measure like a release of pure, spontaneous joy. Something he'd only caught glimpses of watching old MGM movies.

After she capped it all off with a show-stopping flourish of syncopated high kicks and a slick trouper's bow, she rushed back offstage, spotted Josh and shouted, "Oh, golly, you came! But you are gonna see the rest of it, right? Or come back for the matinee? We've got it down now real good."

"Sorry, kid. Got to run."

"But you only just got back. I saw the cab pull in real late."

"I know. But believe me, from what I've seen so far, you are a surefire up-and-coming star."

"Oh, you're just saying that."

"Would I lie? Have you ever known me to lie?" Dropping down on one knee, Josh said, "Boy Scout oath and a double-dog dare you to boot."

"Oh, Mister Josh, you're the best." She leaned over, gave him a kiss on the cheek, said, "Got to go. My next big number's coming right up," and ran off.

Amazed at what had gotten into him, dropping to one knee like that, he left the auditorium as unobtrusively as he'd slipped in. He drove off under the scudding cloud cover down old 70, hooked up with 40 west, then the hell-bent traffic south on Interstate 26 speeding toward the regional airport.

With a few minutes to spare, he parked at the long-term lot, hurried into the modest terminal, got his ticket, waited until his section was called and boarded. From then on, it was a matter of fighting off the fatigue, making his connection with the nonstop flight from Charlotte which, as it turned out, was some thirty minutes off schedule. Regardless, dozing on and off, happy to have procured a window seat, he calculated that under the best of arrival conditions, he'd make it to the warehouse before he totally ran out of afternoon. If by chance J.J. was still there, stocking up and such, there was no way he was going to slough off thanking her in person.

Which, by and large, was how things went as far as going through all the hurdles and driving off under the perpetual scudding clouds for this first leg of his back-in-Connecticut agenda. Navigating the back roads through Paradise Valley, cutting through Terryville and Thomaston, meeting up with Route 8 south, and finally taking the exit ramp into downtown Waterbury.

As if he hadn't quite used up all the good luck due him, he spotted J.J.'s old jeep the second he pulled into the warehouse drive. He parked, got out, and peered across the loading platform, starting with stacks of overflowing wooden cartons of fresh fruits and vegetables at the far corner, over to a large empty handcart and dolly in the center next to the open triple-wide steel rolling door. In no time, she appeared through the darkened recess sporting a gray hooded sweatshirt over faded jeans, clutching a frosty bottle of Corona beer in her right hand, grinning from ear to ear.

"Well there then now, look what blew in."

Gazing up at her, Josh said, "I just dropped by for a second. When I called last night, your aunt Sophie told me how flustered and worried you were, traipsing out there in the dark of night."

"Hold it. You can't go by that. I was only having a smoke by the picnic table, looking up at the sky and kinda wondering how you was making out. She comes over and makes it into some Sunday school thing, like I was praying for you or something. Which is just like her half the time."

"Nevertheless, would it kill you to let me thank you for all you did?"

"Like what? Giving you grief till that creep Vlad laid the wood to you? And showed me you was a standup guy when you got out of bed and went right back in there when I called your bluff? Which then got you boxed-in and hauled off to the boonies? Alls I did was to get Mike finally on the stick and Carmine to give you Mike's number whilst I stayed back and you went through the ringer." Raising her beer bottle high, she said, "So here's to you, pal," and took a long, deep swig.

"Well, missy, I don't see it that way."

"Too bad. Now, I don't know how you busted loose, but I lay you odds somewhere between this Zharko getting whacked, you getting a bead on the goods, and this trucker getting the word out, Sal's operation is down the tubes, and Uncle Fredo is back in business. And that's what counts in my book."

"How do you know this?"

"Guess. What do you think, I got telepathy or something?" She drained the rest of the beer, went over, tossed the bottle into the dumpster and came right back.

"Devlin."

"Bingo. Seems only about an hour or so ago, the three trucks and a gypsy camper were spotted heading for Miami when a trucker gave word on his walkie-talkie to back off till they hit the rendezvous in Key West. That's so's to hit the distribution point and all that like in one raid. I'll also lay you odds that creep Vlad is behind the wheel of the camper. I tell you, man, no sweat, it's all good."

Josh nodded, taking it all in.

"So lighten up," J.J. said, grinning away again. When Josh didn't reply, J.J. came right back with, "I know, I know. You've really had it. So's here's the deal. You go to the inn, sack out for as long as you like. Tomorrow, you're coming over for a picnic. Sophie's whipping up a spread for the whole crew. I'm talkin' the works, including baking a humongous cake. And Fredo's breaking out a case of the good stuff. Monday you can worry about that legal business you got hanging over you and relay Mike the whole story while you're at it. But tomorrow, pal, you got the whole day off. And I ain't taking no for an answer."

The best Josh could come up with was a shrug and a thumbs-up as J.J. began nonchalantly reloading the handcart and dolly. Josh turned away, unable to put off his primary objective any longer.

He slipped behind the wheel, honked the horn, and drove off back to Route 8, hoping against hope there was still an off chance he could pull up in front of Molly's sublet before it was too late. By the time he got there she might be gone or on her way out to see George or have dinner with her fellow school teachers or who knows what.

Hitting the speed limit, he realized he had only a burning desire going for him. But, if by some fluke they could meet even for a moment, he could at least come up with some excuse for being here so she wouldn't think he'd become hopelessly irresponsible. Perhaps telling her that though he'd lost his features position in Black Mountain, Russ Hodges at the Waterbury paper put him on to an opening up in Lakeville. But how in the world could he incorporate his ordeal to account for this belated roundabout trip? And what difference would any of it make if she'd opted for a sensible liaison with George?

Minutes later, as he reached the steep rise at Route 118 leading to the village Green, it came to him that the escapades of Sonny/Josh, Irina, Zharko, and the gypsy camper lodged deep in the woods were like some faded fable based on hearsay. And all that remained was the tail end of Josh's odyssey and his ever tenuous liaison with Molly Hunter.

Coming upon the village center, he skirted the Green and finally reached the pristine cottage as the first vestiges of twilight afterglow glinted low on the horizon. He got out and lingered by the cobbled walkway that led to her front door, having second thoughts, losing his nerve.

A porch light came on and he spotted her silhouette, just standing there motionless, as if she too was lingering, unsure what to make of this.

He took a few steps forward and said, "I'm free now and I just wanted you to know if you ever needed me . . ."

Another step forward, another hesitation. "But I would give anything if only you were. . . if only you could . . ."

Suddenly she broke the impasse and hurried toward him. As she neared, he tried to tell her why he didn't call first, why he was so late in contacting her and what had befallen him. But she kept cutting him off and wouldn't let him speak. All at once she was crying, and then he was crying as she held him tight. And all she would say was, "Welcome home."

ABOUT THE AUTHOR

Shelly Frome is a member of Mystery Writers of America, a professor of dramatic arts emeritus at the University of Connecticut, a former professional actor, and a writer of crime novels and books on theater and film.

His fiction includes *The Secluded Village Murders, Moon Games, Murder Run, Miranda and the D-Day Caper, Sun Dance for Andy Horn, Lilac Moon, Twilight of the Drifter*, and *Tinseltown Riff*. Among his works of nonfiction are *The Actors Studio* and texts on the art and craft of screenwriting and writing for the stage.

He lives in Black Mountain, North Carolina.

OTHER BOOKS BY SHELLY FROME

PUBLISHED BY BQB PUBLISHING

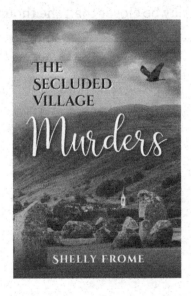

Written in the style of a classic British Mystery with a contemporary young American woman as the amateur sleuth. Entertaining. Keeps you guessing until the end.

From a small, secluded village in Connecticut to the English Countryside, readers are taken on a roller coaster of events and quirky characters as amateur sleuth Emily Ryder tries to solve a murder that everyone thinks was an accident.

For tour guide Emily Ryder, the turning point came on that fateful early morning when her beloved mentor met an untimely death. It's labeled as an accident and Trooper Dave Roberts is more interested in Emily than in any suspicions around Chris Cooper's death. For Emily, if Chris hadn't been the Village Planner and the only man standing in the way of the development of an apartment and entertainment complex in their quaint village of Lydfield, Connecticut, she might have believed it was an accident, but too many pieces didn't fit.

As Emily heads across the pond for a scheduled tour of Lydfield's sister village, Lydfield-in-the-Moor . . . she discovers that the murderer may be closer than she thought.

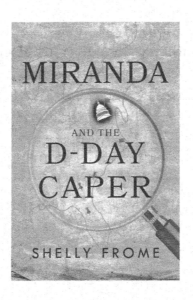

A modern-day mystery with WWII tactics, old-time heroes and values, and the efforts of two amateur cousin sleuths from the Heartland.

On a sparkling spring morning in the Blue Ridge, small-town realtor Miranda Davis approached the tailgate market, intent on dealing with her whimsical cousin Skip's unexpected arrival from New York. It turns out that Skip was on the run and, in his panic, grabbed his beloved tabby Duffy, recalling that Miranda had a recent part in solving a case down in Carolina. His predicament stemmed from intercepting code messages like "Countdown to D-Day," playfully broadcasting the messages on his radio show over the nation-wide network, and subsequently forced to flee.

At first, Miranda tried to limit her old childhood companion's conundrum to the sudden abduction of Duffy the cat. But the forces that be were hell-bent on keeping Skip under wraps by any means after he now stumbled close to the site of their master plan. Miranda's subsequent efforts to decipher the conspiracy and somehow intervene placed both herself and her old playmate on a collision course with a white-nationalist perpetrator and the continuing machinations of the right-wing enterprise, with the lives of all those gathered for a diversity celebration in nearby Asheville and a crucial senatorial vote on homeland security hanging in the balance.